JARDIGO'S CASTLE

Martyn Croft

ISBN: 978-0-9559872-9-8

Dedicated to the memory of Mr Green

'For what shall it profit a man, if he shall gain
the whole world, and lose his own soul?'

(St Mark 8:36)

CONTENTS

1

The New Recruit

Jardigo Batista was rich – very rich by the standards of the local community of Vila Montemor. Though some of his vast wealth had been inherited, he, nevertheless, had acquired most of his assets by somewhat less than legal means. The Castelo no Monte commanded fine views of the rolling countryside to the east of Lisbon, and its owner could count many likeminded individuals under his command. Jardigo was a modern day Robin Hood who liked nothing more than to ensure that those individuals enjoyed all the trappings of his wealth, especially the thirty or so who actually resided at the Castle on the Hill. Though his estate was considered small by some standards, it still occupied over 500 acres of lush green fertile land and, with 44 bedrooms, was the largest such private residence outside of the Portuguese capital and for a hundred miles inland. The castle was not particularly old, having been built in the first decade of the nineteenth century on the site of a former monastery. Jardigo's forebears had acquired the castle after moving the 50 miles from their wealthy Lisbon home to seek a more relaxing lifestyle at the foothills of the mountains. The land around the town of Vila Montemor had provided them with rich earnings, and their investment had brought prosperity to the region that had been traditionally regarded as poor when compared to the wealth of the neighbouring city of Lisbon.

The early summer of 2002 had been a good one for Jardigo and his clan, which some outsiders would have, no doubt, likened to an Italian style 'Mafioso'. Lisbon had become a popular tourist destination for holiday makers from all over Europe with money to spend, both wisely and unwisely, when encouraged by Jardigo's band of merry men. From petty pickpocketing to more organised cons bordering on outright stealing, Jardigo had an organisation that was proving to be far more profitable than arable farming, especially in the summer months when prices at market were so low and unrewarding. When the several protection rackets were added to his mix of capital-making ventures, Jardigo's fortune was becoming a large one, even when judged by national standards.

What Jardigo and his clan really needed, however, was some foreign input into their ranks, as was pointed out to him one morning at breakfast in late June. His first lieutenant and strongest 'muscle', Rafael Cabral, was always quick to offer his advice on such matters.

"Jardigo, my friend, we need an English gentleman; a real toff who can charm his countrymen and women with a silver tongue and a promise of fame and fortune. Then we fleece them dry, eh, boss?"

"Maybe, old friend; the number of British holidaymakers is certainly increasing year by year. Our fortune is growing and soon I will be able to complete my master plan. It would be much to our advantage to have the services of a professional English businessman of some kind, but not just to fleece his fellow countrymen out of their holiday money, for example."

Rafael smiled. His boss had never discussed his 'plan' even with him, his most trusted aide and confidant, but he knew it would have world-shattering implications, whatever it was. One thing was certain, though — there was enough cash within the walls of the castle to finance any project that Jardigo cared to instigate, let alone the several bank accounts in Portugal and elsewhere. Oh yes, Jardigo Batista had enough money even to buy a small country, should he so desire.

"So what would you want him to do?"

"Well, we could definitely do with some contacts in the British banking system; someone who'd be willing to join us and share some inside knowledge and even ...."

Jardigo Batista paused and looked wistfully over the lush green valley from their position on the long covered veranda that ran the full length of the rear elevation of the castle. He took a deep inhalation of his customary after-breakfast cigar and smiled.

"Well, my good and trusted friend, it would be much to our advantage if he brought some knowledge of accounts and certain codes that could be used to, er, how shall I put it — unlock those accounts, eh?"

Rafael Cabral frowned.

"That will not be easy, boss. I mean, up till now we've always acquired our recruits from the low life of society; from the criminal fraternity who've been only too keen to have free food and accommodation in surroundings that they could only dream of, in return for doing, more or less, the same thing they had been doing all their lives. With a professional and honest banker, if that's what we're looking for, it would be a totally different proposition. Finding such a person, willing to give up a lucrative career with stable prospects in exchange for what we do, will be like looking for a needle in a haystack. We would need all kinds of luck and external help."

"We don't need luck, Rafael, my friend, and as for help, there is something that can always be relied on to give us such assistance."

"Oh yeah, who?"

"Not who, but what," replied Jardigo with a broad grin.

"Alright, what, then?"

"Greed, my friend, plain and simple greed."

"Greed?"

"Yes, greed — greed is always there, lurking in the background of these people. For most of them, that's why they became bankers in the first place and the higher they go in their profession, the more they want."

"A lot do it for the stability and status the job gives, and a lot of them do it because they are precisely the kind of people who are careful with their money," said Rafael, doubtfully.

"So we look for the telltale signs, my friend."

"Signs? What signs?"

"There are many, Rafael. Spending beyond their means; gambling; a wife or partner who obviously likes the good life — expensive jewellery, clothes and tastes."

Rafael Cabral reached for a cigar and said,

"Gambling? Now there's a vice; I've seen some of these tourists lose fortunes in the *Las Vegas Casino* in Lisbon."

"And that's where we'll start our search; the high rollers at the casino, and we filter them until we find one suitable who is high up in a major international bank. We'll take enough cash as an investment for our quest. You and I, my friend, are about to become high rolling gamblers ourselves and, hopefully, we will draw potential targets like moths to a flame, eh?"

Rafael frowned.

"Gambling? I don't hold with gambling, Jardigo."

Rafael's boss burst out laughing.

"You don't hold with gambling, eh? That's rich, coming from you, considering you're a thief, a hustler and a thug to boot! I should say that gambling would be the least of your evil vices, my old friend."

Rafael Cabral saw the funny side of his remark and joined his boss in hysterical laughter.

The Castle on the Hill possessed wonderful views of the countryside around and on many a clear night, the glow of the lights from the Portuguese capital could just be seen in the distance to the west. The veranda, on which Jardigo and Rafael often breakfasted alone together, faced north, providing some protection from the heat of the sun during the day and many of the bedrooms also led off it, their ground floor position providing a comfortable sleeping environment at night. The front of the castle was composed mainly of offices and a few rather grander rooms which housed Jardigo's growing collection of antiques and works of art. The first and second floors of the three-storey building had a few further bedrooms as well as a library and other rooms for relaxation; comfortable lounges and playrooms for its residents. Jarigo's private apartment was located on the second floor and occupied about a half of that floor on the west side of the building. Below ground level, there still existed a series of cellars and tunnels that had been put in by the monks, centuries before, which led to one particular cellar of cavernous proportions. This cellar had been recently extended by Jardigo in order to house the 'vault' which contained his growing fortune in cash and gold. Its precise position, reached only by a further series of tunnels, was known only to Jardigo and Rafael. It was generally known, however, that the vault was not directly under the castle itself but deep below ground a few hundred yards beyond the walls. Only Jardigo and Rafael knew the actual piece of the castle's grounds below which it lay. It was thus pointless for anyone to attempt to burrow below the surface from the grounds themselves; no one would have a clue as to where to commence digging.

That morning, after breakfast, Jardigo made his customary visit to the vault while his chief henchman began organising a motley crew of the castle's employees for their daily excursion into Lisbon for the various 'projects', from simple pickpocketing to collection of protection dues. Jardigo loved nothing better than to spend an hour or so inspecting his fortune; feeling the piles of carefully ordered banknotes and admiring his collection of gold, whether as crude ingots or as jewellery. He had long since ceased trying to count his piles of notes; that total was carefully recorded in his ledger, hidden in his private rooms, to which he made entries whenever any cash was deposited in the vault.

The idea of visiting Lisbon's finest gambling establishment appealed to Jardigo and, while he was down in his vault that morning, he placed a few piles of banknotes to one side for the intended purpose. He took a good ten minutes to decide how much to take, eventually erring on the side of modesty — he did not want to attract attention from the authorities who might want to investigate any large sums of cash he might gamble. After much debate with himself, he decided on 500,000 escudos as a suitable amount, with no denomination higher than a 1000-escudo note. True, the sum was more than most people earned in a year, but they needed to attract someone with, as Rafael had put it: '*More money than sense*'.

Being mid-summer, the *Las Vegas* was, as usual, packed with gamblers the following Saturday evening; the last in June. Jardigo and Rafael had arrived early for their initial recce, neither really expecting to find a likely candidate for their cause. Dressed in very dark, indeed, almost black suits with white shirts and sombre ties, they both looked the part — business-like and serious punters. However, to the casual observer, their swarthy complexions and, in particular, Rafael's black moustache, gave them a rather sinister air; an air of businessmen used to getting their own way by whatever means possible, whether legal or illegal. As soon as they were inside the plush casino, they headed for a quiet corner to discuss tactics and their modus operandi for the evening. Jardigo had obviously thought carefully about the plan of action, and after they had accepted a couple of colourful cocktails from a passing scantily-dressed waitress, he began to share his ideas with Rafael. They had taken up a position leaning against the red leather-clad walls with a perfect view of the casino floor.

"You know, Rafael, old friend, we should try the roulette wheel first. It will be easy to tell from the stacks of chips who is doing well and who is not."

"And, indeed, who has real money, Jardigo," replied Rafael. "I'm beginning to look forward to the evening now."

"Yes, you may be, but you are not going to attend the table, Rafael, I'm afraid. I have other plans for you."

"Oh?"

"Yes, I want you to go on patrol and scour the floor for any other possible targets."

"And how will I know if they are going to be willing to listen to our proposition?"

"You'll know, believe me, you'll know. You have an eye and an ear for these things. You haven't spent the last thirty years, since you were a young teenager, mixing with the gullible, without being able to spot someone who can be easily and willingly led to the honey pot."

"Ah, yes, you may be right, boss, and I guess I wasn't that keen to try my hand at roulette; I have never played it before and wouldn't know where to begin. I never was any good with numbers."

"Exactly — you are to be the eyes and ears of the operation this evening, while I try to attract some interest at the wheel by placing some large and somewhat reckless wagers. If you get chatting to anyone, you might like to encourage them to come and watch me as a first step. Do you think your English will be good enough to do some gentle persuasion, my friend?"

"It will suffice for the purpose, Jardigo. Anyway, I'm good with my hands if I need to emphasize my meaning."

Jardigo Batista laughed out loud. He hoped his first lieutenant wouldn't over use the physical side of any persuasion! He had seen in the past what Rafael's hands or, at least, his fists could do. Of course, they were not going to use any such violence that evening. It was definitely going to be a case of '*softly, softly, catchee monkey*'. His chief henchman grinned. He would exercise his charm and not his muscle as he was quick to point out to his boss.

"Of course, I will the height of discretion and charm, Jardigo. You can rely on me. My English may not be up to your standard, but it will be good enough. I have picked up much by mingling with the tourists over the years, even though I don't have the benefit of three years working in England like you."

"It was hardly working, Rafael," replied Jardigo with a smile. "More like some gentle relaxation as a lady's consort and escort."

"Consort, eh, boss? The word gigolo springs to mind, I think!"

"That's enough of that, Rafa!" said Jardigo, sternly. "Now let's get started. Give me about fifteen minutes at the table before you commence your search. Meanwhile, here's a little play money for you to try your luck — maybe the one-armed bandits will take your fancy and be at your level, eh?"

Rafael's boss handed over a thick wad of notes and ushered his deputy away with a smile. After he had gone, he felt inside his jacket for the secret pouches secured to the lining and he immediately felt his excitement rise at the evening's prospects. Nothing like a flutter when you could afford to lose, and lose many times over, at that, especially when he was only carrying a drop in the ocean compared to the fortune of cash back at the Castelo no Monte. Oh yes, win or lose, he was going to have a good evening. It was an investment in the future; the first rung on the ladder that one day would take him to the top and enable him to complete his master plan.

The roulette table was busy when Jardigo sidled over in order to size up the players. He quickly realized that all of the gamblers were only small-time players, with no one investing more than a couple of hundred escudos on any spin. There were eight of them altogether; four women and four men, composed of at least two pairs of spouses. With only three or four watching bystanders, Jardigo was easily able to position himself close to the table, ready to quickly replace any of the eight. He didn't have to wait long as the couple immediately to his right were clearly on the verge of an argument. The woman seemed particularly angry.

"Now, Stan, *that* is enough. Please don't gamble anymore. You've must have lost over a hundred pounds already. It's only our first night here, for goodness sake."

"Just one more spin, Di — then I'll quit. Twenty-eight is bound to come up this time; I just know it."

"Oh, yeah? Well, I'm going to the bar and you'd better join me soon or I'm back to the hotel."

With that, the young blond girl pushed back her chair and turned to smile at the waiting Jardigo.

"There you are, sir, it's all yours."

Jardigo smiled back pleasantly, even though the girl's thick accent caused him to do a double take when she spoke.

"Pardon, madam."

"I said you can have my place, sir."

"Oh, thank you, madam," replied Jardigo.

"And don't follow my husband; he's hopeless."

"Oh?"

The young blonde brushed past Jardigo, causing him to blush and giving him thoughts of the female companionship he lacked. He sighed inwardly as he caught a whiff of cheap perfume. After a brief pause, while he glanced casually at the blonde's retreating rear, he took his seat just as the croupier called,

"Rien ne va plus!"

Jardigo watched as the blonde's husband tried to place two 100-escudo chips on twenty-eight. The croupier barked,

"Rien ne va plus!"

The young man's chips were pushed back to the side. Stan was too late; he had been too busy listening to his wife's conversation with the new dark-suited punter.

"Damn," he swore. "I bet it comes up now."

Jardigo smiled. It always happened like that, he thought.

The wheel was set in motion and the ball released in the opposite direction. Jardigo could sense that Stan was anxious; 200 escudos was a big bet for a tourist. It also looked to be his last chips. The wheel was slowing. The croupier bent over the table. The ball wobbled and came to rest.

"Vingt-huit, noir! Twenty-eight, black!"

Stan swore under his breath and slung his chair back. Jardigo placed a hand on his arm, and in rusty and halting English, said,

"No good luck, my friend."

"No, I just knew that would happen — I'm off, mate. Good luck."

Jardigo's hand brushed the young man's light cotton jacket.

"Thank you, sir, I try."

Stan walked quickly away while Jardigo offered up ten 1000-escudo notes to the croupier's assistant who quickly returned a pile of chips of various colours.

The croupier called out,

"Fait vos jeux!"

Jardigo started to arrange his chips into four stacks of fifties, hundreds, five-hundreds and thousands, while the remaining six players placed their bets on the table. He smiled inwardly at the young man's bad luck in missing out on a win of 7200 escudos; over £500 in sterling. Later, however, Stan would find some compensation when he removed his jacket to find a 1000-escudo note in an outside pocket. The croupier reiterated his command.

"Mesdames et monsieurs, fait vos jeux! Ladies and gentlemen, place your bets!"

Jardigo relaxed in his chair. He was not going to bet just yet; not while there were only small-time gamblers at the table. Also, he liked to watch the wheel and the order of the numbers over a few spins. He had a powerful memory for the purpose.

"Rien ne va plus! No more bets!"

Jardigo studied the table. There looked to be no more than about a few hundred escudos down. The wheel started spinning. The ball was set in motion. He was almost certain he knew what was going to happen. A few seconds later and he smiled as his silent forecast came true.

"Vingt-huit, noir! Twenty-eight, black!"

The elderly couple opposite Jardigo sighed in unison.

"I told you it would come up again, Fred. Why didn't you put a chip on it?"

The lady's husband said nothing. He shook his head in disbelief and stood up, indicating to his wife that it was time to go. There were two vacant seats at the table. Maybe, thought Jardigo, one of them would soon be re-occupied by someone who could be persuaded to join his cause.

It had been a week of recovery for David Marks; a consolation for the recent divorce from his wife, Gaynor. He had spent the first six days of his seven-day recuperation, relaxing and sightseeing in the Portuguese capital from his base at the plush Hilton International Hotel right in the centre of the city. The London Provincial Bank had granted him as much leave as he wanted from his position as one of their top international fund managers. Now, it was Saturday evening, and he was due to return to his flat in Esher the following day. He was going to indulge his passion that evening, no matter what, knowing full well that his gambling addiction had been the prime cause for his marriage breakdown. He didn't care; he was single again and in charge of his own destiny. There were no children to worry about and the settlement had been easily bearable for him; Gaynor kept the house in St Albans and he kept his London flat, which they had owned ever since his promotion to one of the top jobs at the London Provincial. It had been vital accommodation when the need to work late arose, and was ideal for its close proximity to Heathrow or Gatwick for his countless trips abroad each year. Unbeknown to his former wife, its position was also ideal for secretive visits to several London racecourses — Sandown, Epsom, Kempton and Ascot were all within half an hour in his Jaguar XJ12 and even his favourite course at Lingfield Park took not much longer with the thrill of opening up the 5.3 litre engine on the A21 to delight him as well. Though his salary had coped well with his excesses in the past, things had recently taken a downturn, with several heavy wagers failing. Though the Portuguese escape had been paid out of a recent bonus, his debts overall were beginning to weigh heavily on his shoulders. David Marks was in need of a quick injection of cash and he was determined, that particular Saturday evening, to try his luck in Lisbon's premier casino to aid the recovery. He kept reassuring himself that, even if he blew all his remaining bonus money, he would just work that bit harder on some foreign transactions to make up the loss. As far as he was now concerned, even the possibility of a few shady deals was not completely out of the question — money could easily be made when you had the right information. Life owed him a thing or two after his losses — financial or otherwise.

David Marks had set out from his hotel at six but he didn't get to the *Las Vegas* until gone eight; visits to several bars on the half mile walk to the casino had slowed his progress, as well as his speech by the time he signed in at reception. He was in bullish mood when he finally reached his favourite gaming table and he found his luck was in — there were two empty seats close to the roulette wheel. A smartly dressed man in his forties nodded from the other side of the table. For the first time in a while, David Marks felt underdressed when compared to the handsome and swarthy gambler opposite.

"How's your luck, hombre?"

Jardigo smiled at the clichéd appellation; he'd been called worse.

"I have not tried it yet, sir."

"Well, stick with me, chief and you'll make money."

By this time, only two other people remained at the table; four had just left when they sensed that a couple of professionals had arrived. Apart from Jardigo and David, the foursome was completed by two men in their twenties who both seemed rather the worse for wear, judging by their slurred speech. They appeared to be winning heavily.

"Come and join us, mate," said one of them, addressing David as he sat down. He was a short and rather fat individual with tattooed arms. "We can't lose at the moment," he continued.

"Yeah," said his friend, an equally scruffy individual with a shaven head that had obviously seen too much sun in recent days. "Karl here has won at least fifty quid. I'm Wayne by the way."

'*Karl and Wayne*', thought David Marks. "*Girlfriends called Sharon and Tracy, no doubt*'. He did not reciprocate with his own name.

"Nice to meet you, boys. Now let's spin that wheel, Mr Croupier, if you please."

Jardigo said nothing; he was still sizing up the new player. This could be the one, he thought. His clothes looked expensive and he had an air of sophistication mixed with and easy-going nature that might be moulded in the right direction. Just then, the croupier sensed that the players were ready to start and that no one else was going to join them.

"Fait vos jeux! Place your bets, gentlemen!"

Jardigo waited while Karl and Wayne placed their chips, noting that they each staked about 200 escudos. He looked at the smart young man opposite. David Marks exchanged a few notes for his chips. Jardigo counted about 5000 in chips — it looked promising. Jardigo smiled and said,

"After you, sir."

"No need to be so formal; I'm David, and you are ...?"

"My name is Jardigo Batista, David."

"Good to make your acquaintance, Jardigo; may I compliment you on your English."

"Thank you. I am pleased you understand me."

"Now let me see," said David. "A simple bet to start with, I think."

He placed a 1000-escudo chip on red and sat back in his chair. Karl and Wayne seemed to take extra breaths. This was already out of their league. Jardigo remained calm and fiddled with his stacks.

"Fait vos jeux!"

The croupier was insistent. Jardigo took five 1000-escudo chips and placed them next to David's single on red. In addition, he placed another of the same value on twenty-seven. Now, Karl and Wayne let out audible gasps. David Marks smiled.

"Rien ne va plus! Rien ne va plus. No more bets."

The wheel was set in motion. Jardigo still had a calm and relaxed posture. David and the two young men bent anxiously over the table to watch the spinning ball. It wobbled and came to rest.

"Vingt-cinq, rouge; twenty-five, red!"

Wayne and Karl sighed in unison; they had won nothing. David beamed and said,

"Excellent, eh, Jardigo. We both win. Shame about your number. It was close, though."

The croupier slid 5000 in chips towards Jardigo and 1000 to David.

"Our luck's in, chief," said David.

Karl and Wayne got up from their chairs.

"Time to go, son," said Wayne. "Let's get a drink while we've still got some money left."

"I'm with you," replied Karl.

David winked at Jardigo, and as soon as the boys were out of earshot, he said,

"Small time gamblers, eh? Now we big boys can do our stuff."

Jardigo nodded. This was indeed looking promising. Suddenly, out of the corner of his eye, he caught a glimpse of his deputy, Rafael, strolling towards the table. Not wishing David to hear any likely conversation between them, Jardigo got up from his seat.

"Please excuse me for one moment. I will return."

He looked directly at the croupier and added,

"Do not make the next spin, please."

The croupier nodded at the command that was obviously not to be ignored. He was well acquainted with Jardigo's influence and power in the local area. Jardigo turned and headed for his advancing henchman. Fortunately, Rafael was still a few yards away when Jardigo managed to usher him into a quiet corner.

"What's up, boss. You've started gambling. Any luck?"

"Maybe, Rafa, my friend. However, I do not think I need your services for an hour or two. Go and enjoy yourself wherever you will. Here, take this."

Another wad of notes was thrust into Rafael's hand. He smiled; unlike him, his boss had clearly identified a target. He quickly pocketed the cash and strode away. Gambling wasn't the only pleasure the *Las Vegas* offered for discreet customers who had money.

On his return to the roulette table, Jardigo found that his order to the croupier had not been obeyed and it was evident that it was due to David Marks' insistence that they should continue without him. The croupier received a dark stare from Jardigo; he would deal with him later. In the meantime, he had a fish to hook. He began to fix the bait to his rod.

"Ah, how did you do, David, my friend? What number appeared?"

"I doubled up on red and thirty-two came up," he beamed; a large drink was now at his side. "I'm 3000 up already."

"Well done, David," said Jardigo. "I think that red may be on a roll, as you English say, eh? Why not double up again and I'll join you there. Croupier, give me 100,000 in chips, please."

David Marks stared at his fellow gambler. He started to open his mouth but nothing came out. Jardigo handed the croupier a thick wad of notes and he glanced at the Englishman.

"Time for some real betting, my new friend."

At last, David managed to find his tongue.

"That's out of my league, I'm afraid; I'll just leave my 4000 on red,"

"Oh, but you must join me, David," said Jardigo, grinning. "I insist you take some of my chips. If you win, you can pay me back out of the winnings; if not, call it an interest-free loan to be paid back when you can — no pressure, David."

Jardigo didn't wait for David to respond and looked at the croupier.

"Give him half my chips; 50,000 each, please."

The croupier duly obliged. Inside, David Marks' stomach was churning and his heart was racing. He had nearly £4000 in front of him. His mind was in a whirl; he could make more than that on one deal back at home. He placed the five chips on red. Jardigo followed quickly and said,

"There, that was easy, David. Croupier, spin that wheel.

"Rien ne va plus! No more bets."

David Marks bent his head towards the wheel, hardly noticing that a small crowd had gathered behind him; they were watching in anticipation of the two gambler's audacity. The wheel started its rotations; the ball likewise. Jardigo smiled inwardly; the fish had taken the bait. If he didn't land it this time, he could always try again, he thought. The ball was jumping across the numbers; it hesitated on seven; David Marks gasped in anticipation, but his luck was out as it tripped forward and settled in seven's neighbour, twenty-eight.

"Vingt-huit, noir. Twenty-eight, black."

"Oh no!" mumbled David. "That's nearly four grand I've lost."

Jardigo did not smile openly.

22

"Bad luck, my friend. Croupier, more chips, for my friend, please. Give him 100,000 and the same for me."

More and tastier bait was being fixed to Jardigo's line. Just how wealthy was the young Englishman? Would he bite? He handed another wad of notes to the croupier.

"Oh no, I couldn't possibly take it; it's too much," spluttered David Marks.

"Don't worry, David, your credit is good with me and the deal still stands — pay me the 150,000 out of any winnings or some time later when you can afford it. You can afford it, can't you; you look an affluent man to me."

David did not reply; he hadn't noticed how good the Portuguese stranger's English seemed to have become the longer the evening had gone on. The harsh accent and faltering sentences had all but disappeared. Jardigo had just added more bait; flattery was a powerful weapon in his armoury. David Marks at last managed to speak.

"When?"

"When what, David?"

"When would you want your money back?"

"I'm not going to answer that, my friend, because you are not going to lose. You have a lucky face, I think."

The croupier seemed anxious for the two gamblers to place some more bets, as did the small crowd behind them. Two stacks of ten 10,000-escudo chips were poised in front of his slide.

"Well, sir? Fait vos jeux. Place your bets, please."

Jardigo took one pile of ten chips and placed them immediately on red.

"Second time lucky, David. Come on, I'll make it easy for you; you can have a month to pay me back if you lose, but just think about winning."

The fish bit. Whether it was the drink or just out of sheer bravado, David Marks nodded at the croupier who slid the second pile of chips across to him.

"Well, here we go, then; red it is."

The bait was swallowed; 200,000 escudos rested on red. David Marks was in debt to the tune of about £11,000. He was getting into serious trouble and he was blissfully unaware that he was being subtly controlled by the dark-suited and smooth-talking Jardigo Batista.

"Rien ne vas plus! No more bets!"

This time, the ball showed no hesitation as it reached its final resting place.

"Dix-cinq, noir. Fifteen, black."

The small crowd gasped. David Marks' head dropped to his shoulders; Jardigo smiled. The fish was in the net for good.

"I am sorry, David. Do you want me to lend you some more chips? I could let you have another 100,000, but that's all, I'm afraid. It would then be 250,000 that you would owe me."

David Marks did some mental calculations. He quickly made his decision. '*In for a penny, in for a pound*', had always been his motto and, anyway, it was going to be almost exactly £20,000 — it was a nice round figure.

"Well, alright, but that's it, Jardigo."

"Of course, David; it's your choice, my friend."

A couple of minutes later, the croupier made his call.

"Rien ne vas plus!"

Jardigo had placed 100,000 on red; David had put 80,000 on black. This time, he was not going to follow his benefactor. In addition, he placed 20,000 on the group one to six. He and Jardigo had realized that the 100,000 all on red or black would not be enough to make the 250,000 needed.

The croupier started the wheel; even he now looked anxious for the two gamblers. David Marks was soon to learn his fate. The ball wobbled a little over four and then jumped several slots to rest finally on sixteen. David Marks hardly listened to the croupier's call.

"Dix-six, rouge. Sixteen, red."

Jardigo had made 100,000 escudos; David owed him 250,000. He was in his power.

2
Gentle Persuasion

There was only ever going to be one place that David Marks was going to retire to after his disastrous and somewhat embarrassing sojourn at the roulette table, and his new 'owner' was only too pleased to accompany him. Unlike some losing gamblers, David could remain cool when his pride had been badly hurt and he rose from his chair with some dignity, albeit forced.

"Well, I'm done here, Jardigo. Care to join me at the bar? We can discuss our financial agreement."

"Of course, my friend," replied Jardigo. At least his prey was not wriggling free from the net, he thought, as he joined his new friend who was already moving quickly away from the table. As he did so, some people in the small crowd passed a few well-chosen comments. Jardigo immediately placed a sympathetic arm round David's shoulders.

"I know the best bar on the next floor; it is for members and their guests only. We will be able to talk in private and make the necessary arrangements. It is very unlikely that there will be anyone who speaks English there; it is for local VIPs only."

"O.K., Jardigo."

David's new master continued to keep his arm somewhat firmly on his young protégé's shoulder; a casual observer might have easily remarked that the Englishman appeared to have a forced escort in his walk across the floor of the casino.

The first floor of the casino was clearly much more luxurious than the ground; the carpets were softer and the furnishings considerably more opulent. David made immediate comment when they emerged from the lift.

"Wow; very nice, Jardigo."

"Yes, it is the best in all of Lisbon and Portugal. Membership is expensive and very exclusive."

As the lift doors slid softly to behind them, Jardigo removed his arm from David Marks' shoulder. He would find it difficult to run away now, should he have the balls to try; he'd already had a quiet word with one of the security staff on their way to the lift. He led the way to the bar which ran the full length of one wall of the private room. Jardigo smiled at the tall, muscular barman and, continuing to speak in English, said,

"Now," said Jardigo. "What can I get you for a drink? Gordon makes some nice cocktails here, don't you, my friend?"

"Yes, Senhor Batista; only the best in Lisbon."

David was immediately taken aback. The barman spoke perfect English with a faint cockney accent. He began to relax a little, not realising that Gordon Donovan was an ex-conman from Bethnal Green and was, in addition to his front as senior barman at the *Las Vegas*, on Jardigo Batista's permanent payroll. He was always on hand as necessary muscle whenever any contractual negotiations took place in the private member's bar between his boss and any clients he brought with him. Quickly recovering his poise, David replied,

"Whisky, please; a double Jamesons on the rocks."

"And I'll have one of your evil cocktails — a *Las Vegas* bombshell, I think."

"Coming right up, chaps — in need of some medicine after a bad evening downstairs, eh?"

Jardigo's looked sternly at the barman.

"Something like that, Gordon; just bring the drinks over to my table and less of your comments, please."

"Yes, sir, Senhor Batista; coming right up."

David's first drink took only a few minutes to disappear and Jardigo instantly ordered another. They had sat in silence to begin with; David unsure how to approach the matter of his debt and Jardigo waiting while the pressure became too much for the Englishman to bear. It had the desired effect as, with second whiskey in hand, David Marks started to grovel.

"I really don't know when I'll be able to pay you back, Jardigo. I have just been through a divorce and my financial situation is not good at the moment."

"I think I said you could have a month, David," replied Jardigo, his friendly smile disappearing suddenly from his face.

"And if I can't get you the money by then?"

Jardigo Batista held up a clenched fist.

"Well, shall we say I have ways of ensuring that you do?"

"I don't follow."

"Oh, come now, my English friend. Do you really think I would lend you a sizeable some of money if I didn't have the power to make sure you paid it back. I'm not a philanthropist, you know."

The young Englishman still seemed somewhat naive.

"What kind of power?"

"The power that can exact all kinds of punishment, David."

Jardigo paused while his words took time to settle in David's mind.

"You understand?"

"Ye-es."

"But, hey," Jardigo continued. "It's not going to come to that, is it?"

"No, but I ...."

"Well?"

"I was going to say that we had no written agreement about the loan or the timescale for paying it back and — we didn't shake on it, so we don't even have a gentleman's agreement."

Jardigo started to laugh.

"But, David, my friend, I'm not a gentleman and you are more of a fool than I thought you were if you think I am."

David looked hurt.

"You think I'm a fool, then?"

"All gamblers, who cannot afford to lose, are."

David took a swig of his drink. He was cornered.

"So, I think you are threatening me, Jardigo. I need to be clear on this. Am I right?"

"Threats come in all sorts of guises, David."

"How do you mean?"

Well, for example, when you take out a loan with a bank, do they not threaten you with extra charges if you default on your repayments?"

"Ye-es, I suppose so."

Jardigo grinned. He put out a feeler.

"But you would know that, wouldn't you? You look like you're a businessman of some kind. Am *I* right?"

"Yes."

"So what sort of business are you in?"

"International banking and fund management."

Jardigo's expression did not change, even though his heart started to beat faster. This was too good to be true.

"Oh, I see. Does it pay well, David?"

"Not bad – it depends on lots of things; the markets; exchange rates and so on."

"Obviously you earn enough to be able to gamble quite freely, even recklessly, though?"

David Marks was silent. Jardigo put out a second feeler.

"And, no doubt, you get bonuses when things go well?"

"Yes, I do."

It was time to offer the real bait. The line soared into the air and hit the surface of the water.

"Well, I think I can offer you a bonus, David; a bonus that will wipe your debts off in a flash; a bonus that will also ensure that you will never have to worry about money again, no matter how hard you gamble."

Jardigo let his words register in the Englishman's mind. The fish's mouth was open.

"Wha-what do you mean?"

'*Steady*,' thought Jardigo. '*Play the fish along the surface.*'

"Sometimes debts don't have to be honoured with money. There are other ways of repaying your dues, David."

"Such as?"

"Well, for example, if a diner cannot afford to pay for his meal, the traditional forfeit is to wash the dishes for the restaurant owner; to work his bill off, eh?"

Jardigo could tell from the expression on David's face that his proposal was beginning to dawn on him.

"You mean, I come and work for you? What do you do, Jardigo?"

The fish was hooked — now to get it into the keepnet.

"Well, like you, David, I make money."

"Are you in banking, too, then?"

"Not exactly — but I do have a lot of money in them."

"I guessed that," said David, ruefully.

"Let's just say I have many enterprises going that bring in more money per day than you would probably earn in a year or even several years."

"Oh."

The keepnet was wide open.

"You say you've just been through a divorce, so you are now on your own; with no one to please but yourself, eh?"

"Yes, that's so true."

"And you're obviously willing to take a gamble?"

"If the odds are stacked in my favour, yes."

Jardigo laughed again.

"They weren't stacked in your favour earlier this evening, were they?"

"That was different; it was just for fun."

"Well, I'm deadly serious about my proposition. If you were to come and work for me in one of my enterprises, you would earn three or four times your salary now."

"Really?"

The fish was at the mouth of the net.

"Yes, really, my friend. What have you got to lose? I'll even give you a year of your present salary upfront on top of wiping your debt off. Come and have some fun for a year at my expense and see how much you can earn. At the end of that year, you can then choose to go your own way or stay on with me. A year's trial would be your only commitment."

"Sounds like an offer that's too good to refuse."

"It is, my friend. What do you say?"

"I say, buy me another drink and we'll discuss the fine details," replied David, with a smile.

"So that's a yes, then?"

"I need that drink first, Jardigo, please."

The fish was in the net. Would he wriggle out? The next few minutes would tell. Jardigo placed a hand on David's shoulder.

"Of course, my young friend. Let me get you that drink, but, remember ...."

"Remember what?"

"The offer is only open tonight; after that, normal payback procedures will be in place — cash or pain."

Jardigo stood up and headed for the bar. David Marks glanced at the two men, one Portuguese, and one English. They both looked like the kind of men that could inflict pain if their requests were not met in full. The net began to close.

Jardigo took a good few minutes to bring David his drink; he seemed locked in deep conversation with the cockney barman. When he did return, he was quick to seek a response to his unusual proposal.

"Now, my new friend, what do you think? Are you going to come on board?"

David took a sip of his drink; he felt lightheaded and under pressure. The deal sounded too good to be true. Was it the several whiskeys that made it so attractive? He still didn't know what it involved. He began to exercise some caution, despite the unveiled threats.

"I can't make a decision until I know what my responsibilities will be. What do you want me to do for you?"

Jardigo began to get a little tetchy.

"Oh, David, I've already said I'd give you a year's salary for doing nothing, so why worry about your duties?"

"I would have thought it was a natural question for me to ask," said David. "How do I know I have the skills you require?"

Jardigo's mood changed back. He became his former urbane and smooth-talking self.

"Believe me, David, you have the ability to the job; I wouldn't have suggested it otherwise."

"But you only met me tonight; you hardly know me. How on earth can you know what I can do?"

"Because of your present occupation, my friend."

"What — banking?"

"Precisely."

"But you don't own a bank, do you?"

"No, but I make money, and your knowledge of the banking system would be invaluable to me, David. You have access to certain information that I could use to my advantage. Indeed, if you did come to work for me, I would want you to continue with your bank for a few weeks in the first instance. Do I need to spell it out?"

The penny began to drop.

"So your operation isn't entirely legal, then?"

"Well, let me put it this way — I often liken what I do to your Robin Hood; I distribute money and assets more fairly by whatever means at my disposal. You would be just one of those means."

David Marks smiled at the analogy. It sounded romantic and a just cause, but it was the last decade of the twentieth century, for goodness sake, and you couldn't do things like that anymore, could you?

"What sort of information do you think I have — or could get?"

"There are many different kinds of things that would be useful; from being able to anticipate changes in market conditions to more specific things like ...."

David held up his hand.

"Let me guess," he said, with a knowing nod. "Things like details of bank accounts and so on; codes, passwords et cetera. Am I close?"

It was Jardigo's turn to hold up a hand as he put a finger to his lips.

"David, David, you make it sound as if I'm involved in outright stealing."

"Well, you are, aren't you, and you want me to help you?"

"All I want is for you to share a little specialist knowledge with me. You are not really stealing."

Here, Jardigo reached for his drink; he seemed to be searching for the right words. He took a large gulp of liquid, cleared his throat, and continued,

"David — some people in our world just have too much money and most of it lies idly doing nothing in bank accounts when it could be put to much better use, for the good of all mankind. In that sense, it is not stealing; it's making that money work for the better good. If, say, a rich man has billions in his bank account, he's hardly going to miss a few million, is he?"

"You make it sound a just cause. What do you do with *your* money? After all, you must have a lot resting 'idly' in your own bank account."

"That is no concern of yours, David; you just have to accept I will eventually put it to good use. In the meantime, you will have to take it on trust that you would be helping me in a worthy cause. Now, I must have an answer. Are you with me or not? Because, if you're not ...."

Jardigo gave a knowing glance at Gordon Donovan behind the bar. David read the intended meaning of the look. He took another sip of his whiskey. The obvious illegal nature of Jardigo's operation didn't really bother him as much as his possible inability to get any information that his new boss would require. On the other hand, what did he have to lose? He didn't really have an exciting life at that moment and Jardigo's proposal definitely sounded exciting.

"Well, David, do you have more questions?"

"No, I have made my decision."

"Which is?"

"I would like to accept your offer; I will come and work for you for at least a year, Jardigo."

The fish had stopped wriggling; the net was closed tight and it would swim no more in its own river. Jardigo reached across the small glass and metal table, grabbing David's hand in genuine delight.

"Oh, congratulations, my new friend, and welcome aboard!"

Jardigo turned to George Donovan.

"George, your finest champagne, if you please!"

34

3
Introductions

The black Mercedes wound its way through Lisbon's backstreets with Jardigo's new employee slumped in the rear seat, drifting in and out of sleep. He and Jardigo had consumed more than a bottle of Dom Perignon after David's acceptance of his host's strange offer. Although Jardigo had, on the face of it, drunk an equal quantity of champagne and other cocktails, David Marks was unaware that the so-called 'Bombshells' were nothing more than fruit juice with suitable spices added to give the appearance and aroma of strong alcohol. He had also failed to notice that his host's one glass of champagne had lasted him as long as the six or seven that he himself had drunk. Oh yes, Jardigo was sober; a fact that his driver had been fully aware of when he arrived with the big S550 limousine. It was one of five expensive cars that Jardigo owned, and though he rarely drove it himself, he did like to be seen in it when it was driven by his chauffer, Leon, a former getaway driver for a rival protection operation in the city. Leon Carvalho was also one of his most trusted employees; in a small group of four under the command of his deputy, Rafael. For his part, Rafael did not return to the Castelo no Monte that night; a welcoming bed of a wealthy middle-aged woman from Chicago had proved too much to resist, another fact that Leon had soon become aware of after picking Jardigo and David up just after three in the morning. He had been quick to joke about it with his boss.

"Rafael up to his old tricks again, boss?"

"I suspect so," replied Jardigo. "I spotted him with a platinum blonde as we went upstairs for a drink. He seemed to be heading for her suite — she looked expensive, too."

"Ah, he will not have to pay for her services, eh?"

"As usual, Leon, he will find a way of relieving *her* of some money for *his* services. No doubt, he will make his own way back to the castle in the morning."

"Yes, if he can stagger to a taxi, eh? said Leon.

The two men laughed as the Mercedes began to quicken; they had reached the inner ring road that would lead them to the highway for Vila Montemor.

"Our English friend seems to have dropped off to sleep, boss," said Leon, as he glanced in the rear-view mirror. "What plans do you have for this one?"

"Now, you know better than to ask that, Leon Carvalho. Only Rafael is aware of how he can help us."

"So he is definitely hired, then?"

"Oh yes, Leon, he's one of us now."

"Did you have to do much persuading?"

"No, he was an easy catch. Has Mariana prepared a room?"

"Yes, boss, he can have the one next to me."

"Good; it is at least as good as any at the Hilton International where he was staying."

"Didn't he want to go back and collect his things?"

"He didn't seem bothered. As you can see, he is out of it at the moment. I will send someone to collect his belongings later today before any suspicions are raised. He has given me his room key and we will settle his bill for him in cash at our expense. If anyone from England tries to investigate where he has gone to over the next few days, while he is initially still here in Portugal, there'll be nothing to trace him to us. He will have just disappeared off the face of the earth. Apparently, he has just gone through a divorce and so maybe people will just think he needs more time to recover and get himself together. In any case, I am soon going to send him back to England to gather certain information for us, so nobody will eventually be any the wiser as to his new job with us."

"Wha', where am I?"

David Marks had stirred. The Mercedes had reached the highway out of the city.

"Speak in English; I can't unnerstan' wha' you're saying, chaps."

"Our friend is awake, Leon," said Jardigo, still in his native tongue. "I'd better reassure him. You concentrate on getting us home safely."

"Yes, boss; I will not be able to contribute."

Jardigo turned on a map-reading light above him and turned to look at their passenger.

"How do you feel, my friend?"

"Like death warmed up; too much to drin', I suppose. I'll be fine af'er a few hours sleep."

"Good — no regrets?"

"No, none."

"Excellent — everything is sorted; you will have several days to find out about our operations and your private room awaits you at my castle. Now you can relax and go back to sleep; we'll be there in under the hour."

"Castle? Now you're talkin' — a cas'le, eh?"

And with that slurred remark, David Marks returned to his dream of wealth and glory with visions of knights and damsels in distress. He was a happy man.

David Marks slept like a baby until the sun was almost at its zenith, despite Jardigo checking on his protégé several times from nine the following morning. His new boss seemed to need the minimum of sleep, having only retired four hours earlier. Finally, on his fourth visit, the slumbering Englishman showed some signs of stirring. Jardigo stood beside David's bed and said, gently,

"Come on, David, it is a beautiful Sunday morning and we are serving lunch outside on the back veranda."

The young Englishman opened his eyes and immediately wished he hadn't as bright rays of sunlight stabbed them like darts. He groaned his objection.

"Oh, my head; I need some water."

"There is a jug beside your bed, my friend. I will leave you to come round. Take a nice cold shower; your private bathroom is right next door, and when you are feeling better, come and join us. Just go along the corridor till you reach the main stairs and turn left when you reach the bottom. You'll hear us from there."

David grumbled his acknowledgement and sat up to rub his eyes. With an unsteady hand, he poured himself a glass of water and took a sloppy gulp, spilling a good deal of it over himself. A few seconds later, he began to regret his haste in taking a drink of the ice-cold fluid, as his stomach began to heave. Jardigo pointed to the bathroom door and said,

"I will leave you now. Join us when you are refreshed. There is a change of clothes in the wardrobe; there should be something in there in your size."

The shower did a lot to restore David to a semblance of normality. He had been determined to make it a cold one and the shock seemed to revive him almost as much as the water itself. Within half an hour, he was ready to make for the veranda. Whether or not he was prepared for any sustenance would be a decision he would take when he got there. Right then, he wasn't altogether sure that he needed fresh air and bright sunshine. Apart from his clothes of the night before, together with essentials like his watch, wallet and passport, he had suddenly realized that all his other clothes and possessions were still back at the Hilton International in Lisbon. God alone knew how he was going to get them back. As he prepared to leave his room, he also suddenly realized for the first time that he had absolutely no idea where he was in relation to the Portuguese capital.

Dressed casually in a pale blue cotton shirt and light brown slacks, he headed for the stairs indicated by his host, marvelling, as he did so, at the opulent and expensive furnishings. The corridor was lined with all kinds of works of art, from some paintings that looked like genuine old masters to a curious mix of modern ones, some of whose style he thought he recognised as being by relatively famous artists. The paintings seemed to be hung in a completely haphazard fashion, with no apparent feeling for good taste. In short, the corridor was nothing more than a vulgar display of the trappings of wealth and would have made an art connoisseur cringe at the horrible juxtaposition of colour, shape and form. It was a hideous exhibition of incredibly bad taste. One thing was sure, however — Jardigo Batista was a very wealthy man.

Apart from Jardigo, there were only two other people on view when David eventually got to the rear veranda. To his great relief, it was in deep shade, and with a pleasant breeze blowing, it at least felt bearable after the previous night's excesses.

"Ah, our guest has surfaced!" said Jardigo, loudly. "Come and let me introduce you, David."

David smiled at Jardigo's companions; one tall and muscular with a heavy black moustache and one short and squat with a balding head, surmounted by an expensive looking pair of sunglasses. Both had got to their feet immediately on David's arrival. Jardigo turned to the two men and said, in Portuguese,

"Rafael, Eduardo, this is David Marks who has joined us today."

The two men nodded politely at their new guest. Jardigo ushered David to a seat and reverted to his perfect English.

"David, this is Rafael Cabral and Eduardo Rivaldo. Rafael is my deputy and Eduardo is his assistant. We will talk in English now, boys. Please sit down, David."

Rafael and Eduardo remained standing until David had taken up Jardigo's invitation.

"Thank you," said David. "I have no Portuguese, I'm afraid; just a smattering of Spanish."

"No problem, my friend; Rafael speaks a little and Eduardo is learning. Now please help yourself to cheese and croissants. There is also some nice refreshing juice and some hot coffee."

The thought of food made David's stomach churn again, and he reached for the jug of fruit juice.

"Just fruit juice and black coffee will be fine, thank you, Jardigo."

Though not fully alert, David still could not help but notice that both Jardigo's senior employees had not taken their eyes of him since he had sat down. While understandable, it, nevertheless, made him feel distinctly uncomfortable. It was like he was being sized up for a prize fight or something similar.

"Now, David, did you sleep well?" asked Jardigo.

"As well as could be expected after last night."

"Good — Rafael here overindulged last night, too, didn't you Rafa?"

"Pardon, boss."

"I said you did a few naughty things last night, eh?"

Rafael's head dropped in embarrassment.

"Yes, boss."

Eduardo grinned from ear to ear. His English was just good enough to understand Jardigo's jibe at Rafaels's misdemeanours. David began to relax; his new employees seemed friendly enough.

"Well, it's certainly a beautiful day," said Jardigo to no one in particular, as David noticed that his two henchmen had finally taken their eyes of him and were enjoying a private joke between themselves. Jardigo looked sternly in their direction.

"Rafa, Eduardo, I think you have some matters to attend to, don't you?"

Jardigo's intention was obvious — he wanted to talk to his new recruit on his own. His aides needed no further instructions and they quickly got to their feet, almost military style. Their subordination to their boss would have been all the more complete if they had saluted him as well. They disappeared inside the castle without a word.

By this time, David had managed two large tumblers of juice as well as a small coffee and his natural colour had started to return. Jardigo looked somewhat relieved at his recovery.

"Right, my friend, I think a nice walk in the grounds is called for. I have some things to discuss with you and I can show you the estate as well. Come, let us go."

David followed his host off the veranda and onto the sloping lawns that stretched a few hundred yards down the hillside towards a small lake in the distance. He was anxious to ask about his clothes and other possessions back at the Hilton International in Lisbon. Jardigo seemed to have read his mind.

"You have no need to worry about your stuff back at the hotel, David; I have sent Rafael and Eduardo to settle your bill and collect everything. Big hotels like that take no notice if a bill is paid by someone else. Your key is their authority."

"Oh, good," replied David. "It would be nice to have my own clothes, at least."

The gradient of the hillside was quite steep and David had to be careful of his step; his recovery was still only partial and out of the shade, his head began to throb a little again. The day was hot and the breeze seemed to have dropped.

"We can take shelter from the sun in the summer house by the lake, David," said Jardigo, as David paused for breath and to wipe the sweat from his forehead. "It will be cool in there."

The walk took longer than David had imagined and by the time the two men reached the haven of the stone-built summer house, they were both ready for some liquid replenishment, courtesy of a fridge stocked with water and other drinks. The summer house had both light and power and Jardigo's description of the building didn't really do it justice. The interior measured at least thirty feet by twelve and was open on the side facing the lake. With a purpose-built bar and gas barbeque, it was obviously used for serious entertaining and enjoyment. Beach chairs and loungers lay scattered across the floor and its white stone exterior provided a coolness even more equable than the veranda they had just left. Jardigo went behind the bar and brought back two cold bottles of beer. At first, David made as to refuse, preferring to drink water instead, but he could tell from his new employer's face that it would be churlish not to join him and he took the bottle of *San Miguel* with relative enthusiasm, given the circumstances. The two men sat side by side in two loungers and Jardigo began to talk.

"After a few days, David, I want you to return to England. When are you expected back?"

The thought of going back to London caught David a little off guard and brought him back to the harsh reality of his situation. In his mind, he had already burnt his bridges, so to speak.

"Oh?"

"Yes, David, your job starts there. Now when are you expected?"

"Anytime, really. I told them to expect me some time next week, but why do I need to go back, Jardigo?"

"I'm coming to that, my friend. I will get Eduardo to arrange your flight for Wednesday."

Jardigo finished his bottle of beer and tossed it idly into the lake, no doubt joining several hundred others.

"You see, David, I need you to provide us with specialised information from your bank and contacts throughout Europe — the London Provincial, isn't it?"

"Yes, but how did ...?"

"How did I know who you worked for? Simple — I did some investigating while you were asleep through some friends I have in the banking system. Apparently, you are quite well known in certain circles."

Jardigo eased himself out of his lounger and went to the bar to get another beer. He continued talking.

"So you see, David, I know what you can do for me and we must not raise any suspicions just yet. You need to go back as normal, or as normal as can be expected after your divorce. Indeed, it may be an ideal time for extracting and processing the information I need since the pressure will be off you as your superiors allow you to ease back into your job. Am I right?"

"Possibly," replied David, thoughtfully. "I'm not completely clear as to what kind of information you can use."

"Ah, well, let me see."

Jardigo paused and smiled.

"It's simple, really — I want you to do some money transfers for me."

"Money transfers?"

"Yes, David, money transfers. You have access to accounts which have large sums of money resting in them; accounts which are rarely touched or even checked by their owners; accounts where no one would notice money missing for a long time. In short, I want you to fleece those accounts and skim them, depositing the froth, as I would call it, into bank accounts I shall designate for the purpose — accounts that are untraceable to the authorities; offshore and the like. The money will just disappear and I'm sure you have enough knowledge of computers to perform such tasks without generating any suspicion until it is too late. Do you understand your role now, David?"

"Oh, yes, Jardigo, I understand fully. You want me to rob people."

"Not rob, David, just redistribute; it's much nicer word, I think."

David Marks smiled; he understood and, surprisingly, he didn't feel as guilty as he might have done. Jardigo made the operation sound almost like they were doing society a favour! However, he thought, he might need some technical help in such a 'fleecing'.

"Alright, redistribute, then."

"Well," replied Jardigo, sternly. "That's what you have to do for me if you are to clear your debt, my friend."

"No problem, Jardigo; I'll have a go."

"Good — your first problem, as I see it, is to identify those accounts which are suitable for the purpose, given what I said earlier."

"That can be done, Jardigo; I already have one or two in mind."

"Splendid — just so long as the account owners will not miss any substantial sums, perhaps for a while, eh?"

"Oh, they shouldn't miss a thing, immediately, Jardigo. They have too much money for their needs anyway, especially the ones who never use their fortunes to contribute anything to society."

"Excellent! Now you're talking my language. I feel you're already a part of my band of merry men. Now have another beer and let's enjoy ourselves, David."

It was to be late afternoon before the two men left the summer house for the stiff climb back up the lawned slopes to the castle. Fortunately for David, the fridge was stocked with nothing stronger than beer and though he drank a good number of bottles, he was reasonably sober by the time he returned to the veranda. They had spent the hours by the lake getting to know each other, and despite coming from opposite sides of the tracks, they had found that they had much in common, from a love of horse racing to tastes in music and literature. David had risen out of a life of poverty as the youngest of five children in the backstreets of South London where his parents had survived as market traders, dealing on both sides of the law. Jardigo had had a head start to success, his family having been wealthy landowners in and around Vila Montemor for several generations. Unlike David, he was an only child who had inherited the Castelo no Monte when his parents had been tragically killed in a car crash in the mountains over ten years previously. Other than a couple of female cousins who now lived in America, he had no close family. However, it was rumoured in the locality that he could claim to be the father of several children by different women — women who now seemed to enjoy an affluence beyond their apparent means, courtesy, it was said, of Jardigo's desire to keep such affairs quiet.

Despite their different backgrounds, the two men had begun to form a bond that afternoon; a bond formed out of similar aspirations, whether it was a love of making money or their inherent hate of waste and the inefficient use of that money. On the surface, David Marks and Jardigo Batista came from different cultures and classes, but there was no doubt that they had found a soulmate in each other and were both looking forward to furthering a common cause — making as much money as possible. Time would tell if their second mutual aspiration would be fulfilled for both of them. It would be a long time before David Marks would really be aware of his new friend's driving ambition for the use of his money. From his own point of view, his immediate and sole motivation was to clear his debts both to Jardigo and to his several creditors back in England.

Dinner that evening gave David much more of an insight into the workings of the Castelo no Monte. It was soon apparent that Jardigo ruled the castle with a rod of iron and was a stickler for discipline and corporate identity. No less than twenty-seven people sat down for the lavish meal in the long dining room on the ground floor at the front of the castle which faced the long drive from the main road below in the valley. Everyone one of them had stood up when David was given a formal welcome and introduction, with one or two even applauding warmly. Jardigo's 'family' was indeed a motley bunch, but it was abundantly clear that they were as much a natural family of likeminded individuals as if they shared common blood. They shared common ideals and those ideals provided them each with their individual responsibilities, each family member knowing their place and the importance of their roles in the smooth running of the whole operation of the castle. By the time David eventually retired to his room just before midnight for some much needed sleep, the realisation had begun to dawn on him that most of the castle's family had already come to regard his place and role at the castle as being close to the top of its hierarchy; some even commented among themselves that Rafael had better look to his laurels as Jardigo's deputy. Whatever had been said to them earlier, David Marks was already a respected and revered member of the castle's staff.

4

A Racing Reminder

L isbon airport was very busy when David Marks arrived for his two-fifteen flight on the Wednesday afternoon. Fortunately, because he was carrying only hand luggage, his check-in for British Airways flight L207 was quick and smooth. He had enough clothes back at his flat in Esher for what he surmised would only be a brief stay in England, and his flight bag and laptop were all he needed until he got back there.

The previous three days had been tied up with getting to know the workings of the castle and one or two of its more lucrative projects; petty pilfering and 'street cleaning' were not to number amongst his responsibilities. Indeed, he had spent most of the previous day in Jardigo and Rafael's company while they visited several prominent businesses in the city to collect certain moneys that seemed to be due on a regular basis. In one case, the money, in cash, was handed over under the seemingly disinterested gaze of a senior Lisbon policeman. In addition, David had met nearly all the remaining staff and most, if not all, seemed to show him immediate respect. Since his new role was unique among those other staff, he had spent nearly all of his time with Jardigo and Rafael and, to a lesser extent, Eduardo, who seemed to be in charge of the technical aspects of the day-to-day running of the castle. His role seemed to be very much akin to that of a traditional estate manager of a large country house in Britain, as well as providing support to Rafael when certain organisational tasks needed to be sorted out quickly. Jardigo's driver, Leon, and Eduardo had escorted David to the airport earlier that Wednesday morning. Before Jardigo had said goodbye at the castle to his new employee, he had thrust a wad of notes into David's hand and said, '*It's just your expenses till you get home, and you also ought to check your bank account when you get there.*' Later, when David counted the notes, he found over £1000 in mixed currency of Euros and Sterling.

In his excitement, the second piece of Jardigo's parting sentence had hardly registered in his mind.

After check-in, and with over an hour to kill, David took the opportunity to sample the luxury of BA's Business Class lounge to await the call for his flight departure. With its private bar and member's club, it was a haven for tired businessmen on trips to and from the Portuguese capital and Jardigo had instructed Eduardo to purchase a first class ticket for his return to England. He made straight for the bar where he ordered a double Jamesons and then he retired to a quiet corner of the lounge. Apart from a couple of young men in grey suits sitting at the bar, the lounge was empty of any other passengers. He quickly opened up his laptop — he was anxious to check his bank account after he had suddenly recalled Jardigo's slightly cryptic comment to him as he had been leaving the castle. As far as he could recall, he had been less than a hundred pounds in credit when he had left England ten days previously. With fingers that were trembling a little, it took him three goes to logon successfully with the correct passwords. When the relevant window eventually opened, he had to refocus his eyes carefully to take in what he saw. He actually spoke the words out loud, as though trying to convince himself of their veracity.

"Bloody hell! There's over fifty grand in the account."

And then he remembered Jardigo's words at the casino:

'*I'll even give you a year of your present salary upfront ....*'

David smiled; the man had been true to his word, but how on earth had he done it? He hadn't furnished Jardigo with his bank details; that was going to come later when he returned to Portugal along with the other banking information. His wallet containing his bank cards had never been out of his sight at the castle — he'd always carried it in his back pocket except when asleep, when it would have been on his bedside table and no one had been in his room when he'd been asleep — or had they? Of course, he thought, Jardigo himself had woken him up that first morning and he'd even said he'd been in

48

several times before to see if he was awake. That was how he'd done it — he'd opened his wallet and copied down his bank details, making the transfer subsequently via his local bank or even over the internet. However it had been done didn't really matter to David Marks at that particular moment in time, because, more importantly, it meant that he could clear all his other debts and still have well over half of the money left. He quickly logged out of his account and closed his laptop. He was a very happy man as he walked to the bar to order another whiskey. He nodded pleasantly at the two well-dressed young men at the bar but felt quite insulted when both of them stared right through him with disdainful expressions on their faces. They carried on their private conversation and David could not help but sense, dressed casually as he was, that they had assumed he was just another tourist and clearly not their equal. With a small whiskey in hand, he returned to the anonymity of his quiet corner. The snub had been a new experience for him and for almost the first time in his life, he no longer felt a part of the class-orientated society that he and thousands of others like him had enjoyed since it had developed under Margaret Thatcher, twenty years previously. Indeed, he began thinking that his new association with Jardigo Batista had already changed his outlook on his previous life; a life where personal gain, promoted by greed, was all important. His new friend's vision of a more 'equal distribution of wealth' appealed to him even more as he sipped on his drink. Robbing the very rich, or the parasites that climbed on their backs, was a mission that he wanted to be a part of, despite having no knowledge of his boss's intentions with his increasing wealth. For himself, he wanted to contribute to Jardigo's 'Robin Hood' operation in the truest sense of the old-fashioned ideal.

Flight L207 was on time and landed at Heathrow at five past five. David was immediately thankful for the weather in London, being at least twenty degrees cooler that when he had left Portugal. Within forty minutes, he had collected his

Jaguar from the parking lot and was heading for the M4/M25 interchange. For no apparent reason, other than for the pleasure of driving the big coupe with the top down, he swung the Jag off the M25 and took the M3 south. It was still rush hour, with London's orbital motorway slow-moving, and he wanted to avoid being stuck in traffic further up. Taking the motorway south for a few miles and then cutting across to the A3 was a much longer way to get to his flat in Esher, but it would be less frustrating and Glendower Mansions was only a few hundred yards from the end of the dual carriageway. It was a perfect English summer evening and he had cash in his pocket; several hundred pounds after exchanging all the remaining Euros. A thought suddenly entered David Marks' head — it was perfect weather for an evening at the races. David glanced at the dashboard clock: 18.28. His train of thought developed further. Was there an evening meeting at Ascot? He was coming up to the M25/M3 interchange, where he could take the B389 that went through Virginia Water and on to Ascot, a few miles further on. He knew the route like the back of his hand and he could be at the course in ten minutes; in time, no doubt, for four or even five races, with racing light lasting well beyond nine o'clock. He patted his trouser pocket and slowed for the exit. Once again, he had money to lose. After all, he would have over thirty thousand pounds left in his bank account even after all his other debts had been paid. What a great way to finish off his holiday, he thought!

David's luck was in when he discovered that the famous Berkshire course was indeed staging one of their summer evening meetings. It was clearly a minor one at that, judging by the ease with which he was able to find a parking space in the closest section to the member's entrance. A bowler-hatted steward nodded amiably and held a door open as he made his way through the Queen's Stand and out onto the green lawns adjacent to the track; David was well known at one of his favourite courses. It was five to seven and there were five minutes to the third race of a seven race card. He headed for the bookmakers by the rails, glancing at his Timeform racecard as he did so. The seven o'clock race was a one mile four furlong handicap and the betting seemed to be wide open with the favourite at 9/2.

"Let's have your bets, please! It's 6/1 bar one."

Reg Smith called out the odds in his cockney twang.

"Yes, sir?"

"Two ponies each-way on number six, please."

"Yes, sir; thank you sir. That's a ton, sir."

David handed over five twenty-pound notes and took his ticket. He turned away and crossed the lawn to return to the Queen's Stand where he took an isolated aisle seat near the top. It was a poor meeting with very few class animals running and prize money of only a few thousand per race. By listening to a few conversations near the bookies stands, he had gleaned that, in addition to some important World Cup games that evening, Epsom were also staging one of their premier evening meetings with an Abba tribute band playing into the night after racing. The anonymity of a moderately deserted Ascot suited David, especially given the fact that several of his bank colleagues could well be at Epsom — he had encouraged and nurtured a passion for the sport of kings in at least four of his close friends and he was not yet ready to face any of them after the previous ten days. He would have found it difficult to answer questions like: *'Well, what have you been up to, David?'* and *'How was Portugal? Visit any casinos?'*

The race commentator droned on.

"Still four out of line."

David studied the runners in his racecard. His decision to back *Casino Royale* had been an easy one. Apart from the name's timely reminder of his meeting with Jardigo Batista, he had also used his favourite method of selection for handicaps of more than twelve runners — there were fourteen. It was a simple rule: Back a horse each-way when the favourite was at least 4/1 and choose one exactly half-way down the betting, and if it was also about half-way down the weights as well, so much the better — a kind of anonymous selection, hidden in the middle of the field, where the price would be good and the horse would have a reasonably light weight to carry. *Casino Royale* was 16/1 and had 8 stone 5 on its back. The favourite, *Blue Horizon*, was top weight and had been backed down to 4/1. It was going to have to lug 9 stone 12 around the track, whose going was officially good to soft after recent rain in the London area. A stone and a half difference might well prove too much for the 4/1 chance.

"One to go."

David looked up from his racecard.

"Stand by."

He glanced to his left at the mile and a half start. They were all in the starting gates.

"Orders, and off!"

It was an even break as the fourteen runners made their way away from the enclosures and onto the side of the course to David's left. He checked his horse's colours — yellow and green cross-halves and a white cap. Jockey Darren Morton had the three-year-old filly in mid-pack, on the heels of the leaders.

"Old Man River leads by the best part of a length; Fleur is second and The Charmer third. The favourite is well back and Call It A Day is almost doing just that — the old-timer is already trailing the tails."

A derisory cheer went up from the small crowd in the public enclosure — *Call It A Day* had gone off at 100/1. David Marks raised a smile.

"Into the back straight and Fleur moves up to eyeball The Charmer; Blue Horizon has made giant strides and now goes easily in third; Dancing Mystique is on the outside of Belle Epoch in fourth and fifth and the jockey is already getting to work on Pulgatha who is slipping back through the field. They're well

strung out now and in Indian file. Approaching Swinley Bottom and the favourite joins Fleur and The Charmer, three-abreast across the track."

David shaded his eyes to try and pick up *Casino Royale* — she was still down the field in seventh or eighth. Suddenly, the commentator gave him some encouragement.

"Climbing out of Swinley Bottom and the one that's going the best in behind the leaders is this Casino Royale from the in-form David Bartlett stable. Upfront, the favourite takes over with under five furlongs to run. Gavin Prentice is going to try and make Blue Horizon's stamina tell. He's going for home from a long way out, though."

Casino Royale was now a clear fourth and David's heart began to beat faster as the familiar adrenaline pumped through his veins. He needed third for a well-earned profit.

"He's all out on this favourite to maintain his advantage but The Charmer is not going to go down lightly. Fleur is beating a retreat as Casino Royale closes. You can forget the rest. Call It A Day has called it a day."

Another derisory cheer as David began muttering his instructions to Darren Morton.

"Keep pushing Dazza; ease her into it. Don't go too soon, mate."

"They're turning in; less than three furlongs to go and it's a war of attrition upfront between Blue Horizon and The Charmer with Casino Royale hunting the pair up. From the back, Montelabria has got a second wind and is now only four lengths off Casino Royale."

"You've got 'em, Dazza!"

David was shouting now.

"Inside the two, and The Charmer has got the favourite in trouble; two lengths back to Casino Royale with this Montelabria, fresh from last week's triumph at Windsor, still closing behind."

"Let her go, Dazza!"

"A furlong to go, and Casino Royale joins The Charmer to fight it out. Blue Horizon is now well beaten in third and Montelabria's effort has petered out in fourth. It's a dozen lengths back to the fifth, who is a staying-on Caldiceron."

David was on his feet now, punching the air as he urged his horse on.

"Less than fifty yards and Casino Royale is getting there with every stride. They hit the line together. It's on the nod; I can't separate them. It'll be down to the judge. Blue Horizon is third and Montelabria will be fourth."

David Marks clenched his fist in triumph; he just knew his horse had made it.

"Photograph! Photograph!"

The grandstand announcer confirmed the commentator's view. David skipped down the concrete steps and onto the lawn, his head carrying out the mental calculations. *Casino Royale* had drifted out to 20/1 at the off, but he had taken 16/1 and the bookie did not give 'best odds guaranteed'. Nevertheless, he still made it £1100 to come back, with ¼ the odds for the place part of the bet. The evening would have begun well if the photograph confirmed what he honestly believed.

"Here is the result of the photograph. First: Number six; second, number ten and third, number one. Officially placed fourth was number twelve."

David headed for bookie Reg Smith. As he queued for his winnings, the announcer gave full confirmation of the result.

"Here is the full result of the London Pride Handicap. First: Casino Royale; second, The Charmer and third, Blue Horizon. The distances were a short head and three lengths. Weighed in. Weighed in."

At first, he didn't notice the man who sat down next to him on the wooden bench on the lawn in front of the Queen's Stand. He was too busy studying the form for the last race — the nine o'clock. The rays of the setting sun had made him narrow his eyes as he looked at his racecard, and it wasn't until the man leant forward that a shadow suddenly appeared on his open page, causing him to look to his side.

"Have you had a good evening, mate?"

The accent had a faint American twang. David shaded his eyes and looked into the stranger's face. It seemed familiar.

"Not bad. I was well up after the first race but have lost a bit since then."

"Got any tips for this one?"

"The favourite's got a good chance, but at 4/6 it's not really worth a punt," replied David, still trying to work out where he knew his questioner from. He studied the man's face more carefully.

"Have we met?"

"Not officially, David."

"How ...?"

David Marks sat bolt upright and his racecard slipped off his lap to the ground. The man bent down and picked it up.

"Don't be alarmed, David; I'm your friend."

"My friend? Who the hell *are* you?"

"Allow me to introduce myself; I am Henry Madison, originally from Chicago but currently residing in Portugal."

The man placed a hand on David's left wrist and winked. He could feel the hairs on the back of his neck stand up.

"Oh," said David. "You mean you ...."

"Yes, my friend, I work for Jardigo Batista."

"But I don't understand — how did you know I'd be here? I only made the decision to come here a couple of hours ago. To all intents and purposes I was going home."

"Esher?"

"Yes, but ...."

"Jardigo knows a lot about you, David Marks, including where you live; your shoe size and so on."

"So have you been following me, then?"

"Of course, my friend. Did you seriously think that our boss would allow you out of his sight without some kind of chaperone? I was on your flight from Lisbon."

So that's where he'd seen him, thought David. He hadn't seen him at the castle, though. He said nothing as Henry Madison continued.

"When we landed, I followed you to your car; I even held the bus door open for you on arrival at the parking lot."

"But how did you manage to follow me then? Did you have a car waiting?"

"No, not to begin with, but we have other ways of knowing where you were going, David."

"What other ways — I drove quickly from Heathrow."

"Tracking device on your car."

"Oh yeah, how?"

"One of Jardigo's London operatives fitted it this morning. Jardigo can get any information he wants for the right money. All airports have a record of passengers who leave their cars while abroad and car parks can be bribed for that information; your car is very distinctive, isn't it?

"But why do I need an escort. I'm a big boy now. I can look after myself."

"It's for your own good."

Really? In what sense?"

"Has it not occurred to you that you have a lot of Jardigo's money in your possession? You have already been well paid for your services, which you have yet to carry out. What is to stop you just disappearing and never coming back to

Portugal? My presence here is to ensure that that idea never enters your head as a serious possibility. Jardigo Batista's net spreads wide throughout the world."

"I see," said David. "And will you be escorting me all the time I am in England?"

"There are others, David. My initial job was to see you safely back to number 14A Glendower Mansions, Esher. After that, you will have a couple of other chaperones who live in London and are employed by Jardigo on a sub-contractual basis. I will escort you back to Heathrow when you have completed your tasks. You understand?"

"Yes, completely, but you might like to tell Jardigo, if you are in contact with him before me, that the idea of reneging on my responsibilities had never even entered my head — O.K?"

"Naturally, David. I am due to report your safe arrival late tonight. Jardigo is already aware that you are here at Ascot. Cell phone technology is wonderful, isn't it?"

"Well, you can tell him also that I will have his information by the weekend at the latest. I just need access to the main computers at the London Provincial when I go there tomorrow."

"You do not need to tell me more, David. I am not privy to your precise role within the operation, so the less I know the better. I am just here to see that you come to no harm, whether or not it is self-inflicted."

By this time, the runners for the last race were trotting past the stands; it was less than five minutes to the off and David was anxious to have one last bet.

"Well, Henry, I hope you won't mind if I leave you now."

He stood up and began to walk away but hesitated when Henry Madison called him back.

"Of course not, and remember, David ...."

"Remember what?"

"You and I are on the same side, my friend — alright?"

"Yes, I'm sorry, Henry, if I seem a little put out by your presence here. When I gave Jardigo my word as a gentleman that I would work for him and perform the task he asked me to, I did not expect that commitment to be questioned, that's all — alright?" David mimicked his chaperone.

"No problem, mate. Just remember I'm your friend and you might need that friendship some time soon. I'm here to help."

David smiled and finally walked away from his new 'companion'. The starting stalls were already being loaded and he was still some distance from the rails bookmakers. He broke into a trot, refusing to glance behind him to check if Henry Madison was stuck to him like a limpet. Then he remembered they had a tracking device attached to his car and such a concern was therefore irrelevant.

"Last bets, please!"

Reg Smith's voice boomed out across the lawns. There were two other punters in front of him in the queue.

"Three more to load!"

The announcer's voice echoed in the back ground.

"Come on, mate," shouted David. There was just one person in front of him.

"One to go!"

The punter put his £20 bet on and moved away, annoyed at David's impatience

"A monkey on number three, please, Reg."

"£500 to win on three, Bert," repeated the bookmaker. "And the best of luck, sir."

David took his ticket.

"All in — stand by."

David relaxed and headed for his seat in the Queen's Stand.

"Orders, and they're off!"

David checked his racecard; he'd got the number correct. It just had to be number three — *Warning Shot* was such a fitting name after his 'chat' with Henry Madison. Strangely, as he watched the seven horses sort themselves out over the first few furlongs of the two-mile handicap, and despite his earlier misgivings, David Marks felt comforted by his new employer's concern for his welfare. Any worries, that he was being watched as if he were a schoolboy, began to recede from his mind. He was going to enjoy the last race with £500 riding on the fourth favourite at the generous odds of 9/1. And enjoy it he did as, in a little over three minutes, the commentator finally called,

"*It's all too easy for Warning Shot; he's going to win with his head in his chest — Darren Morton is easing him right down to a canter. He's some horse, defying that weight in this ground.*"

David Marks got up from his seat, grinning from ear to ear. Henry Madison's warning had proved very beneficial to him; *Warning Shot* would have been one of the last horses he would have backed. He strolled triumphantly to Reg Smith to collect his £5000 in cash. The day was just getting better and better. He had quite forgotten that he was still under careful supervision and that, in some sense, he was no longer his own man; he was now owned by Jardigo Batista.

David Marks got home rather late that night — after a visit to the *Mulberry Bush*, just a stone's throw from Glendower Mansions, from whose car park he would collect his car some time the following day. He failed to notice the small middle-aged man who drank slowly at the bar, occasionally glancing in his direction until he left at eleven-thirty. In his slightly intoxicated state, David also failed to hear the footsteps that echoed behind him on his way home via the late night takeaway across from his flat.

He slept like a baby that night, totally unaware that any phone calls that he might make from his flat were being recorded for his Portuguese host's interpretation. Jardigo already knew a bit about David's ex-wife, with whom, at her instigation, her husband had had a brief conversation just before midnight; an event that often took place at odd and random times, despite their divorce having been rather less than amicable. Often, she would just phone to gloat over something or other when she had imbibed one too many gin and tonics and she wanted to rant and rave at him. Secretly, David suspected that she still loved him, and her rants said more about that than any outright and continuing hatred of him. He invariably ended up putting the phone down on her, especially when she became quite nasty; nastier even than when they had been together, and that was saying something. He just wished she would leave him alone. Still, he thought to himself that night, she would not be able to contact him for some time after the weekend and that could only be a good thing. How long he would be out of England would depend on how the next few days would pan out. Whatever happened, it was going to be an exciting period in his life and the risk-taking side of his nature was going to be exercised to the full.

5

The London Provincial Bank

The international headquarters of the London Provincial Bank was located at Canary Wharf and occupied the top two floors of the skyscraper that was Canada House where David Marks' office possessed fine views over Cabot Square and the Thames. He rarely used the Jaguar to make the daily journey to East London; it was much quicker and more efficient to take the train to Waterloo and the Jubilee Line tube direct to Canary Wharf. On a good day, and with the right connections, he could be in his office less than forty minutes after leaving his ground floor flat in Esher, which was conveniently situated only a quarter of a mile from Esher's mainline station and adjacent to Sandown Park. This last fact furnished David with the regular opportunity to attend several evening race meetings there, often directly after a hard day's work at the office, without the need for him to go home first. One or two work colleagues often accompanied him, Matt Sampson being particularly keen on trying his luck. Matt was thirty-four — five years younger than David and also single. He and David had been good friends ever since they had joined the bank on the same day six years previously. Matt had a much more junior role in the bank, being one of their computer processors and had been hired for his IT skills rather than any financial knowledge. He knew how the bank's information was processed but understood little of its significance. As soon as Jardigo had outlined his assignment to David, it had been Matt he had thought of — he realized that he might need his expertise in securing any confidential information from the computer system.

David was understandably a little late for work the morning following his return from Portugal. In any case, his P.A. seemed surprised to see him at all that day — he had telephoned her the previous Sunday to say he was extending his holiday by at least a week and that she should expect him when she saw him.

As soon as he entered his office which he shared with another fund manager, a red-headed Irishman called Gerry O'Dowd, she came strutting down the corridor from her room adjacent to his.

"Oh, Mr Marks, I wasn't expecting you back today."

"No, I know, Jean, but I've got to get back into the old routine as soon as I can. Before you bring me any updates, I would like you to make me a nice strong coffee, please."

"There's nothing much to report, sir; the markets have been quiet and Mr O'Dowd has covered most of your cases. He's on vacation this week and next."

David Marks smiled both at the news of his colleague's absence and at his P.A.'s formality. Jean Needham was the only one he'd come across at the bank who had always insisted on addressing him and Gerry thus. Despite asking her to call him by his first name, she had stubbornly refused to do so. She was definitely old school; a spinster of indeterminate age who had been with the bank when it had still been based in the city. Some people even said she had started before Britain had decimalised, over thirty years previously. Absolute discretion and loyalty were her two strongest and most admired qualities. Many had been the time that she had covered for him with his immediate superiors when he'd taken an afternoon off, and her typing and word-processing skills were legendary; David rarely had to correct any of her documents and she would be distraught if he did. There was an attractiveness about her that David and Gerry both found difficult to describe. It certainly wasn't a sexual attraction — Jean Needham was short, plump and greying. Nevertheless, whether or not it was their need as single men to have a mother figure to look after them, they both adored her.

"Thank you, Jean," replied David eventually. "Now I need that coffee, please."

"Yes, Mr Marks, I'll get it straightaway."

As she turned to go, David suddenly said,

"After that, Jean, will you ask Matt Sampson to come up? I'd like to talk to him."

"Yes, Mr Marks. Shall I tell him what it's about?"

"Just say it's a technical problem with my computer."

"Certainly, sir; I'll get that coffee for you."

After Jean had gone, David eased himself into his black leather chair and turned on his desktop. Things were going well, he thought, particularly with his colleague away for another ten days. He would have the office to himself with no one to observe what he would be doing. He would have to be careful with Matt, though. He sat back in his chair and swivelled it to look at the panoramic view outside. He needed an excuse to ask his friend some questions about passwords and how to login to the 'special' accounts.

Five minutes later, when the ebullient Matthew Sampson strolled into David's office, he had to delay any immediate delicate investigating as his friend seemed more interested in what he'd been doing during his leave. Unlike David's tall, dark and handsome physique and appearance, Matt was of medium build with seventies-style long brown hair tied with a band at the back. A product of a large comprehensive in Birmingham, followed by a minor polytechnic also in England's second city, he had a pronounced Brummie accent. He dropped himself at once into David's swivel chair and spun it with some alacrity to face David who was standing gazing out of the window.

"Well, mate, what have got to tell me?"

"Huh? Oh not much, Matt."

"Oh come on, David, a week in Lisbon and free and single again; I'm all ears. That is why you sent Jean hotfoot to fetch me, isn't it? I bet you had a bostin' time."

"Yeah, not bad. And I did need to see you."

David turned to face his friend; he knew he'd have to give some kind of a report.

"Won a bit at the casino," he lied. "Hotel was full of American tourists so I spent a lot of time in the city's bars and squares just chilling."

"I bet you did a bit more than chillin', eh? All those Portuguese young ladies at your disposal and you're telling me you just played it cool."

"I'm afraid, Matt, that after Gaynor I didn't want any female companionship while I was there.

"Who said anything about companionship? Just some healthy exercise, eh?"

"Well, I didn't indulge, old boy, but I didn't ask you up here just to report on my holiday."

"Oh," said Matt Sampson. "That's sounds a bit formal."

"No, not formal; I just need your help on the IT front."

"Your new Dell playing you up again?"

"No, it's fine, I think. I've only just turned it on."

"So what do you need from me? Skim a few accounts?"

David immediately turned back to look out of the window. He felt a little giddy. His friend's last jibe had caught him off guard.

"You alright, mate?" asked Matt, getting to his feet. "Here, you better have your chair. I bet you overindulged on the alcohol front, eh?"

"Yeah, I expect so." replied David. His composure had returned and he sat down formally in his chair. "I also shouldn't look as long out of my twentieth floor window; it can make me giddy."

David tapped a few buttons on his keyboard and said,

"Right, Matt, let me explain what I need."

"I'm all ears; it sounds important."

David gathered himself.

"Bob Mckellar is worried, Matt."

"Worried? Why should he be worried? He earns twice what you do and all he does is sit in his office all day, when he's in, that is, while you and Gerry do all the real work. He may be a senior executive but he does bugger all."

"I know and that's probably why he has time to worry — too much time on his hands and not enough to do."

"You're not wrong there, mate. So what does the old fart want?"

"Identity fraud," replied David, simply.

"Oh yeah? What, his, or the bank's?"

"The bank's."

"Well you can reassure him from me that our system is one of the most protected available. It's almost impossible to break into it and steal information. Even I would find it difficult."

"I know and that's exactly what I told him, but is it possible?"

"Yeah, it's possible."

Matt Sampson looked puzzled.

"I'm still not sure what he wants you to do, though."

"He wants me to do a dummy run."

"How do you mean?"

"He wants me to test the system out."

Matt's frown deepened.

"How?"

David looked nervously all round his office as though checking to see if anyone else could be eavesdropping on their conversation..

"This must go no further, Matt; you understand?"

"Of course, mate; you can trust me. I see and hear lots of things down in the computing department that I probably shouldn't."

"Good — basically, Mac wants me to see if we can break into the system by ...."

"Go on."

"He'll select some accounts and I will have to see if I can open them up and transfer money into other dummy accounts that he'll set up. If and when I can do it, we'll simply put the money back into the correct account with no one the wiser. If the owners of the accounts check their statements, it will just look like a temporary computer glitch has occurred. Afterwards, he'll no doubt come down to you guys with the evidence of how it was done and ask you to close the loopholes. And you will then be able to tell him precisely how it was done, eh?"

"And I'll probably already have the solution since, as you say, I will know how the virtual fraud was done in the first place," said Matt, with a sly smile beginning to form on his chubby face.

"Exactly. Well, can it be done?"

"And you'll have the account numbers?"

"Yes, of course."

"Well, that's one hurdle out of the way," said Matt. "I'm liking this, mate. It's like something you read in a book. I hope the old woman gives me a hefty bonus when I present my findings to him immediately after the experiment."

"Yeah, but not too soon afterwards; I'd like him to think that I did most of the work, so we both gain, right?"

"Right!" said Matt, with a wink. "I'll scratch your back if you scratch mine."

David Marks nodded. His plan was taking shape. If only he could tell his friend.

"So when will you get the account numbers, Dave?"

"What? Oh some time later today, Mac said. I'll buzz or email you when I've got them; and Matt ...."

"What?"

"Absolutely no one else must know. Mac was insistent that only he and I should be aware of the test. He says he would have done it himself but his IT skills are so bad he just had to involve me. I'm doing you a huge favour by entrusting you with the information. You know how news spreads round these floors. After all, it's only like a practice fire drill, not a real fire. The experiment must be held under controlled conditions; controlled by Mac and me — O.K?"

"Reading you loud and clear, mate. My lips are sealed. I'll be up as soon as you call me."

"Second thoughts, Matt," said David, just as his unwitting conspirator was leaving the room. "I'll email you on your private address, so check your inbox regularly during the day."

"No problem, Mr Bond!"

His friend closed the door slowly behind him, his gentle action seeming to be all part of the secrecy that now existed between them. David Marks turned his chair back to face the panoramic view over London. Jardigo's task had begun and one of his best friends had been sucked into his plan. At the same time, David Marks felt both triumphant and guilty — guilty that, in a few days time, his friend would find that he had been used in probably the biggest scam of the new millennium. And, at that particular moment, it seemed all too easy. He had discovered a new part of his character; one that enjoyed the excitement of working on the edge, manipulating people and situations like one of the very best conmen around.

As his protégé was gazing contentedly out of his window in Canary Wharf a thousand miles away in England, Jardigo Batista was gazing over his rich green lawns and down to the lake in a similarly relaxed mood. He had dwelt long over his breakfast on the rear veranda and, as he pointed out to his deputy, things were going well.

"The reports from England appear good, Rafa."

"He is behaving himself, then?"

"Oh yes; Henry says that his warning to him was probably unnecessary and that he had no thoughts that he could tell of pulling out of his mission."

"Good," said Rafael Cabral. "He'd better not, eh? What else did the yank say?"

"Just that he had stopped off at Ascot racecourse for some evening entertainment; he was successful, apparently, with my money. It seems like he had a better evening than last Saturday."

"When do you expect him to make contact?"

"Oh, maybe by the weekend. We haven't been able to track his movements since he arrived at the bank earlier this morning; we have no one inside his office building or any way of tapping his phone there. We did, however, get some information late last night from the tap at his apartment."

"Oh?" queried Rafael.

"Yes, apparently his ex-wife called him and she was not happy. They argued quite vehemently."

"Do we know much about her?"

"No; just that she's called Gaynor and still lives in the former marital home in a place called St Albans."

"Is that near to our friend?"

"Not too near — about the same distance as from here to Lisbon."

"Could she be a worry to us?"

"I don't know yet. I have someone in England checking on her for us. We don't want David to be put under any unnecessary emotional stress."

"I thought they had just got divorced, though," said Rafael, quizzically.

"They have but beware a woman scorned, my friend. I suspect there is still some fire burning in that one."

"Why did she call him? I thought you told me that the divorce settlement had been agreed reasonably amicably."

"Just to rub salt into his wounds, I guess, but whatever the reason, I don't want an irrational woman interfering with the smooth running of his task."

"Yes, boss."

"Now," said Jardigo, stretching out his body to its full length in his chair. "We have work to do, Rafa, my friend. You and Eduardo need to see Senhor Montelobo about his late payment. I have some phone calls to make and some things to arrange with a Swiss bank or two."

Rafael Cabral nodded perceptively. His boss was laying the ground for the completion of the young Englishman's mission.

The email read simply:

> '*You are required.*
>
> *Mr Bond.*'

Matt Sampson had heard his computer ring out the familiar sound as the message came through just after he had eaten his sandwich lunch. His heart had immediately started to flutter. He had spent a good deal of the morning checking through the bank's files and programs in order to write and rehearse the software he would need — he more or less knew how he would use it. He picked up a small case and headed for the flight of stairs that led to the top floor.

A floor above, David Marks was excited and nervous. He had selected two accounts to pilfer for his dummy run; for that was what it was going to be that afternoon. It wasn't going to be the real thing yet; he hadn't contacted Jardigo and would need the bank accounts that he would provide for the real transfer. He was going to use his own private offshore account that he'd opened years before and which had lain untouched for months with only a minimal balance to keep it in the system. If he was honest, the thought of doing exactly what he and Matt were going to do that afternoon had crossed his mind many times in the past, like many people in similar jobs to his own. Some had even tried it but, to his knowledge, only one had succeeded; a junior bank official in Germany, who had been on the run for the last eighteen months with five million Euros of the bank's assets missing. The two accounts he'd chosen to perform the temporary skim hadn't been touched in over a year, and should

Matt be able to process the transfer, he would just use them for the real switch later that week. Each contained over two hundred million Euros and that should satisfy his boss, surely. He would try to shift just a million that afternoon. Just as he'd finished going through all these details in his mind for the umpteenth time, there was a gentle knock at the door.

"Yep, come in!"

Matt Sampson's cheery face appeared round the door.

"Ah, we meet again, Mr Bond!"

"Come in, Matt, and lock the door, mate."

David's friend turned the key in the lock and strode towards the desk.

"Where's Jean?"

"I've given her the afternoon off and Gerry is not back till next Monday, as you well know."

"And where's Bob?"

"In his office, I presume, but we don't need him."

"O.K., so tell me what you want me to do."

"I have two accounts at our bank from which we will temporarily move a small sum of money to a dummy account which I have opened."

"With the London Provincial?"

"No."

"Who with, then?"

"I'd prefer not to say, Matt. You don't need to know, do you?"

"No. What about the two accounts? Are they current, deposit or bonds?"

"Deposit."

"Right, let's get into your computer."

Matt produced a couple of discs from his leather case and sat down in David's chair. He inserted one into a drive.

"What's that for?" asked David.

"Oh, it's a program that can find the initial customer numbers to access any of our deposit accounts."

"God, Matt, how did you get that?"

"You forget, mate, that one of my first jobs here was involved in setting up a password system for customers. I made a copy of the disc."

"So could you have transferred money before, then?"

"No, not really; you need another piece of software for the entry password and I've only just written that this morning."

"Wow, you have been busy!"

"Right, the first account number, please."

David passed a small piece of paper to his friend who typed it into the computer. He tapped a couple of keys and then said,

"So, we have the customer number; now we insert the other disc and, hey presto, we'll be in."

Matt hurriedly scribbled the twelve-digit number down on his friend's slip of paper. A few nervous seconds passed while the screen went blank.

"What's happening?" asked David, anxiously.

"My program is working; just be patient. It is going through millions of combinations."

Seconds later, the screen brightened to reveal the six-digit entry-pass number. Matt scribbled the second number down beside the first.

"We're in, mate!"

He returned to the original screen and typed in the pass number.

"Right, now you can take over. I don't want to know what you're going to do next, Mr Bond."

They swapped seats and David perused the familiar account screen, identical to the one for his own deposit account with the bank. Matt walked to the window while his friend made the transfer, his fingers trembling as he typed in the seven-figure amount. He pressed the *amount to transfer* key and then his

71

own offshore account number. Finally, he hit *transfer* and the deed was done. He sat back in amazement as he checked the details of his own account. He was, for a few minutes only, a Euro-millionaire!

"Bloody fantastic, Matt!"

"Yeah, now put it back, mate."

David reversed the process and within a couple of minutes the status quo had returned.

"So, could you do it on your own with all the accounts that Mac wants you to test?" asked Matt.

"Yeah, I think so; I just need the two discs, right?"

"Right, Mr Bond."

David was thoughtful for a moment.

"So the system can be broken, then?"

"Yes, it appears so, with the right software, using a routine like the one I wrote this morning."

"So," said David, after a pause. "When Mac comes to you guys to tell you that I breached the system, how will you fix it for him?"

"That's easy, mate — you forget that I wrote the code breaker. I can also write a protection against it, but there could be another problem."

"What?"

"Will Mac really believe that you were able to break into the accounts all by yourself?"

David smiled inwardly at his friend's hypothetical question. Oh, if only he knew what was really going on!

"I'll tell him anything he wants to hear. I'll tell him it was easy and if a mug like me could do it, so could anyone. He'll come running to you in a screaming panic — you could even be on a quick bonus and all for undoing something that you've created. You'll be able to name your own price."

"I'm really liking this now, Mr Bond."

"Good, now while you're still here, let me see if I can fleece the other account. Give me the two discs."

David sat down at his computer and five minutes later, he shouted in glee,

"Done it; Mr Solomon Arthur Meickelberg is quite a few Euros light in his deposit account!"

"He has a wealthy sounding name, Mr Bond. Now put it back."

Quickly, David once again reversed the process and closed both accounts. He beamed in satisfaction. Depending on how much Jardigo wanted him to skim, he could just use the two accounts he had identified or, if not, he would have to find some others on which to apply Matt's discs.

"So, Matt, I'll keep the discs for a couple of days — alright?"

"No problem, Mr Bond, and remember, I know nothing. I just hope that Mac doesn't ask you where you got the discs from."

David Marks smile got broader.

"He won't Matt; believe me. I can absolutely guarantee that he won't."

"Well, on your head be it. He won't be able to trace the discs back to me. I can absolutely guarantee that, too."

After his friend had gone, David took some time to rehearse the transfer process a couple of further times. He had been slightly curious at Matt's parting remark but concluded that he had probably designed the discs to work only on his computer, and if Bob Mckellar used them on another one, they would probably self-destruct. He looked at his watch. It was gone three and he quickly made the decision to finish early; no one would miss him and he still needed to collect his car from the *Mulberry Bush's* car park. He might even see if Epsom, Kempton or Sandown had an evening meeting on; he would leave it till the morning to contact Jardigo with news of his progress. Perhaps his boss would have details of the receiving bank accounts by then and he could finish his mission more quickly than he had anticipated. He had already found himself missing Portugal and his new life at the Castelo no Monte. Jardigo would certainly be pleased that his new employee was ahead of the planned schedule. He had barely made the decision to leave early when his internal phone rang. He hesitated before answering it, hoping that it was only his friend, Matt. He nearly dropped it when Bob Mckellar's Glaswegian accent boomed down the line.

"Davy lad, will you pop up and see me in five minutes, please."

"Oh right, Bob. No problem. What's it ...?"

But the line had already gone dead.

6

Gaynor Marks

David's boss was approaching retirement, though you would hardly guess it to look at him. Married three times, the Scotsman's current spouse was twenty years younger than him and he often said it was Marie who had helped him to keep his youthful looks. He had met Marie at a conference held in his native Glasgow five years previously where she had been working as a temp for a big oil company. After their marriage, Marie had formed a strong friendship with David's wife, with whom she shared many similar interests as well as being of a similar age. Gaynor's naked ambition for David within the bank was probably another reason that she had been keen on a personal association with the boss's wife and one of the things, no doubt, that had contributed to her and David's divorce. Bob Mckellar had encouraged the friendship, thankful that his new wife had someone of her own age to associate with when he was at work. He had even tolerated the expensive shopping trips that the two women frequently made to the West End; another contributory factor to David's spiralling debts.

Bob had a worried look on his face when David entered his boss's executive suite after the peremptory,

"In!"

"You wanted to see me, boss" said David, rather nervously. Had Matt said something to him?

"Yes, laddie — sit yourself down."

David noticed the green personnel file open on Bob's desk in front of him.

"Now, Davy, how are we?"

"Fine, Mac."

"Good, I'm glad you seem to have got through your divorce and feel able to take up the reins again. How was Portugal?"

"Great, boss; just what the doctor ordered."

Bob Mckellar got to his feet and stretched himself to all of his five foot six. Fortunately his slim build disguised his rather short stature and his silver grey hair gave him a distinguished and presidential look that belied his humble beginnings in Glasgow. He approached David and sat casually on the corner of his desk.

"Marie has had Gaynor on the phone several times during the last week or so, laddie."

"Oh?"

"Yes, they seem to be as thick as thieves over your divorce, you know."

"I know, boss."

"Well, Marie says that Gaynor appears to be worried about you."

"Worried? Why?"

"Wanted to know where you were last week as she tried to phone you but there was no reply. Did you not tell her you were going to Portugal?"

David gave a puzzled and slightly exasperated look.

"No, why the hell should I?"

"I agree, laddie, and Marie told her just that, but it didn't seem to make much difference, she said."

David sighed audibly.

"She phoned me last night when I got back; must have been nearly midnight."

"Everything is alright, isn't it? You two haven't made the wrong decision?"

"Well, I know I haven't, boss. I can't speak for Gaynor. She was the one that wanted it."

"Mebbe, she's regretting it now."

"Maybe; I don't know, but it may be something else."

"What?"

"I have a nasty feeling that she's out for some kind of revenge and ...."

Bob Mckellar leant forward and looked into David's eyes. David felt uncomfortable. Why was he being interrogated like this?

"She's just pestering you to annoy you, you mean?"

"Yeah, something like that."

"Marie was adamant that she seemed genuinely concerned about you, Davy. Thought you might be going off the rails and were about to do something stupid — those were more or less her exact words."

"How the hell could she have got that impression?"

"I don't know, laddie. Maybe you should have told her about going to Portugal and perhaps the apparent secrecy of the trip worried her. Perhaps she hasn't yet got used to the idea that she hasn't got you around anymore and can't check on you like she used to. Maybe, also, it's just women's intuition; like twins can know what each other are going to do even before they do it. You know how difficult it can be to fathom how women's minds work sometimes."

"Yeah, I know — or at least I thought I knew."

"Maybe she's jealous."

"Jealous, boss?"

"Yeah, jealous of the fact that you appear to enjoying life and your freedom again. Maybe she had hoped that you would be thoroughly miserable after the divorce; at least for a few months anyway."

"She's got her freedom again as well," said David in an unsympathetic tone.

"True, but as I say, she may not want that freedom. I know Marie is getting a bit fed up with the constant phone calls and requests to go out with her; it's nearly every day now. Maybe you should go and talk to her and put her mind at rest about how you see your future."

"Yeah, maybe I will, Bob."

His boss leant even closer to him and placed a hand on his shoulder.

"And Davy, lad ...."

"What?"

"You're not going to do anything stupid, are you?"

"No, of course not, boss. I'm fine."

"Good, because you're too valuable a member of this bank's staff to lose."

Bob Mckellar stood up and almost nonchalantly, said,

"I'm retiring in a year, Davy; just remember that."

"I will, Bob."

"Good, now take it easy for the next few days. Go home early if you want today, or any other day. No need to tell me, O.K?"

"O.K., and thanks for the warning about Gaynor. I'll check on her sometime."

The uncomfortable meeting was at an end and David took his leave. On his journey home, he thought about his boss's words: '... *do something stupid ...*' and '... *women's intuition*'. It was the first time since making his momentous decision that he'd considered what the aftermath of that decision might be, and how his colleagues and friends would react when they discovered him missing, let alone when one or two of the bank's richest depositors found huge sums of money missing from their accounts, too! He quickly tried to dismiss the uncomfortable thoughts from his mind and, by Waterloo, he had made up his mind to relax that evening — he would pick up his car and go for a drive and even if there was not a convenient race meeting on, he would still find a nice country pub and have a good meal. By the time he had reached the *Mulberry Bush* car park, he'd also convinced himself that he was not going off the rails or doing something stupid either.

Gaynor Marks, née Cavendish, had enjoyed the kind of upbringing that was at the opposite end of the social scale to that of her former husband. The

Cavendish family had been gentlemen farmers in one of the most affluent parts of Hertfordshire for generations, going back to at least the early part of the nineteenth century. Educated at St Albans Ladies College and the London School of Economics, she had initially trained as an actuary in the city but, by the time she was twenty-five, she had returned to the family farm near to Buntingford. Soon, she was to use assets other than those provided by her intelligence and education to provide her with an alternative career. Her natural good looks, fine bone structure and long blond hair had got her noticed on the country circuit within the county where she was able to make an independent living as a high class model favoured by several national magazines devoted to the aristocratic life in the shires. Her father had already bought her a penthouse apartment in St Albans for her twenty-first birthday from which she had commuted for her three-year stay in the city. During that time, she had met and briefly dated David after meeting him by chance at a mutual friend's party. Though it was not really a serious relationship for either of them, they had stayed in touch by email and phone. After not seeing each other for a couple of years, David had spotted her photograph in an Ascot race programme and had re-established contact. This time, the relationship blossomed with David renting out his Esher flat while he moved in with Gaynor in her flat in St Albans. In less than a year, they were married, a perfect looking couple; both tall — one blond and one dark. Soon after the wedding, they had bought an elegant Edwardian detached house in one of St Albans' classiest areas. David had kept his flat for the times when he needed to work late in the city or for travel abroad. That had been June 1992 and the marriage had lasted all but ten years, for the last two of which, Gaynor had become a lady of leisure, only occasionally taking up modelling and photographic assignments. As well as Bob Mckellar's wife, she had many childhood friends in and around St Albans with whom to occupy her days and her mother and father always welcomed her up at Wood Green Farm, a short drive up the A10. With the couple's disparate lives, and hailing from different backgrounds, 'the marriage made in heaven' was inevitably doomed to eventual failure. With David's gambling, too, the end had come quickly, earlier that summer, apparently to their mutual relief.

Having picked up his Jaguar, David returned briefly to Glendower Mansions for a shower and to change from his suit into some casual clothes. To his disappointment, Ceefax had confirmed that the only evening race meeting was at Newmarket. The Suffolk course was just too far and the diversion he needed was thus no longer there. Almost immediately, thoughts of Bob Mckellar's remarks about his ex-wife returned. It didn't take him long to make up his mind to pay her a visit; a visit that might provide the last time that he would see her for a very long time; a visit that he needed to make to confirm that that part of his life was behind him for good and a visit that would hopefully determine what Gaynor's problem was.

He knew the route to number 3 Princess Gardens like the back of his hand: A3 to the M25; north to the M1 exiting on the A10 and a few country roads to St Albans. He had done it in forty minutes but even at an hour he would still be there by seven — perfect for dinner at the *Royal George*, whether or not Gaynor chose to accompany him. If she wasn't in when he called, then at least he would have tried. He had decided not to phone her beforehand in case she tried to avoid him — he would surprise her and take it from there.

It had been a very strange phone call. The voice had been a man's with a soft American or Canadian accent. Gaynor had spent the afternoon with her mother at Wood Green Farm and had only the minute before returned to her house in St Albans when the phone rang.

"Hello, who's calling please?"

"Oh, good afternoon, am I speaking to Mrs Gaynor Marks?"

"Yes, who is it?"

"Oh, my name is Fred Collingwood and I work at the London Provincial in personnel."

"Is it about David?"

"Yes it is, Mrs Marks."

Gaynor sighed down the phone line.

"What's he done now?"

"Oh, nothing, Mrs Marks, he's fine. This is just a courtesy call to reassure you that he has settled back into his job and that we have one of our counsellors keeping an eye on him. We suspected that you might have been anxious for him."

"Really? I couldn't care less actually. He's a free agent now and can look after himself, I'm sure."

"Of course, Mrs Marks; it's just that we'd like you to know that there's no need for you to worry about him — his future looks extremely bright."

"Well, good for him," Gaynor said, impatiently. "Now was there anything else, Mr Collingwood?"

"No, that was it, Mrs Marks; he just needs his space over the next few days as he has some very important business to undertake for the bank. I hope you understand."

"Thank you for your advice, Mr Collingwood, if that's what it was. Now I bid you a good afternoon. Goodbye, sir."

Gaynor Marks slammed the phone down. How dare they call her? And why had personnel been involved? Was her ex-husband having problems that they thought she could solve? Well, not anymore, she told herself as she headed for her bathroom for a shower to wash herself clean of the memories and any lingering regrets. She'd never heard of a Fred Collingwood but one thing was certain — she would have to refrain from sharing her innermost thoughts with Marie Mckellar who, no doubt, had shared their private conversations with David's boss. The more she thought about it, the more annoyed she became at the bank's unnecessary interference, and before showering, she headed for the kitchen to open a bottle of wine. She needed to calm down and enjoy *her* new freedom. It was a quarter past six.

The M25 turned out to be a slow crawl and David didn't make the A10 exit until nearly seven. It took another twenty minutes before he entered Princess Gardens, a cul-de-sac of only seven houses, each individually designed in the first decade of the previous century. His luck was in — if luck was needed to see his ex-wife — as he spotted her silver BMW parked on the drive. He carefully pulled the big Jaguar beside the M3 and steeled himself for his visit. He didn't need to ring the bell as Gaynor was already on the doorstep when he approached his old front door.

"What the hell do you want? Checking up on me like Mac," she bawled, loudly enough for her words to echo in the quiet suburban street.

"No, I just thought I'd pay you a courtesy call as I was in the area, Gaynor," he lied. This had not started well and his ex-wife seemed a little intoxicated as well — he could smell the alcohol as he reached the threshold. "Can I come in for a few minutes?"

"I suppose so"

She stepped aside to allow David to pass into the hall.

"I'm in the kitchen."

Her tone seemed to have mellowed as she followed him into the familiar room. He sat down at the large rustic oak table.

"Have a glass of wine, David?"

"Thanks, I will; it's been a hard day."

He poured a glass from the second opened bottle and tried to relax.

"I gather from Bob that you may have been worried about me, Gaynor. I must admit it didn't sound like that when you phoned last night."

"Yes, I'm sorry about that. I suppose I haven't got used to it yet."

David didn't inquire as to what the 'it' was and said,

"Well, I just wanted to come and tell you that I'm fine, O.K.?"

"That's not quite how the bank sees it. I had someone from personnel on the phone earlier this evening, more less telling me the same thing and that I was not to worry about you."

David's ears pricked up. He didn't know anyone in personnel. Surely they could not be involved, unless Mac had ....

"Oh, who?" he asked, hesitantly.

"Some American sounding guy, a Fred Collingwood, I think."

David was now on his guard as a scene from Ascot the evening before flashed in front of him.

"What did he want?"

"You know him, then?"

"I know of him," he lied.

"He just wanted to reassure me that you were O.K. and that personnel had a counsellor keeping an eye on you."

"Why did he think you needed reassuring; we're divorced now, for goodness sake."

"Maybe I said too much to Marie, David, and she blabbed to Bob. They're obviously concerned for your welfare — this Collingwood fellow said you had some important business to attend to over the next few days and, to put it crudely, that I should leave you alone. I don't know why they think that they have the right to interfere in anything that I choose to do. I'm really quite cross about it all."

"I'll go and see Fred in the morning. I agree absolutely that they're out of order over this. I don't need protection and, if anything, they should be as equally concerned for you. We both went through the same divorce, after all."

"Thank you, David, that's thoughtful of you."

David smiled; Gaynor never usually gave thanks like that. Divorce had mellowed her, perhaps.

"No problem; I was going to invite you out for a meal this evening but I think it might be best if I just share another glass of wine with you and then go. You look tired."

Gaynor appeared to take no offence at the euphemism for her intoxicated condition.

"Yep, I want an early night, David. I'm glad you're O.K. Looks like you've got a bright future, according to Mr Collingwood."

On the drive home in the gathering dusk, David's mind was abuzz with what his ex-wife had said. There was no doubt in his mind that the man who had phoned her calling himself Fred Collingwood was none other than Henry Madison, employed by Jardigo to warn Gaynor off interfering in his business by causing a distraction while he was in England. As well as his own, it meant that his ex-wife's movements were being closely monitored, too. He had handled the situation well, he thought. He could have easily blurted out his ignorance of a Fred Collingwood, thereby probably ensuring that Gaynor would have contacted the bank in the morning to warn them of an impostor who was causing problems. At least now, Gaynor might leave him alone, despite her attitude to him that evening being rather more pleasant than it had been for some time. He must not let that distract him from his mission and, clearly, Jardigo held the same opinion. Once again, he felt, at the same time, both comforted and a little apprehensive that he was no longer his own man.

Gaynor cried herself to sleep that night. A bottle and a half of wine had had its effect, exposing the raw nerves that had been on edge from the very first day that she had determined to end her marriage to David. Only she knew that an idle threat had snowballed into an avalanche which had culminated in the divorce. David had wanted his freedom, of that there had been no doubt, but she could have tolerated that within the marriage, as she had done for a couple of years anyway. Though she would never admit it, she did miss his presence around the house and in her life, despite it being irregular owing to his job and his gambling exploits. The tears that night were an outpouring of those emotions, which included the near certainty that David did not apparently feel the same way about her. It was also clear to her that the London Provincial Bank regarded him very highly; enough to be extremely concerned for his welfare. It was a pity that no one seemed to be concerned for *her* welfare.

7

Froth

Other than the usual superfluous spam, there were only two important emails waiting for David when he returned to Glendower Mansions. One, remarkably, was from Jardigo Batista and one, perhaps less surprisingly, from Bob Mckellar. Though he'd never really understood how some online companies seemed to be able to get hold of personal email addresses, he was even more puzzled to learn that his employer in Portugal should have done so. He hadn't given his to Jardigo, that he had been aware of, but once again he soon came to the conclusion that his laptop must have been tampered with when he had been asleep the first morning at the castle. He read its contents with some excitement. It was brief and to the point.

> *DM,*
>
> *Please confirm by return that you have two targets and take the froth. Your lucky numbers are:*
>
> *9610-3478-29158773 and 8871-5454-21839268*
>
> *They are ready for this weekend's draw. Both should involve a different 5,000,000 Euro prize. Please confirm that you will use these numbers tomorrow. FC will escort you back here when you are finished.*
>
> > *Jardigo*

He instantly understood the significance of the final two initials and smiled at his new boss's reference to Henry Madison's alias. He also recognised, he thought, the prefixes of each set of numbers; one could belong to a Swiss bank and the other had to be from Portugal. The rest of the rather-less-than cryptic message was easy to decipher: Five million Euros were to be taken from each his two identified accounts and placed separately in Jardigo's as specified. He was being instructed to do the transfers the following day, Friday. He sat down at his laptop and typed his reply.

JB,

Message received and understood. Have the targets and the froth will be lifted tomorrow as requested. Can confirm the lucky numbers will be entered into the draw.

DM

The email from Mac was even briefer and far less informative.

Davy,

Please see me in my office at 8.30 sharp tomorrow morning.

Bob

Both emails in their own way made his heart skip a little. Five million Euros was a huge sum of money to skim from any account no matter how much it contained to begin with. In addition, Mac's email sounded too formal to be just an ordinary briefing; the timing was very early for such a mundane meeting. He suddenly felt hungry as he realized that he hadn't eaten since lunchtime and it was nearly ten o'clock by then. As he headed to the kitchen for some beans on toast, the familiar sound of an incoming email chimed in his ears. He rushed back to his computer. It was from Jardigo — he must have been waiting by a computer. The message was simple and explicit enough and provided him with a realisation of the finality of the step he was taking as he glanced round the familiar surroundings of his flat.

DM,

Great news! When the froth has been dispersed, make your way to your new home to celebrate your winnings. My band of merry men awaits you! FC will make contact tomorrow in CS with your travel arrangements and flight ticket as soon as we have verified your numbers have been entered in the draw.

    JB

So that was that, thought David; he would do the deed straight after his meeting with Mac and then email Jardigo to confirm the transfer. Henry Maddison, alias Fred Collingwood, would meet him in Cabot Square adjacent to his office building with his ticket back to Portugal. They had thought of everything. That night could be the last he would spend in England for some time and he would, no doubt, be a wanted man from the following day to boot. Suddenly, baked beans on toast seemed the wrong kind of meal for such an occasion and an Indian takeaway and some cold beers seemed far more attractive.

After a couple of drinks in the *Mulberry Bush* followed by a curry, the harsh realisation began to sink home that it was probably going to be his last night in Glendower Mansions. Jardigo's email had provided a finality to his present situation and while he was excited by the prospects of his new one, he was also a little scared of the repercussions of the following day's actions. He knew what he was about to do was purely and simply stealing, and if caught, he would likely face many years in prison. After a couple of large Jamesons, however, his mood lightened as his mind turned back to Jardigo's 'Robin Hood' philosophy. It had to be right; robbing the idle rich to help the poor and if he made money along the way, so much the better. He then started to think about the practical issues of his permanent flight to Portugal. He would travel with the absolute minimum of luggage, he decided; just his laptop and a carry-on bag together with the necessary passport and wallet. He still had some clothes back at the castle and he could soon furnish himself with a new wardrobe once back there. He would leave his car in its parking space and post the flat keys through the letter box after locking the door. He would take the train/tube combination to work as usual, see Mac and then complete his mission. Surely he would be back under the protection of the castle before anyone spotted any discrepancies in the bank accounts. In the end, he slept soundly and woke refreshed at six sharp. It was Friday, July the 5th and it had been less than a week since the apparently disastrous, but certainly, life-changing night at the *Las Vegas* casino in Lisbon.

Bob Mckellar seemed amiable when David entered the senior executive's office at a minute before the scheduled time.

"Come in, laddie. I have a job for you."

David tried to put an interested expression on his face.

"Really, boss?"

"Yes, I want you to go to Brussels for the bank, Davy."

"Brussels?"

"Yes, there is a conference on the ERM and how it might affect the banking system. I would go but it's our wedding anniversary."

"No problem, Mac — when?"

"Today, laddie. That's no problem, is it?"

David's internal disinterest changed immediately, as he stammered,

"Er — no, I don't think so."

"You'll need to go home and pack some things, no doubt — it's a weekend conference starting this evening. Take a cab back to Esher and charge it and any other expenses for the weekend. You can take Monday off to write a brief report at home, if you like."

David said nothing as Bob Mckellar passed him a glossy brochure and what looked like his travel documents. This was just unbelievable, he thought. It was a diversion, yes, but it might also provide the authorities with a nice distraction after his imminent crime. His boss brought him back to his reality.

"Your flight is for two this afternoon and you are booked in at the Hotel Flambard close to the conference centre for two nights so enjoy yourself, Davy. I'm sorry it's such short notice — my fault entirely, I'm afraid. I was going to tell you about the weekend just before you went on leave but I didn't want you to have to think about it. It slipped my mind again until last night."

"Heathrow or Gatwick?"

"Gatwick, as I recall."

Even better, thought David; his Lisbon flight would be from Heathrow.

"Right, I'll just check my emails and see Jean and then I'll be off, boss."

"Jean's gone to a funeral this morning so you can get off straightaway, if you like."

"Will do; just the emails and calls, then."

"Good — have a good weekend and I'll see you Tuesday."

David got up from his chair and turned to go. He hesitated near the door.

"I saw Gaynor last night and things there are sorted now, I think. She seemed much happier. I think she'll be O.K., so you don't need to worry. I would be grateful, however, if Marie could keep a weather eye on her for me. I may not be able to see her for some time."

"Will do, laddie; now get yourself organised for your trip."

After he got back to his office, David wasted no time in turning on his desktop. His hands were trembling as he pulled the two discs from his flight bag which he'd previously lodged out of sight under his desk. Bob Mckellar would have been quite surprised, if not shocked, if he had known that the bank's conference delegate was already prepared for a flight to mainland Europe. Hopefully, he would have his alternate flight arrangements and ticket within an hour or two. However, before he had time to use the discs, his office door suddenly swung open to reveal his friend, Matt. Instantly, David hid the discs under his blotter and tried to present as normal an expression as he could.

"Nudge, nudge; wink, wink, say no more. About to do the test, Dave?"

"I have no idea what you're talking about, Matty," replied David, with a smile. He had to appear relaxed even though his heart was pumping. "What can I do you for?"

"Just wanted to see if you fancied a night at Sandown. There's a meeting on tonight and we could go for a couple of beers afterwards."

"I can't, I'm afraid — the boss wants me to go to Brussels for the weekend; a boring conference on the ERM. Sorry, mate."

"Bit short notice, isn't it? Are you sure he isn't just using you, now you're single? I hope he's paying you double."

"Just two nights in a luxury hotel and the usual expenses."

"Can't be bad. What about Tuesday night; there's a Hawaiian evening down at Lingfield? Are you up for it — you must have a flowery shirt or two?"

"Yep, sounds good. Anyway, was there anything else, Matt?"

"No, mate, I just popped in about tonight. You're a bit touchy, aren't you?"

"Sorry, Matt, I just want to get organised for Brussels. Gotta go home and pack some things, O.K?"

"So you won't need the discs over the weekend, will you?"

They were inside his office now and David knew he had to think quickly. He only needed a few minutes. Matt stood looking at his friend, expecting an answer to his awkward question.

"There are a couple of things on them that I need today," he continued.

"Oh, right, no problem. I'll drop them down when I go, Matt."

"Can't I take them now? You won't need them till next week, will you?"

David felt the odd sweat droplet fall down his neck. He felt a little lightheaded. He suddenly had a brainwave. It was an obvious solution, if a little contrived.

"Sorry, they're locked in my cupboard and the key's in my locker in the changing rooms down the corridor. I'll get it in a minute and bring you the discs before I go. Now, if you don't mind, I've one or two things to sort out here before I go."

Matt gave him an odd look, as if to say: '*What the hell did you do that for?*', and for one awful moment David thought his friend was going to try the cupboard door — he would have found it unlocked.

"I need them in a few minutes, mate, so, if *you* don't mind, I'd be grateful if you could do it right away and bring them down to me."

Matt didn't hear David's affirmative reply, as he'd already left his office, obviously a little put out by his friend's diffidence. He would report later, when interrogated, that his friend had seemed a little odd and not quite himself on the morning in question.

David moved quickly. He turned on his desktop and found two blank discs in his open cupboard. Within five minutes he had copied Matt's disc onto his own. He breathed a sigh of relief and headed for his locker — he had to make his excuse look genuine. After wasting a few seconds in the changing room, he returned to his office, picked up Matt's discs and took the stairs to the floor below. Matt was apologetic when David entered the IT suite.

"Sorry about that, Dave; I know you must have your mind on your trip."

"That's alright; I won't need the discs till later next week, anyway. We'll go to Lingfield on Tuesday as well, Matty."

"Good, now sod off and let us real workers do some work!"

David smiled and gave the appropriate sign.

"See you Tuesday — Mac's given me Monday off."

"Part-timer!"

Despite hands that could hardly hold a disc, let alone insert it into the drive slot, he completed the two transfers in less than ten minutes. It had gone as smoothly as before. It was nine-seventeen and he sat back in his chair and tried to relax. What was to happen next? Jardigo's last email had said they would need to verify the transfers and Henry Madison would meet him in Cabot Square. Should he go and wait there? He tried to busy himself, tidying up his office and checking one or two things on his computer. He glanced at his watch again — it was twenty to ten. He would have to go soon anyway, if he was to appear to make the Brussels flight, with check-in no later than midday. His finger was poised over the on/off button when the email came through. It was the signal.

DM

Congratulations! Your numbers have been successfully entered into the draw. Please proceed to CS for your instructions.

JB

8

Dead Man Walking

One thing that David neglected to do that morning before he left for Cabot Square would later have dire consequences for his friend, Matt Sampson. In his haste to get away, he stupidly left one of the copied discs in his computer and the other lying on his desk, in full view of even a casual glance at its top. His bridges were burnt and there was no need for him to look back at the other side of the river.

He found Cabot Square to be reasonably deserted at that time of the morning when he eventually emerged into the bright sunlight from a nervous trip down the twenty floors in the lift. It was still too early for mid-morning breaks for the staff from the various offices crammed into the skyscrapers surrounding the concrete haven. The sun was warm and David headed for a bench shaded by some trees in one corner of the square. Though hidden from view from his office building, he still felt exposed and would find it difficult to explain his reason for idly sitting there if anyone from the bank had passed by, particularly someone who knew he was supposed to be on his way to Brussels. He prayed silently that Henry Madison would not be long.

"I see you're ready for your journey, my friend."

The American emerged from behind one of the trees, smiling and carrying a large brown envelope in one hand and a slim leather case in the other. David turned round with a start.

"Where the hell did you spring from, Henry?"

"Oh, I've been here since just before you arrived earlier this morning, David."

"How did you know when I'd be finished? You might have had to wait all day."

Henry Madison sat down beside David.

94

"Marvellous things these cell phones, or mobile phones, as you Brits call them, but this laptop was the key. There are countless networks available round here."

"So, do you have my ticket?"

"Of course — but there is no rush, my friend. Your flight is not till four this afternoon. You were quicker than we thought."

"Well, let me have it, please. I don't want to be spotted by one of my colleagues."

David held out a hand for the envelope but the American still seemed reluctant to pass it to the Englishman.

"All in good time, David — the envelope doesn't only contain your flight ticket and itinerary."

"Oh, what else do I need? I have enough money to get to Portugal."

"Well, just think, David. You have just done something very illegal, I understand and you are fleeing the country, probably for good."

"So, it's very unlikely that anyone will discover what I've done for several days. Only Jardigo knows the precise details."

"That is true, my friend but we, or should I say I, have to make certain that no one will be able to trace what you have done back to Jardigo. Airlines keep records of their passengers for several months after they have flown with them. If you were to leave the country under your real name, it would be easy for the authorities to discover where you had gone to after you left the bank, wouldn't it?"

"I suppose so, yes," said David. He had guessed what was coming.

"From now on, you are Mr Colin Fenner and you are going on a nice relaxing weekend break to Barcelona."

"Barcelona?"

"Yes, Barcelona — have you been there before?"

David was getting anxious to leave and be on his way. This just seemed to be a distraction. He wasn't going to Spain. Henry Madison was only one of Jardigo's minor employees. What right had he to tell him where to go?

"No, never, and I'm not going there now."

Henry Madison moved closer and said,

"Look, Colin, you will follow Jardigo's orders to the letter or suffer the consequences of disobeying. We have to cover your tracks and by going to Spain for a few days we may be able to create a temporary smokescreen for your eventual destination. It will only be until we are sure it is safe for you to travel on to Lisbon, and that will probably overland as well."

David understood. He knew what 'the consequences' might be.

"I see, so what documents do I have."

"A new passport; you may remember Jardigo organising your mug shot for his records when you first joined his operation at the castle."

David nodded. They had everything on him.

"Also, your flight ticket to Barcelona and details of your accommodation there. I think you'll be pleased with it. Then there are some maps and a brief personal history of your new identity, including things like a medical card, social security number, new credit cards, family history and so on."

"Jardigo is thorough."

"He has to be."

"A forged passport? Won't it be spotted at the airport?"

"No, we only use the best forgers in Europe. Yours cost over 5,000 Euros to produce, my friend."

"So, I am now this Colin Fenner?"

"Yes."

David looked thoughtful.

"And does this Colin Fenner exist in real life?"

"Not anymore."

"You mean ...?"

"Colin Fenner died tragically in a car accident barely a month ago. Most of his records are still live, shall we say. You are — how shall I put it ...?"

"A dead man walking?"

"Precisely!"

David Marks smiled; he really was a new man with no past and only an exciting future to look forward to. It was the stuff that dreams were made of. From then on, he had to think of himself as Colin Fenner.

"I understand, Henry — now give me the envelope.

"Not so fast, Colin. You will please give me everything you are carrying."

"Everything?"

"Everything but the clothes you are wearing — your wallet, passport, credit cards, laptop and flight bag."

"No, not my laptop; it has all my private information on it."

"Precisely, Mr Fenner and it is all totally irrelevant to you now and must be destroyed along with all your other possessions. You will be given suitable replacements for your bag and laptop at Heathrow. The envelope contains everything else you will need until you reach Barcelona. The credit cards are in the name of Colin Fenner and are signed on the back. Pin numbers are also in the envelope."

"You've thought of everything, haven't you?"

"We try. Now how were you thinking of getting to the airport?"

"I wasn't; I was going to take a taxi into the city first and buy one or two things."

"You will not take a cab anywhere, my friend — too easy to leave a trail that can be followed at a later date. You will only use public transport. Did you tell the bank where you were going this morning or did you just leave without saying?"

"Well, the ironic thing is I'm supposed to be flying from Gatwick to Brussels this afternoon for a conference over the weekend and they had given me time to go home first to pack so, fortunately, I will not be missed until they check the delegates. For the next few hours, the bank will just assume I'm on my way."

"That is indeed fortunate, my friend. Pity you weren't flying from Heathrow, though."

"Does it matter?"

"No, not really, but you must go straight to Heathrow from here — tube all the way, I presume. It will provide exactly the right anonymity."

"O.K."

"And, Colin?"

"Yes."

"Look behind the trees over there."

David/Colin looked beyond Henry Madison to where he was indicating. In the distance, he could just make out the two men who were leaning idly against the trees. As if on cue, he thought he noticed them nod imperceptibly.

"I suppose they'll be escorting me to the airport?"

"Yes, so take your time and don't try to lose them. They are very experienced, and in more ways than one. Just take the tube as you would normally do. You have plenty of time and, as I say, you will be provided with everything you need when you get to Heathrow. Have you any further questions?"

"No, I understand."

"Good, now empty your pockets and place your wallet and everything else in your flight bag. When you've done, take the envelope and get up and walk slowly away. Just leave your bag and laptop on the seat. We may meet again some day when I return to Portugal. I suspect by then, however, that I will not recognise you, Colin."

Henry Madison placed the brown envelope on the bench and watched while Colin placed all his loose possessions and evidence of his old identity in the flight bag. Leaving his past life behind him, and without saying a word, he picked up the verification of his new one. He then gave a cheeky 'thumbs up' to his two tails; stood up, and walked confidently across the square towards the Canary Wharf tube station and his future life.

Jardigo Batista was happy — his young protégé had performed the miracle that he had thought might be well nigh impossible. He had robbed two wealthy men of a combined sum of 10 million Euros and though it was still at least another two hours until lunch, he had opened a bottle of his finest champagne to drink in the relative privacy of the castle's rear veranda. Apart from Rafael, all his other staff were engaged with their normal duties. His deputy and chief confidante had been at the computer for most of the morning so far, waiting and watching for news from Henry Madison in London and relaying David Marks' movements to his boss at regular intervals. The Englishman had been followed from his flat to the bank with Jardigo's American operative being informed at a little before nine. Now, it was just after ten-thirty and Henry had sent an email to report that Colin Fenner had just left for Heathrow for the flight to Barcelona. At ten-forty precisely, Rafael appeared once more on the veranda with the news that Mr Fenner had boarded the underground at Canary Wharf with two experienced tails in tow. They were following Jardigo's orders to the letter and would make absolutely sure that their mark would board the flight for Spain. Senhor Fenner would be met at Barcelona airport; escorted to his hotel and finally reminded once again of his responsibilities by one of the castle's part-time operatives in Spain.

"So, boss, are we very much richer?" asked Rafael, spotting the expensive Dom Perignon at Jardigo's side.

"A little, Rafa; just a little."

"Senhor Marks seems to have followed your instructions carefully, eh?"

"Yes, he is a good man, that one, Rafa, my friend. I have more plans for him when he eventually gets here. We must wait to see what happens when the authorities in England find out what he has done."

"And just what has he done, boss?"

Jardigo's face broke into a broad grin.

"Good try, Rafa — you know better than to ask me that."

"Well, I'm not stupid, Jardigo. It has to involve movement of large sums of money somehow, judging by the champagne you are drinking."

"Then you do not need to ask more, Rafael — agreed?"

"Yes, boss."

"And Rafa?"

"Yes, boss."

"Our former English friend no longer exists, so do not even mention his name anymore — do you understand?"

"Boss?"

"Mr David Marks has disappeared off the face of the earth. We won't go so far as to provide the police with the evidence of a body. Though, if necessary, that remains an option. When he arrives in Barcelona, Mr Colin Fenner will be undergoing some physical changes; some temporary, some permanent."

"Permanent, boss?"

"Don't look so squeamish, my friend. The alterations this time will not involve any surgery — just some changes to his hair colour and facial appearance. We are not butchers and beards are easily grown. Add a few tattoos and he really will be a new man!"

"Got 'cha, boss. Do you want me to get rid of all his clothes and belongings from his room?"

"Definitely — we must erase all trace of David Marks from the castle as soon as possible."

"I'll get it organised today, boss."

"No, Rafa, you will do it yourself."

"Yes, boss."

"And then you can tell everybody else that Mr David Marks failed in the assignment I gave him and will not be returning from England. You can let them draw their own conclusions as to what has happened to him. If you put it in a certain way, it will serve as a timely reminder as to what can happen to anyone who does not carry out my orders completely."

"Yes, boss."

"We will smuggle Senhor Fenner into the castle at night when the time is right and make further changes to his appearance, if need be — before anyone sees him. I will decide if those changes are necessary after I see what will have been done in Barcelona — O.K?"

"Yes, boss."

"Yes, Rafael! Now go away and leave me in peace. If anyone wants me, I'm not available for the rest of the morning. I may well go down to the lake or visit the vaults."

"Yes, boss."

"Rafael, vamoose!"

"Yes ...."

Mr Colin Fenner was feeling lost; a stranger in his own body and mind, let alone his native country. At that moment, he didn't belong anywhere and as the tube pulled into Waterloo, another feeling returned to haunt him — he was downright scared. One more stop and he would get some much needed air at Westminster where he could change to the circle line for Paddington and the Heathrow Express. He knew he had plenty of time, with check–in at Heathrow not until two. He would have a stroll round Westminster to soak up the atmosphere of the city one last time before he left England — possibly forever.

How much time did he have to waste? He glanced at his bare wrist — bare of his gold watch, a wedding present from Gaynor. He'd even been persuaded to leave that with Henry Madison. He strained his eyes to look at a neighbouring passenger's wrist.

"Can I help you, Senhor?"

Colin sat up straight at the foreign accent. He stammered,

"Oh, have you got the time, please?"

The middle-aged man glanced at his watch. He looked somehow familiar.

"Just gone eleven."

"Thank you, sir."

"No, problem, Colin; you have plenty of time."

"You're ...."

The man held a finger to his lips and, as if to gain his tail's approval, Colin continued,

"I'm getting off at the next stop."

"So are we," replied the man and his eyes turned left to look at a similarly dressed man sitting on the other side of the aisle. "Though you have plenty of time, please behave yourself," he whispered.

"Of course."

Strangely, the brief conversation with his 'escort' had lightened his mood a little; at least he felt protected and part of something again. Previous thoughts of the enormity of what he had just done less than two hours earlier receded from his mind. Now, not everyone he looked at was a plain-clothed policeman. He sat back in his seat and began to relax, clutching the brown envelope to his side. He would have a stroll round Westminster before carrying on to Paddington. He would aim to get to the airport by one, meaning he could take an hour's break at the next stop. He had very little cash on him — the envelope had contained a single five-pound note — not enough to get him all the way to Heathrow, even without a much needed coffee or something stronger to calm any lingering nerves. He would try out one of his new credit cards when he got off the tube; no doubt, this had been Henry's intention in any case.

Emerging into bright and warm sunshine, Colin thought about the irony of the situation, as fifty yards to his left stood the Westminster branch of the London Provincial. He'd even done some of his early training there and guessed that there might be still one or two people working there that he had known. Fortunately, however, there were two ATM's outside and he would not have to face any awkward questions if he was recognised. As he approached the machines, he took out the remaining contents of his envelope; a credit card, a bank debit card, his new passport and the flight documents. He hurriedly ditched the empty envelope into a waste bin as he passed. Carefully distributing everything in his pockets, he verbally rehearsed the relevant pin number which he'd committed to memory on the tube. The ATM on the left was conveniently free and his hand shook nervously as he inserted the debit card into the slot. He smiled like a gambler whose horse had just come in as he withdrew £200 in new twenty-pound notes. This was like a licence to print money. Before removing his card fully from the slot, a thought suddenly occurred to him: '*How much money was there in the new account in the name of Colin Fenner*?' The Visa debit card indicated it had been issued by Crédito Agricola, one of the largest banks in Portugal. He pushed the card back in.

"Hurry up please, sir."

The familiar voice echoed behind him as the account balance appeared on the screen. Colin Fenner carefully removed his card and turned to face his tail with a grin that stretched from ear to ear.

"Just needed some cash, my friend, and now I'm going for a drink, alright?"

"Of course, Senhor; I can recommend the *Red Lion* in Parliament Street."

Colin said nothing as he brushed past his tail. He knew the *Red Lion* well enough from his short time at the bank whose machine he'd just used. He wanted to get there as quickly as possible now to calm his fluttering nerves, particularly after seeing his balance on the screen. He'd wanted to go back and check he hadn't dreamt or misread it but his tail was still there getting cash. He had just won the Scoop 6; five numbers plus the bonus up on the lottery; a six-horse accumulator — the list could be endless. The figure he'd seen had been £200 short of half a million. He was almost skipping into Parliament Street with ecstasy. Any perceived worries about his new situation and life seemed to evaporate into thin air as he started to come to terms with his new fortune. He needed his favourite Irish tipple — he had enough money never to have to work again or, at least, for a very long time. As he turned off the street to enter the *Red Lion*, a voice seemed to whisper in his ear.

'*Remember who you work for, Senhor Fenner.*'

He turned round abruptly — but there was no one there. He looked up to see one of his tails a good distance away across the other side of the wide thoroughfare. He was hearing voices now. He definitely needed that drink.

The public bar was fairly crowded, even at that hour; a mixture of thirsty tourists, workers already on lunch and heading for an early weekend and the odd minor politician trying to appear anonymous. Colin ordered his double Jamesons, thankful that the barman had not recalled his face from previous visits. He headed for a quiet corner which contained the useful distraction of a familiar fruit machine. If nothing else, it provided him with something to concentrate on and with his back to the bar it also gave him some useful cover should there be any of his old bank colleagues there. He had a three or four pounds in loose change with which to feed his habit. Though the ten-pound jackpot was small, it gave him the mental exercise he needed to relieve his tense mind.

"Dave, is that you, mate?"

Colin's body stiffened. He did not turn round. He could get away with it, surely. It had been over ten years. The man came round to his side and looked into his face.

"Dave Marks? It's Rory Cullen — you must remember me."

Colin glanced briefly to his right.

"Sorry, mate, my name's Co ..., I mean, Corrigan, Mike Corrigan."

He'd been quick to invent the name. If he'd used his new one, the guy, whoever he was, might have recalled it if and when the news of the bank fraud leaked out.

"Oh, I could have sworn you used to work round the corner at the London Provincial; about ten years ago it would have been, I think."

"Not me, mate. I live abroad most of the time."

"Are you sure?"

"Well, that's a pretty stupid question. What do you want me to say — no, I'm not sure who I am, eh?"

Colin glared at the man who seemed to be about his own age.

"Well, you're the spitting image of Dave Marks; he must have a double, that's all I can say."

Colin said nothing as another jackpot spilled into the drawer. He could certainly prove he wasn't David Marks, if he had to, but that would mean he would have to reveal his real identity.

"Sorry, mate, I live and work in Sweden. Now please leave me alone — O.K?"

The man calling himself Rory Cullen backed away. It was not a name that Colin remembered.

"I apologise, Mike; I must be getting senile."

"No problem, mate," replied Colin, without taking his eyes of the spinning reels. He reached for his drink from on top of the machine. He had to go — it might get even more awkward. His astute mention of a home in

Scandinavia would hopefully provide some more cover should Rory Cullen be alerted when any news broke about his former bank colleague. Keeping his head down, he made for the nearest exit, emerging into a deserted side mews. He turned right to present himself as quickly as he could in Parliament Street — he did not want the embarrassment of his tails rushing through the *Red Lion* searching for him. Turning back right to the front entrance, he gave a military style salute to the tail who had spoken to him on the tube. He had been just about to go into the pub. The other tail joined his colleague from his position on the other side of the road. The two men stood next to each other and with arms folded, they were clearly indicating that he should be back on his way to the airport. Taking their obvious hint, he started towards them and, nodding as he passed, he began his return walk to Westminster tube station, barely glancing at the 'Mother of Parliaments' as he did so. He wanted to get back to the anonymity of the tube and, judging by the closeness of the footsteps behind him, Jardigo's men also wanted him in a more confined environment.

Reaching the foyer, Colin took the opportunity to buy two things from a street vendor's stall just inside; a leather wallet and a cheap digital wristwatch would make him feel a man again. Feeling a little more complete, he made for the line that would take him to Paddington. In no time at all, he found himself able to relax a little as he waited on the appropriate platform for the next train west. While his tails now watched his every move from close quarters, he carefully inserted the remaining notes and the two credit cards into the wallet. It was five minutes past midday.

Though he had no bags with him on arrival at Heathrow, Colin made his way directly to the British Airways desk for check-in for the four o'clock flight to Barcelona. The young woman behind the counter seemed somewhat confused when he announced that he had no luggage to go on board.

"You have some hand luggage with you, then?"

He hesitated before replying. The assistant looked dubious. She stared momentarily at his work suit.

"No, I travel light."

"Are you going on business, then, sir?"

The question had been asked casually enough but Colin still wanted to tell the girl that it was surely none of her business — she wasn't passport control. He thought better of it.

"Yes, I am staying with friends who live in Spain. With this weather, they told me to bring nothing — better to get appropriate clothing when I got there, they said."

Colin knew it was an odd reply but the girl seemed satisfied enough with it.

"Well, I hope you have a nice time, sir. You're our first check-in. You will be called at about three-thirty and departure is from Gate 27."

"Thank you, young lady."

As he walked away, he offered up a prayer that the assistant would not have the chance to talk to anyone at the boarding gate; he would have a flight bag and laptop by then, if Henry Madison had been correct. With tight security measures in place, it would be a cause for concern if he suddenly turned up with possessions; especially if they thought some other party had brought them to the airport. He would have a hard task convincing anyone that he had packed them himself! He shrugged his shoulders — surely Jardigo's men would be aware of the possibility — and headed for the nearest bar. He hadn't noticed either of his tails get off the Heathrow Express but suspected there were others in the vicinity. Jardigo's foreign operatives seemed to be limitless.

The expected approach was made at Terminal 2's Wetherspoon's outlet, a familiar drinking hole for Colin on numerous previous visits to the airport. He had just finished a revoltingly greasy cheese burger washed down with a pint of lager — he had decided against another Jamesons as he thought he might continue to need his wits about him. Out of the corner of his eye, he noticed someone sit down on an adjacent stool. He also noticed that two black leather bags had almost miraculously appeared on the ground next to him. Taking a better look at the stranger who had obviously been responsible for the bags, he decided he was surely too young to be one of Jardigo's men; more like the typical teenager bound for the Spanish sun. The boy said nothing as he got up and walked slowly away. He had just made fifty pounds from the tall foreign looking stranger that had assigned him the simple task of delivering Colin's hand luggage.

He turned round nervously. Had anyone observed the delivery? No one was looking his way.

"Another one, sir?"

The barman had clearly seen nothing, too.

"Er — no thanks, mate, I'm fine."

Colin gave the barman the chance to walk to the far end of the counter before he left his stool. Reaching down to pick up the two cases, he headed for the nearest Gents to discover what he had been provided with.

Once in a cubicle, he opened both bags. The flight bag contained pretty standard items, ranging from a comb and some boiled sweets to further details of his hotel in Barcelona. In addition there was some reading material, including a thriller about Inspector Perkins of the Met's fraud squad — Jardigo's little joke, no doubt, thought Colin. The laptop was a top of the range Dell; the latest and more powerful version of his previous one. It would be interesting to play with it on the plane, especially if Jardigo had added anything to it. He quickly packed everything carefully away and looked at his watch. It was nearly three and time for more anxious moments as he still had the worry of negotiating passport control.

He found he had a business class seat at the front of the plane in a section containing about twenty similarly dressed individuals. Passport control had presented no problems — he had looked like hundreds of other business travellers, with accompanying laptops. For almost the first time that day, he began to relax as he seemed to have been left on his own with no obvious following protection. Presumably Jardigo was of the opinion that once on the plane, he could not escape until he was through passport control in Barcelona and, no doubt, his new boss would have someone waiting there to meet and greet him.

The three hour flight went without too many alarms as he tried to ignore any attempts at conversation with neighbouring passengers other than a brief yes or no. Once they had reached cruising height, he was able to open up his laptop and study what was on it. Apart from the usual software, there was one message in his new inbox from Jardigo. It took a little time for Colin to interpret all of its contents as his boss had presumably been aware of the possible scanning techniques at any security control which might involve checking emails and suchlike. It read:

My Dear Friend Sixteen Red,

Your client is most appreciative of your efforts to redeem his faith in your company. Our business is thriving this year and we look forward to receiving your technical support in our venture. I am pleased to say that your promotion is very well deserved and I look forward to seeing you in a few days.

Please enjoy your stay in The City of Counts at our expense where our representative, Señor Castilla will be your guide and where we hope you will enjoy many years of success.

From your friend, All On Red

Colin read the cryptic message with a smile. Jardigo had been careful not to mention any names and Señor Castilla was probably a pseudonym. The reference to their last numbers at the roulette wheel reminded him of how he had got into Jardigo's operation in the first place and was, no doubt, Jardigo's way of saying, *'you're one of us now.'* He was, at first, a little puzzled by the indication that he was going to be in Barcelona for years but, in the end, he put it down to another diversionary tactic to cover his real destination. Only one thing bothered him about the tone of the email. Though he was heartily in favour of Jardigo's 'Robin Hood' philosophy with regard to wealth and its fair and equal distribution, he had not fully realized that he was now a part of that operation on a permanent basis and not just as a means to pay of his debt to his boss. In addition, he had seen little, if any sign so far of this particular Robin Hood giving any of that wealth to the poor and needy. Was Jardigo Batista just a thief, plain and simple?

9

The City of Counts

It was hot, unbearably hot and taxis were at a premium outside El Prat, Spain's second, but busiest airport. Though its air-conditioned interior and marble floors had provided a comfortable environment after landing, the apron in front of the main entrance was like a furnace as the evening sun continued to burn down. The digital thermometer on an overhanging awning read 32°C. Mr Colin Fenner, late of Esher in Surrey, and currently of no fixed abode, wanted a shower and a change into some cool clothes — his suit was damp with perspiration, despite it being only about five minutes since he had emerged from the terminal building. He had walked slowly through the concourse, expecting at any moment to be stopped by Señor Castilla, or worse — the police, but no one had approached him and it seemed he had to make his own way to his hotel in the centre of the city, more than six miles away. *'Oh well,'* he thought. *'What will be, will be,'* which quickly became, *'To be or not to be,'* after he glanced up and back at the terminal building — where, emblazoned in giant letters, was *Terminal 2B*. He was just amusing himself with his play on words when a gruff voice called to him from the taxi rank where a silver grey Audi had just pulled up. It was clearly a private car with no markings or advertisements on its sides. A thin-looking black-haired man of about his own age had leant out of the driver's seat to hail him.

"Need a ride, señor?"

Colin Fenner needed any kind of transport, whether the man was just touting for illegal business, or not. Maybe it was his guide at last. The man got out of the car to approach him. He was tall — well over six foot and Colin noticed the slight limp in his gait.

"Are you going to the city — I'm staying at *Le Meridien* on *Las Ramblas*. Do you know it?"

"Si, Señor Fenner. Welcome to Spain."

"Oh, thank God for that," said Colin. "You are from our mutual friend, aren't you?"

Although the man knew his name, he had to be sure he was the right person. He was standing directly in front of him now, his eyes staring down into his own — he had to be at least six foot six.

"Our friend said I was to ask you why you don't always bet on red. He said you would understand."

"I do. Am I glad to see you; it's so hot here."

"It is worse in the city, but you will get used to it. My name is Manuel, by the way. May I take your bags, Señor Fenner?"

His English was good — very good; just the occasional word in his native tongue. He was holding a rear door open now and Colin could already feel the Audi's powerful air-conditioning before he got in.

"No, I'd rather keep them with me in the car."

"Of course."

Manuel pulled the big A8 away from the terminal. It was sheer unashamed luxury; leather upholstered comfort.

"Your English is good, Manuel."

"Si, I mean, yes, sir. I have lived in London in the past — a waiter, you know."

"Whereabouts?"

"Just off the Regent Street in Cornwallis Road. It is called *Barrafina*. Do you know it?"

"No, I don't. How long were you there?"

"Ten years; I went to London when I was twenty-two."

"How did you come to work for our ...?"

It seemed silly to still be referring to Jardigo so secretively and Manuel interrupted Colin.

"You mean Jardigo Batista?"

"Yes."

"He was working in London at the time and ate regularly at *Barrafina* — he was fond of our sea food. I used to be a gambler and I owed him money from a poker school we used to hold on a Saturday night after the restaurant was closed. I lost heavily and he needed someone to work for him in Spain. I think you must understand — no?"

"Oh yes, I understand," replied Colin. "And what do you do for him here in Barcelona?"

"This and that; this and that. I do lots of things. *Las Ramblas* is popular in summer with the British tourists and I run a small operation for Señor Batista. We like to talk to the wealthy ones and relieve them of things — you follow?"

"I follow, Manuel."

They were in the city proper now and Manuel swung the big limousine onto a narrower thoroughfare.

"Only five minutes now, señor. *Le Meridien* is very nice — one of Barcelona's finest."

"Good; I'm ready to change into something more appropriate."

"We have arranged all you need to be delivered to your room, Señor Fenner. I hope you will be satisfied with our service. Señor Jardigo likes to keep his best and most senior employees happy."

'*Best and senior*' sounded good to Colin. His new life had started well. Maybe that evening he would celebrate his new-found status and indulge his passion. His guide was sure to know where he could do just that.

"Manuel?"

"Señor?"

"Do you know of any nice casinos ...?"

They had thought of everything, from two or three sets of shirts and slacks to a personal DVD player and a selection of DVDs. The welcoming bottle of champagne and tray of fruit and hors d'oeuvres were enough to satisfy Colin's immediate thirst and hunger. Looking more closely at his new wardrobe, he began to wonder how long they were expecting him to stay in Barcelona. His estimate of a few days might have to be revised to a few weeks. Still, it wasn't much of a hardship to be living in such air-conditioned luxury. He could put up with it!

By nine o'clock, showered and dressed casually in a trendy floral shirt and white slacks, Colin Fenner, formerly David Marks even began to look different to his previous self. He'd always detested white trousers, let alone the effeminacy of flowery shirts. Perhaps his boss had known that, from observing him and absorbing their several chats over a drink or two down by the lake. However he felt about his personal appearance, it was time to sample the city's nightlife. Manuel Castilla had pointed out the upmarket casino down in the port area. *The Gran Casino de Barcelona* was the city's finest and stayed opened each night until 5 a.m. It was a short stroll from the hotel. His guide had even provided him with temporary membership for the length of his stay; it was a gambler's dream — more money than he knew what to do with. He just had to gain his revenge on a roulette wheel. The drug was flowing through his veins again with no one to counsel him against it.

It was just after ten when Colin Fenner flashed his membership card in front of the uniform doorman who saluted respectively, almost seeming to know that the tall black-haired Englishman had a lot of money to invest. Unlike Manuel, his English was somewhat less than perfect.

"Welcome the Grand casino. Please to good time, señor."

"Thank you; I intend to."

"You have been graded up to VIP pass. Go the stairs for best tables and service."

So his membership had been upgraded, he observed. Had someone alerted the casino that he was coming? Perhaps Manuel had reported back to Jardigo and he had done the rest. However it had been done, Colin Fenner headed for the stairs marked *VIP Members Only*. This really was too good to be true and when he was immediately lubricated with his favourite drink, attended by his personal waitress, he really did think that he had died and gone to heaven. How much to take out of his new bank account — that was the question? The man in the banker's booth soon provided the answer. He spoke perfect English with the hint of an American accent.

"Your credit is good, Mr Fenner. Casinos in Spain are using the Euro now and the table limits are 10,000 Euros per single bet; more only by private arrangement. Your bank account will be debited or credited at the current exchange rate."

"So I don't need cash to take to the table?"

The young assistant's face burst into a smile."

"Of course not, sir. The croupier will keep you informed of your status at any time. Have a good evening with us. Maria will serve you with drinks and light refreshments."

"Thank you, er ...."

"Don, sir."

"Thank you, Don; I intend to enjoy myself tonight."

The young man called Don gave a knowing grin — it said: another sucker with foolish intentions to make easy money. For his part, Colin had no intention of becoming just another 'sucker'. He would find it much easier to do his calculations in Euros than previously with the Portuguese Escudo in Lisbon.

Unlike in Lisbon or at any other casino where Colin had played roulette, the one that Marie took him to at the *Gran Casino* was in a small private room with space for only six players. It had a small bar in one corner from which Maria and another girl plied the VIPs with their chosen drinks. No other people seemed to be allowed to watch the players, all of whom had the air of the experienced gambler about them. There was one vacant seat when Colin arrived and if he'd thought about it more carefully, he might have suspected that the evening had been prearranged for him. He could not, however, fail to notice two small wall-mounted cameras positioned at opposite ends of the room. Every move that was made in the room was being monitored elsewhere in the building. Colin sat down in the vacant seat.

"Welcome, señor; my name is Suzy. How many chips would you like?"

Colin's jaw dropped — he hadn't really looked at the croupier up until she had spoken. She was the most beautiful looking woman he had seen in a long while. Short black hair enclosed a round face of faintly oriental origin with full red lips and dark brown eyes. Her bust was high and full and she wore a bright red silk kimono split impossibly above the thigh to reveal more of her smooth olive skin. Like the young man at the cash desk, she spoke with an accent that was part American, part Asian. Inevitably, Coin stammered his reply.

"Oh, erm — I'll start with 20,000 Euros, Suzy."

"You have credit of 20K, sir."

Suzy made a note in a small book in front of her.

"Fait vos jeux, gentlemen. Fait vos jeux."

Colin glanced round at the other five players — all older than him and all clearly Spanish and wealthy judging by the heavy bets that were quickly placed on the table. One, at least, had been winning heavily. The memory of his last time at a roulette table came back to him. He placed two 1000-Euro chips on numbers one to six.

"Rien ne va plus! Rien ne va plus!"

Coiln's night began as Suzy spun the ball round the wheel. Exactly nine seconds later, she called,

"Quatre, noir; four, black and even."

He had won 12,000 Euros. Suzy dragged all chips away except for his. His neighbour, a cigar-smoking fat man of about sixty grunted his approval.

When, after four further spins, Colin's pile of chips had gone beyond 100,000, the fat man shook his head in disbelief at the young Englishman's luck — the wheel had delivered the numbers: 4, 6, 5, 28 and 3, giving Colin four wins out of five by continuing with the first six numbers and a few side bets on the colours. After another half an hour, however, the same man was smiling to himself as he watched Colin give all his winnings back. He was back to where he started and was about to ask the Suzy for some more chips when something made him think twice about continuing. It was the news he didn't want to hear. The fat man leaned towards Colin and, in broken English, said,

"You English lose money easy. I see a big bank has lost millions today."

Colin looked questioningly at Suzy in case he'd misheard the Spaniard. His heart was pumping.

"Yes, one of your largest banks has reported a big loss, sir."

Now his head was throbbing, too. He barely dared ask the next question.

"Which one?"

"I don't recall," replied Suzy. "One in London, I think."

Colin tried to remain calm — he shouldn't look too interested.

"Oh, I see. Well, I think that's enough for me before I lose as well, Suzy. I believe I am about level, right?"

"You are 1000 Euros up and your account will be credited with this amount in two working days."

"Thank you — I bid you all good night. I am a little tired."

"Of course, sir — come again soon."

He tried not to leave the casino at a speed that would cause anyone to notice his exit, even pausing for a few minutes at the machines to use up some loose change. Eventually, with the time at a little after eleven, he headed back to *Le*

Meridien at a brisk walk, his head hurting and full of impossible notions. No one stopped him and he made it safely back to his room. Locking the door, he wasted no time in switching on the television. CNN seemed to be the only English-speaking channel and, somewhat to his relief, he quickly discovered that the bank fraud was not one of the major stories. It came on after about ten minutes and Colin flung himself onto the bed with a huge mental release. The reporter was standing outside a branch of Lloyds and her opening words confirmed his supreme joy.

'*It is the biggest quarterly loss for three years for one of the UK's largest banks. A spokesman said it was due to fears about the ERM and the current uncertainty in world markets. Some job losses would be inevitable ....*'

He'd been a fool. Surely no one would have missed the money yet? It would have been an extraordinary coincidence if either of the account owners had looked at their balances by now. As he recalled, neither account had been touched for several months and he himself wouldn't have been missed yet as he was not due back at the bank until Tuesday. Surely no one at the conference would have tried to find out why he hadn't turned up and anyway, if they had, the bank was closed on Saturdays. He leapt off the bed and opened the mini-bar. Without bothering with a glass, he downed two miniature Glenfiddichs in seconds. He suddenly realized how nervous he was — he had to email Jardigo about his anxieties. Perhaps he would be able to reassure him of the next steps in his escape. As soon as he turned on the computer, he realized he had a message. It had to be from Jardigo. It provided some of the reassurance he needed but also raised some other concerns.

Sixteen Red,

I hope Manuel has served you well thus far and that you are settling into your accommodation. You have some homework to do. Attached to this email are all the details of your past, including facts about your upbringing etc. Please memorise everything at once and I will send more later.

Tomorrow, you are to go to 74 Diagon Alle at ten in the morning where Manuel's wife will make some alterations to your appearance. Please do not alarm yourself; they are for your own safety. Meanwhile, I would recommend that you stay in your room as much as possible and use room service. Wear dark glasses and a hat when you go out. Manuel should have advised against you visiting the casino tonight. I reprimanded him when he telephoned earlier. Remember, you are a fugitive at the moment and the less you are seen the better. We do not want people recalling your face when your misdemeanour is discovered.

All On Red

Colin was comforted by Jardigo's concern and the details of his past life seemed easy enough to learn. It was the meeting with his guide's wife that worried him a little. What alterations was she going to make? He knew he wasn't going to shave from then on but what else could she do to him? Since it was a woman going to do it, he presumed that the alterations were of a cosmetic nature. After a few more minutes committing his past to memory, and a couple more drinks, he opted to close the day's events and within ten minutes was sound asleep in his king-size bed.

The policeman was insistent.

"*What is your name?*"

"*I told you — Colin Richard Fenner.*"

"*You are David Marks, aren't you?*"

"*No, I'm Colin Richard Fenner.*"

"Who do you work for?"

"I don't work."

"Oh come now, sir. We both know you work for the London Provincial Bank, don't we?"

"No, no, no!"

He was shouting now.

"Bring him in, constable. Here's someone you know, I think, David."

"Hello, Dave, just tell them what they want to know, mate."

"Who the hell are you?"

"It's me, mate — Matt Sampson, you idiot."

"Don't know you."

"Bring the other gentleman in, constable."

"Davy, what have you been doing? Gaynor's worried sick, laddie."

"Nothing, I've done nothing. I'm Colin Richard Fenner and I'm dead."

"Dead, sir?"

"Yes."

"Where were you born, Colin?"

"Towcester in Northamptonshire."

"When were you born?"

"14th of July, 1960."

"What was your mother's maiden name?"

"Tompkins."

"Where did you go to school?"

"What?"

"Your school, sir?"

"I didn't go to school."

"Who did you last work for?"

"I don't remember; Jardigo hasn't ...."

"Who is Jardigo?"

"What?"

"I said who is Jardigo?"

"I don't know."

"Right, time for some encouragement, constable. Bring the chair in."

"What chair?"

"Oh it's just a little electric device for making people talk."

"But you can't do that."

"Oh yes we can, sir."

"No you can't!"

"Yes we can!"

"No! No! No!"

"Constable ...."

"Aah!!"

He was bathed in sweat; his scream still seemed to be echoing round his room. He sat up, arms raised in panic. It had been a nightmare, but it had seemed real enough to him, even down to the half-remembered facts about his past. He jumped out of bed and rushed to his computer — the dream was fading fast. He had to check while he could still remember. His birthplace — that was it. He downloaded the attachment again and there it was: Born Towcester, Northants. It had all been a horrible dream, sparked off by Jardigo's email.

10

Rail, Road, Track

Sancha Castilla was a well-rounded lady who spoke very little English so her husband had to act as interpreter when Colin eventually made his way to their modest townhouse on *Diagon Alle*, a quiet mews just of *Las Ramblas*. Manuel was clearly enjoying a rare weekend off from any duties provided by Jardigo. The walk had done Colin good; it was much cooler with cloud cover to ward off the sun's powerful rays. He had obeyed Jardigo's instructions and sported a baseball cap and sunglasses. On arrival at his three storey property, Manuel led him into the kitchen, a surprisingly expensively equipped affair with all the latest gadgets that modern technology had to offer. Even Jardigo's apparently more lowly employees were paid well and Sancha clearly enjoyed the best that money could buy. Colin's guide immediately tried to set him at his ease about the alterations to his appearance.

"Now, my friend, Sancha is going to ensure you look different from now on. She is going to change your hair colour and then add a couple of additions to your face and arms."

"Additions?" asked Colin, nervously. Sancha was standing by a large secondary sink. She was pointing at a variety of bottles, smiling as though she knew what her husband was saying.

"Yes — a nice tattoo on each forearm and a scar on your cheek; perhaps running from the corner of your mouth to your ear. It will give you a look of the villain, no?"

Manuel burst out laughing.

"But you are one already, maybe?"

Colin had gone silent.

"Oh, don't worry, my friend; there will be no pain. It will be cosmetic — the kind of thing that actors have."

"Oh, thank God for that."

Sancha had turned on a tap and was filling the sink with water.

"Yes, Sancha used to work at the National Theatre in Madrid as a make-up artist. She is very useful to our operation whenever someone needs a good disguise."

Manuel's wife seemed anxious to begin her work.

"Please," she said. Her voice was warm as she indicated for Colin to sit on a high chair near the sink.

"I will leave you for a while," said Manuel. "You did bring your passport, didn't you; Jardigo should have told you in his message."

"He didn't," replied Colin. "But I always carry it with me, especially now."

"Good — I will need to borrow it for a few hours after we have taken a new photograph when Sancha has finished with you. Good luck!"

Though Sancha had few words of English, she managed with sign language and gentle pushing and cajoling to get Colin to put his head over the sink. She worked quickly; her hands were gentle but strong as she worked the dyes into his scalp. The whole process took less than twenty minutes by which time Colin's neck was aching with the effort and the tension of the situation. Handing him a towel, she stood back to admire her handiwork.

"You dry."

He rubbed his hair vigorously, expecting to see it covered with dye when he'd finished. However, when he looked, there was not a mark on it.

She handed him a small mirror and smiled. Nervously, he held it in front of his face. A new man stared back at him. He was bleached blond; all his black hair colour had gone — his complexion looked suddenly darker.

"Wow, I look like Billy Idol!"

"Please?"

Colin gave Sancha a thumbs-up and winked.

"Excelente!"

"Gracias, señor."

Sancha looked pleased and handed Colin a hairbrush.

"No, señor," she said, as he'd been about to reach into his pocket for a comb. He understood.

"Come, please."

Sancha led the way out of the kitchen to the rear of the house where there seemed to b a one-floor extension to the property. It was kitted out like an artist's studio — Colin grimaced slightly at the prospect of his next alterations. Sancha pointed to a low stool near a long trestle table.

"Please, señor."

He sat down. She bent down and traced her finger across his cheek.

"This," she said, simply.

The process of applying the plastic-like addition to his face took over an hour, with Sancha allowing Colin to stand every ten minutes or so. The applied mixture had a smell that reminded him of the glue he used to use with his model Airfix kits when he'd been a boy. By this time, he was getting hungry and Sancha grinned every time his stomach rumbled its protest.

"We finish," she said, eventually. "See."

He took the mirror again and this time he nearly fell off the stool. Apart from the obligatory black eye patch, the person who stared back at him was a pirate who had spent a life in the sun. He looked evil and the kind of man that no one would mess with. He raised his hand to touch the scar.

"No!" she screamed.

He withdrew his hand, more out of shock at her scream than at her command. Sancha shook her head vigorously from side to side.

"Mañana, mañana," she said in a more controlled voice.

"O.K. — I understand."

Wherever Manuel had been in the house, his wife's scream had brought him running into the studio.

"What is wrong, señor Colin?"

"Oh nothing, Manuel — I nearly touched my scar, that's all."

"Hey, hombre! You're the man!"

Manuel stood, arms folded, and took in his wife's work. He bent down and kissed her head.

"She has done well, my friend. You are a new man. Even your own wife will not recognise you."

"I'm no longer married."

"Your mother, then."

Colin did not reply, as he thought wistfully of his blood family. Would he ever see them again? He shuddered — the reality of his burnt bridges was finally hitting home. They had only been burning up until then and now they had gone forever. There would be no way back.

Colin didn't venture out again that Saturday. After leaving Manuel and Sancha, he returned directly to *Le Meridien* where he spent the rest of the day watching DVDs and using room service for his meals. Despite the coolness of earlier, the walk back from *Las Ramblas* had been hot in the emerging afternoon sun. His decision to stay inside at the hotel was determined by a combination of the attraction of its air-conditioned luxury and the fear of his 'scar' being destroyed by the sun's heat. Sancha had told him that it could take up to 24 hours to harden completely. In addition, he had sensed several odd looks from passers-by on his return walk which caused him to think that, despite his alterations, one or two of them had recognised him from his previous walk. He knew, of course, that this was nonsense but it was better to be safe than sorry.

Though the DVDs provided by Jardigo were entertaining enough, Colin was more interested in any English news bulletins he could understand — his apprehension at hearing of the Lloyds Bank's mega losses was still at the forefront of his mind. He knew in his heart of hearts that the possibility of such a discovery was a slim one but, nevertheless, he was anxious to get back to the safety of the castle as quickly as possible. Jardigo had said that he might be in *The City of Counts* for a few days and the self-imposed confinement to the hotel would be hard to bear if his stay was going to be much longer than the weekend. The next email from Jardigo came through just before he retired to bed that evening and it brought hope of an early start to the next stage of his journey back to Portugal.

CF

I trust Sancha has done a good job for you and that you are satisfied with her service. No doubt you are anxious to return to headquarters and I am pleased to confirm that arrangements are nearly in place for your transfer from your present posting. Manuel will be in contact within 24 hours with your itinerary. In the meantime, you may feel it advisable to remain where you are.

All on Red

Just twenty-four hours, thought Colin — he could manage that. As he went to sleep that night, he prayed that when he eventually left the hotel, no one at reception would query his change in appearance from that when he had first arrived. He had tried his best to avoid lingering in any of the public parts of the hotel and had his room service items left outside his door — at least his voice had not changed, whether over the telephone or when shouting through his locked door.

He awoke early after a refreshing night's sleep, uninterrupted by any dreams similar to the previous night. He wasted no time in turning on the television but was soon relieved to find no mention of his worst nightmare on any of the relevant channels. It had been seven hours since Jardigo's email — nearly a third of the time had gone before Manuel would make contact at the latest.

After showering, he ordered a hearty English-style breakfast — he was, after all, an English tourist so that was one thing he could indulge himself in without the fear of causing any remarks from the hotel staff. He was pleased to see that none of his physical alterations had been affected by the water and by eight-thirty, he had just settled down to watch the final DVD when there was a gentle knock at his door.

"I'm just having a shower; can you come back in half an hour, please!" he shouted, assuming the maid had come to change his bed and clean his room.

"Señor, it's Manuel," came the whispered reply.

"Oh, just a minute. Manuel."

Colin ran to the door — this had to be his instructions. Opening it, however, Colin noticed that Manuel looked genuinely puzzled.

"Oh, I am looking for Señor Colin Fenner. I thought this was his room — is he with you?"

"It is me, you ...."

Manuel burst out laughing.

"Just my little joke, señor! Your disguise is working."

"Ha, bloody ha!"

"Excuse?"

"Nothing, Manuel; I'm just a bit on edge, that's all."

"Of course, señor; I apologise."

Colin indicated for his guide to sit in a chair while he stood and paced up and down the room.

"You have news of how I'm going to get back to Portugal?"

"Yes, señor — or, at least, the first part."

"First part?"

"Your journey will be in two parts — train and car, or should I say jeep."

"Go on."

"First, you will take the overnight 'Costa Brava' train from Barcelona-Sants station to Madrid-Chamartin, which will take nine hours, and then you will be driven by jeep across the border at some suitable point where your entry into Portugal will not be observed by the authorities or passport control. That way, there will be no evidence of anyone of your name ever having reached Portugal."

"I see, and when will I start?"

"Tonight."

"Tonight?"

"Yes, the train leaves at ten-twenty and arrives in Madrid at seven-twenty-one tomorrow morning. I have here your ticket and all the details of what will happen when you get to Madrid."

"And what will happen?"

"You will be met at the station — I can say no more because I know no more. My job is to get you to Madrid. You are someone else's responsibility from then on."

"Jardigo has that many employees?"

"Oh yes, señor, Madrid is central to his operations in Spain."

"And where is the station in Barcelona?"

"I will pick you up at exactly nine-thirty — Sants station is less than three kilometres from here. Bring just one bag and your laptop for Jardigo to be able to stay in contact. You may want to include a change of clothes in case the journey suffers some delays."

"Delays?"

"We may have to try several crossing points into Portugal as the border police have been watching many more of them recently — illegal trafficking takes place in both directions between Spain and Portugal."

"I see," said Colin, with a frown. "This sounds a bit hairy, Manuel."

"Hairy, señor?"

"Dangerous."

Manuel smiled.

"Who knows? You will be moved by one of Jardigo's best men, of that I am sure, señor, and he will know the best place to cross."

Colin didn't look too convinced and Manuel continued,

"Don't worry, Señor Fenner; you will get there safely. Even border police can be bribed if you have enough money, eh?"

The 'Costa Brava' train seemed to be less than half full when Colin boarded at a minute after ten. He and Manuel had shook hands on the station forecourt with the latter wishing him God speed and the promise that they would meet again sometime soon. His couchette was a relatively private affair with a curtain separating it from other similar cubicles. Though it was really nothing more than a seat that extended out flat for sleeping, and despite its apparent lack of comfort and his own excitement, Colin managed to get a few hours sleep before the train pulled into Zaragoza at ten past three. He was half-way to the Spanish capital. He tried in vain to settle back after the inevitable disturbance of passengers leaving and joining the train at the one big city on the route to Madrid and by four, with the early morning lightness starting to filter into the cabins, he gave up on the idea to study the map that Manuel had furnished him with for the journey. He calculated it was at least 250 miles from Madrid to anywhere on the Portuguese border and maybe over 300 if the route by road was as tortuous as it looked on the map. It would well into the evening before he reached Castelo no Monte, provided his illegal entry went smoothly enough.

Breakfast was very welcome when they pulled into Guadalajara with just under an hour to go — his stomach had been making serious protests since he had been woken at Zaragoza. The scenery in the early morning sunshine was more mountainous on either side as the track wound its way between Spain's two largest Sierras. Colin seemed to remember from somewhere in a school Geography lesson that Madrid was over 2000 feet above sea level; an odd fact that had stuck despite his loathing of his teacher, Mr Flicker. He had barely noticed the gentle uphill gradient that had taken place since Zaragoza.

The ride into Madrid went in no time at all and his excitement grew as the train slowed for its terminus at Chamartin station. How would he know who his next escort was? Was his description now so unique that he would stand out in a crowd? Where should he go on leaving the train? All these questions were buzzing inside his head when he began to follow the other passengers to the nearest exit door. All Manuel had said was that he would be met in Madrid.

When he got off, he found the station concourse to be extraordinarily busy with incoming commuters. Like ants, they headed in long orderly lines for the way out — a ritual that had, no doubt, been repeated every weekday for countless years; every person in the vast phalanx moving in time and step with those around them. With his lack of knowledge of the station, Colin did his best to disrupt this perfect and perpetual motion by walking across and sometimes against the flow, causing several irate workers to offer up Spanish obscenities. Anyone looking for him had no chance of spotting him in the vast crowd. After a few vain attempts to make for the centre of the concourse, he gave up the idea and opted, instead, to stay in line and go with the flow to an exit, hoping that a car would be waiting for him outside by the taxi ranks. His decision proved to be the right one as immediately on reaching the roadside, a voice called out to him.

"Señor! Señor!"

The man was short and had a gypsy-like appearance, with black hair and a red neckerchief and beret. At first, Colin was unsure if the man had been shouting to him but when he trotted up to him, he was left in no doubt.

"Señor Fenner, come."

His English was not good as he attempted to introduce himself. His words seemed to have been rehearsed and committed to memory.

I Pedro; you come. Jardigo send me."

Colin began to relax again as he followed his driver to his next transport and this time it was clear that Jardigo had chosen it for its ability off-road and its inconspicuousness rather than for any luxury or comfort. The dusty-green Landrover looked prehistoric and the kind of vehicle that a sheep farmer would use to inspect his flock on rolling hillsides. Presumably, therefore, it would be, suspected Colin, perfect for crossing the border at a remote location where sheep had no respect for national boundaries or the necessity of a passport to make a visit into another country.

The first part of the journey was reasonably comfortable despite the Landrover's ancient and hard suspension. Pedro kept the Defender at a constant fifty-five on the motorway that wound roughly north-west out of Madrid, slowing to forty to negotiate some of the more mountainous terrain. Conversation was difficult and Pedro's standard answer seemed to be: '*Si, señor,*' no matter what question Colin asked. In the end, he allowed Pedro to concentrate on his driving and settled back to enjoy the magnificent scenery of brown mountains interspersed with massive pine forests and rivers. Their first stop was to be the mountain town of Avila, famous for its magnificent medieval walls which Colin spotted from several miles away. The provincial capital, built on a rocky outcrop and surrounded by rolling brown hills was in stark contrast to the lush mountain passes they had been through. Its barren position and 3,600 foot elevation meant it provided a welcome respite from the fierce Spanish sun for those tourists adventurous enough to explore further afield from the Spanish capital. Summers were always short in Avila and Colin was glad of the 60° temperatures when he took a short stroll into the ancient town for something to eat and drink while Pedro refuelled the Landrover and disappeared to some haunt or other. He had indicated to Colin that they were stopping for one hour, an instruction that took some time to convey with sign language and use of both their watches. They would be leaving at eleven-thirty.

The road out of Avila quickly became two-lane and continued roughly west as they descended gently with the mountains receding behind them. By ten to one, they had reached the Renaissance city of Salamanca for their second stop. Again, Pedro gave the same signals to indicate they had about one hour and would be leaving at two for the next leg of their journey. It was warmer again and Colin opted to spend the time at a quiet taverna to sip ice-cold tea — he'd wanted something stronger but had thought better of it with the most difficult and dangerous part of the day still to come. On the short walk from the Landrover, he'd marvelled at the architecture of the city's history-laden buildings and promised himself that he would come back to Salamanca for a longer visit sometime in the future. A glance at his map showed it to be less than seventy miles from the Portuguese border — if Pedro was to take the most direct route. He suspected it would be much longer, given their proposed illegal entry.

The track was dry and rutted and shook every bone in his body. They were in a narrow gorge and Colin soon began to realize that what he thought was a track was actually no more than a dried-up river bed, lined on either side by olive trees and shrubs. They had left the main road near Espeja and for the last four miles had followed the 'track' into a barren and desolate wilderness. It was hot now and the sweat was pouring off both men as Pedro fought to keep the Defender upright. It was nearly four o'clock and Colin estimated that they had another 200 miles to go to reach his destination. As he put his map away, he was suddenly jolted forward when Pedro slammed on the brakes. He muttered something unintelligible in Spanish.

"Whoa, what's up, Pedro?"

"Bandidos!"

Colin peered through the grimy windscreen. He'd understood Pedro's Spanish perfectly and this was confirmed when he caught a glimpse of two men standing about a hundred yards down the track in front of them. They had rifles aimed at the Landrover.

"Baje! Baje!"

He didn't need to translate this command as Pedro immediately took his right hand and forced his head down to his knees. It was a powerful shove and it left Colin in no doubt as to its meaning.

"O.K! O.K!"

Almost at the same instant, Pedro swung the Landrover out of the river bad and floored the accelerator as it jumped and bucked up the dry bank. Colin tried to raise his head to look.

"Baje!"

He ducked down again as the first of several bullets hit the Defender's left side. Pedro was now driving blindly with his head below the dash board. Suddenly, the Landrover lurched right and slowed.

"Keep your foot down, Pedro!" he shouted.

But Pedro didn't hear this command as Colin took in the horror of the gush of blood oozing down his driver's face — he had taken a fatal shot to his head. The Landrover ground to a halt. Mercifully, it had remained upright. The bullets had stopped and Colin moved quickly as he reached across to release the driver's door. With every ounce of strength he could muster, he pushed Pedro's lifeless body out. He could hear the voices now and with the door still open, he jumped into the driver's seat and gunned the accelerator. The response was quick as the Defender leapt forward in a smokescreen of dust and flying grit. The bullets started again but none appeared to hit the vehicle; the bandits aim was useless in the fog of brown dirt. Colin kept his foot down, unable to steer in any particular direction as the wheel responded uncontrollably to the bumpy terrain. After what seemed an age, the steering wheel suddenly became easier to control as the ground flattened out. He slowed the Landrover and glanced in the rearview mirror, praying that the bandits didn't have their own vehicle. Thankfully, they were nowhere to be seen and it dawned on Colin that they had given up the chase and were claiming the second prize as they robbed Pedro's dead body of anything valuable. He offered up a prayer that they would provide a suitable burial for his erstwhile driver, temporary escort and friend.

He was in a bare field now and he slowed to a complete stop to gather his bearings. Judging by the sun, he knew he had to go left if he was to continue in the same direction that Pedro had been taking them but he also knew he would have to ditch the Landrover — its bullet-riddled bodywork and blood-splattered windscreen would hardly go unnoticed. With this in mind, he headed for a corner of the field where there appeared to be a small stone building that looked to be the perfect hiding place for the Landrover. He would worry about how to get across the border afterwards. He had no idea where it was anyway.

The Defender fitted perfectly into the crumbling stone hut and after gathering his bag and laptop, he emerged to plan his next move. The land was relatively flat in all directions and his only clue as to a possible route was a well-marked track that led roughly west from the stone hut. It had to be his best bet on the basis that, '*all roads lead somewhere*'. He hoped the same applied to tracks as well.

Before setting off in the bright sunshine, Colin immediately realized he had another problem — he looked like anything but an Englishman on a walking holiday. His shirt and slacks were reasonable for the role but the two black bags containing his laptop and a change of clothes were not. As soon as he had stowed the Landrover away, he'd tried to get a signal and connection for his mobile phone and computer but without success. A phone call or email to Jardigo would, no doubt, have helped his situation enormously. He went back to the Landrover to rummage through Pedro's paraphernalia in the rear compartment to salvage anything useful for his needs. His luck was in as he unearthed an old grey army looking rucksack and a dirty brown sunhat. Fortunately, his trainers, though new, would soon look like the kind of footwear a walker might use if the terrain was not too rough. With his baseball hat reversed to shield his neck from the afternoon sun, he felt he could just about pass in his role of a rambler on holiday on the Iberian Peninsula. With his laptop and clothes stashed in the rucksack, he started down the track, singing as he did so, his choice of refrain reflecting his mood and circumstances.

> *I'm a rambler, I'm a gambler, I'm a long way from home;*
> *And if you don't like me, just leave me alone.*
> *I'll eat when I 'm hungry , I'll drink when I'm dry,*
> *And if the whiskey don't kill me, I'll live till I die.*

He repeated the chorus several times, almost until his throat became too dry to sing further, reminding him that he'd not had a drink since early afternoon — it was now gone five and he'd walked barely a mile from the stone hut, with no apparent indication of civilization ahead. The only significant change he'd noticed in the track was that it had begun to show some evidence of being repaired in places with a tarmac-looking substance, indicating vehicles other than tractors or 4X4's were accustomed to use it. It held out the hope that it might lead to a real road nearby. He started to walk quicker and soon that hope began to become a reality when, in the distance, he thought he could hear the rushing sound of traffic. He broke into a trot, now sweating profusely, until he breasted a small knoll which commanded a view of the way ahead. There, below him lay the black snake he'd prayed for and it looked to be a major route as well. Within a few minutes, he had negotiated the stiff descent from the hill to the road's right-hand margin which headed roughly west. It was easily wide enough to walk along. Surely he couldn't be far from the border. Would they question his entry into Portugal? Worse still, had news leaked out yet of his crime and had the police forces of Europe been alerted?

Cars and lorries flashed by him and occasionally he stuck out a thumb in the time-honoured fashion of a hitchhiker; something he hadn't done since he'd been a teenager at university. It was to be at least half an hour before he heard the sound of a engine revving down from behind him. A small service truck was pulling up for him. He waited until the driver leant over and wound down the nearside window.

"Você precisa um passeio, senhor?"

Colin recognized the language instantly — the accent and intonation were different from Spanish. His few days in and around Lisbon had been enough to distinguish between the two. The questioner could only be asking one thing, surely. He smiled and, testing his limited Portuguese, said,

"Obrigado, senhor!"

He climbed into the truck and the driver said,

"You English?"

"Yes."

"Where you go?"

The man's English was clearly much better than Colin's Portuguese and Colin replied, cautiously,

"Portugal, senhor."

The man, who seemed to be well into his sixties burst out laughing. He pulled the truck back onto the road and accelerated away. After driving a few hundred yards, he managed to control himself to say,

"Ah, you English, you joke, eh?"

"No, I want to cross the border and visit Portugal. I'm on a walking holiday."

"Yes?"

"Yes."

Colin was getting annoyed by now. Was he missing something in translation? Had he been misinterpreted? The man smiled again and put his foot suddenly on the brake, pulling the truck to a halt by the roadside. He then leant across Colin and opened the door.

"There, you go now."

"No," replied Colin.

"You want to go to Portugal? Well, there is Portugal!"

And then he understood the man's little joke. He was already in Portugal! Somehow, he must have crossed the border on his walk down the track. He was in his 'home' country. The man closed the door and put the truck into gear.

"So, where you go?"

"A big town, please."

"Yes?"

"Yes — it is near?"

"Ten minute, senhor — Vilar Formoso. You eat?"

"Yes, and drink."

"O.K., you try *Tavares Rico*."

"Thanks."

"You say Enrique send you, eh?"

"Obrigado, Enrique."

Tavares Rico turned out to be a café typical of a border town; full of truckers and backpackers seeking refreshment. Enrique had dropped Colin on the edge of Vilar Formoso and after another walk of a mile or so, his immediate priority was to quench his raging thirst. Finding an empty table in the shade of the building, he downed two cold beers in minutes of each other. He ordered a third and began to consider his position and the ghastly encounter with the two Spanish bandits. His first thought, on seeing a telephone kiosk outside the café, had been to call the local police to report Pedro's savage death. However, he soon realized that that was not a sensible option, with his driver being one of Jardio's employees who had been transporting a strange Englishman illegally across the border. What with language difficulties and the involvement of two country's police forces as well, it was an easy decision to make. His second thought was to try emailing Jardigo, but that also was not an option with no internet access in such an isolated spot. The only other course of action was to phone Jardigo to report his employee's untimely death. Surely, given his criminal operations, he was well used to dealing with such matters. Unfortunately, he soon discovered that his mobile didn't have access to any Portuguese provider. His difficulty got worse when he also realized that he didn't have Jardigo's number anyway, as they had only ever been in contact with each other by email. With no alternative remaining, he made for the phone box at the rear of the café. However, after trying the Portuguese equivalent of directory inquiries, and overcoming the language barrier, only to discover that Jardigo was ex-directory; he gave up on the whole idea. He would have to make the last part of the journey to Castelo no Monte under his own steam. Thankfully, he had earlier spotted the signs indicating that Vilar Formoso possessed a railway station — hiring a car, if he could find a garage, was not advisable given he needed to travel in reasonable secrecy. Garages kept records and probably would need to see his driving licence or passport as well. It was ten past seven when he eventually reached what was obviously a frequently-used station, about a mile out of town.

The next train to Lisbon was due to leave at 8.15, arriving at Coimbra at 9.23 and Lisbon at 10.17; a journey of two hours. His three beers had relieved the tension of the afternoon's events and within ten minutes, he drifted off to sleep in his first-class compartment, of which he was the only occupant. He woke just as the train pulled into Coimbra; he was now less than a hundred miles from Lisbon and for the first time in several hours he felt he was going to make it in one piece. Immediately, realizing that Coimbra was quite a sizeable city, he opened up his laptop to see if he could get internet access. The familiar sound of an incoming email provided further relief. It had to be from Jardigo.

> *CF*
>
> *You were expected some time ago. Pedro has not reported in as arranged at the handover at Guarda and your next driver has reported that he is still waiting with his brown Mercedes to drive you back here. Where are you? If you get this message, please report your progress to headquarters.*
>
> > *JB*

No codes now, thought, Colin — his boss was worried. He carefully typed his reply, leaving out the precise details of Pedro's demise.

> *JB*
>
> *Pedro indisposed and unable to drive. Reached Vilar Formoso on foot and have taken train to Lisbon via Coimbra. Expect to arrive Lisbon at 10.17. Currently just leaving Coimbra. Please arrange for someone to meet me on arrival. Will explain all when I see you.*
>
> > *CF*

The reply came back almost instantly — Jardigo *was* worried.

> *CF*
>
> *Message received but not understood. Will await your arrival for details.*
>
> > *JB*

Jardigo himself was there to meet Colin on his arrival at Lisbon's Oriente station though, with his change of appearance, it took him a little time to assure himself he had got the right person. After a quick hug — both men were relieved to see each other — he wasted no time in informing his boss of Pedro's untimely end.

"Pedro is dead, I'm afraid."

"I suspected as much," replied Jardigo.

He did not seem to be too upset.

"We were ambushed near the border."

"Bandits?"

"Yes, he was shot in the head. I had to ditch his body and make my escape in his Landrover. I will give you more details when we're back at the castle. Has there been any news from England?"

"You mean from your bank?"

"No, my friend, not yet. How did you get to the train?"

"I walked to a place called Vilar Formoso — you know it?"

"Yes, it was to be Pedro's preferred crossing for you. Where did you leave his body?"

"About two or three miles from Vilar Formoso; still in Spain, I guess. I hid his Landrover in an old farm building nearby."

"You have done well; we will recover his body and the jeep tomorrow. My man in Guarda can organize it. You will have come through the place where he was waiting for you. You have certainly been through an ordeal today, my friend. You will have a few days to recover at the castle — you deserve a bonus. I am pleased with Sancha's work on you — you look like a new man and in a few days you will feel like one, too."

"I hope so; I am absolutely exhausted and I never want to go through anything like that again, Jardigo."

"I will try to make sure you don't, my friend."

They had reached Jardigo's black Mercedes by now and little more was said between the two men on the journey back to the castle. Extreme tiredness had eventually caught up with Colin and he was to sleep like a baby that night, safe in his new fortified home and with the prospect of some time to enjoy himself again.

11

Suspended

The phone call, when it came, did not produce the immediate panic which such a message ought to have done. The call centre that handled general incoming calls for the London Provincial Bank was located in some part of the Indian subcontinent and the operator had not really been trained to deal with anything other than routine requests for information. It was eight-thirty on the Monday morning, just after Colin had met up with Pedro outside the station in Madrid.

"London Provincial Bank — good morning, how may I help you?"

"Yes, I have a huge problem; some money has gone missing from my account."

"Can I have your name, please?"

"Solomon Meickelberg."

"Your account number, please?"

"28139628"

"One moment please."

"Please hurry, a great deal of money is missing."

"Just getting your details on screen, Mr Meickelberg."

"Well?"

"Ah yes, I see you made a transfer withdrawal on Friday for the sum of 5,000,000 Euros. Is that correct, sir?"

"No, it damn well isn't correct; I made no such withdrawal."

"It was made online at nine-fifteen in the morning."

"I tell you I didn't make any withdrawal. Where was it made?"

"I don't have that information, sir."

"Well, can you get it please?"

"No, you would have to contact the holding branch directly, sir."

"Will this call be logged?"

"Yes, sir, all calls are logged into the system."

"Well, will you kindly notify the Canary Wharf branch that I shall be there within the hour to sort this out? In the meantime, will you please put a block on this account until I can change the password and so on?"

"Yes, sir, I will send an email with the details of your call. Your account is now blocked, too."

"Thank you."

Solomon Arthur Meickelberg was a second generation immigrant from Nazi Germany. He had made his colossal fortune in cheap clothing manufacture in the post-war years and had built up his empire through his range of 500 shops which traded under the name *Quality Suits* and branded simply as *QS*. He was currently one of the UK's top hundred wealthiest men yet still lived in a modest house in the East End where he had arrived in 1943. By nine-thirty that Monday morning, he had parked his gold Rolls Royce directly outside the Canada Building in Cabot Square. After several failed attempts to see someone in a senior position, he was asked to wait in a small private office while his problem was looked into.

Bob Mckellar had heard of Solomon Meickelberg, both because of his high-street shops and because he was by far the bank's wealthiest customer, so when the call came through from twenty floors below, he dropped everything and headed for the lift. The teller had said that Mr Meickelberg was reporting a sum of money missing from his account, but he had refused to say how much. Mac suspected it would not be a trivial sum for him to pay the bank a personal visit.

Solon Meickelberg was pacing up and down the small interview office when Mac opened the door.

"Ah, at last — you are someone in authority, I hope?"

"Yes, Mr Meickelberg — Bob Mckellar. I'm one of the senior executives at the bank, in charge of private accounts."

"Good; well perhaps *you* can solve my problem."

"I hope so, sir. You have reported some money missing from one of your accounts?"

"Yes."

"How much?"

"Five million Euros."

Bob Mckellar dropped his pen and looked absolutely dumbfounded. He rubbed his chin and stared at the clothing magnate.

"Five million? Are you sure?"

"Yes, damn it, five million! Go check my account on your computer, if you like."

But Bob Mckellar had already switched the terminal on and was busy tapping a few keys.

"Account number?"

"28139628"

"Right, let's see what we've got."

Mac sat back and waited for the details to appear on screen.

"When did you notice the money missing?"

"This morning when I checked the balance online — maybe about an hour ago."

"Ah, here we are — a transfer was made on Friday for the amount you stated."

"But it wasn't me, Mr Mckellar; I promise you it wasn't me."

"Well, it can only have been made using your pass numbers, sir. Has anyone in your family got access to them?"

"No, of course not and besides, I have no family. My wife is dead and we had no children. Any remaining members of my blood family still alive live in Germany."

"Could someone who works for you have got hold of them?"

"Again, no; I keep such information entirely in my head. It is not written down anywhere."

"What, even the twelve-digit entry number?"

"I have a good head for figures, Mr Mckellar."

"I see — you understand I have to ask these questions?"

"Yes."

"Well, we will have to investigate this as a matter of urgency."

"How?"

"I will get one of my computer experts to look at what's happened. It looks like it must be some kind of identity fraud to me."

"And how quickly will I get my money back? I presume you're insured for something like this."

"Provided it can be proved that either our system was at fault or ...."

"Or the person who perpetrated the fraud is caught."

"Do you need the money quickly, Mr Meickelberg?"

"What do you think, Mr Mckellar — presumably you've just seen my balance with your bank?"

"Yes, sir — stupid question, I suppose."

"Not stupid; just naïve."

Bob Mckellar's face has taken on a deep shade of red. He was quick to change the conversation.

"Well, it may take a few hours for us to investigate this, so I suggest you go home and I'll call you personally as soon as we have news."

The two men stood up and after a brief hand shake, Solomon Meickelberg left the Canary Wharf headquarters of the London Provincial

Bank, slightly happier but certainly none the wiser as to what had happened to his money. Meanwhile, senior executive Bob Mckellar headed back up to the nineteenth floor — there was only one person that could possibly sort his problem out — computer whizz kid Matthew Sampson.

Matt Sampson had a hangover — the result of an extended Sunday lunchtime session with friends in the Black Bull, near his home in Windsor. However, after Bob Mckellar had marched into the IT suite to share his problem, his head suddenly began to throb for entirely a different reason.

"How much is missing, Bob?"

"Five million. Are you alright, Matthew; you look awful."

"Too much to drink yesterday, I guess."

"Well, you're going to have to get your brain in gear and find out what's happened to Mr Meickelberg's money — O.K?"

"Yes, boss. How was the money taken?"

"Someone or some thing made a transfer on Friday morning, using his pass numbers to get into the account."

"Just when you were testing the security of the bank as well, Bob?"

As soon as Matt saw the blank look on the senior executive's face, he knew what had happened.

"I haven't been testing the security, Matt; I leave that to you boys. What made you think I was?"

Matt Sampson's face went even whiter and deep down he knew he couldn't hide what he knew. He had to come clean there and then.

"I think I know how it was done, boss. Can we go to somewhere private — your office?"

"Yes, Matt; I knew you'd have a solution."

Matt Sampson smiled wryly but said nothing. He followed Mac up to the top floor in silence. Once in the senior executive's office, he flopped down into a chair and said,

"I think Dave has done it."

"Dave Marks?"

"Yes."

"Come on, laddie, what the hell are you talking about? David Marks went to Brussels for a conference over the weekend. He's not due back at work till tomorrow."

And then Matt told the whole story — Bob Mckellar's mouth dropping further with each revelation.

"And you believed this cock and bull story about me wanting to test the bank's security?"

"Yes."

"Why the hell didn't you check with me first?"

"I just trusted that Dave was telling the truth."

"And you actually stood and watched while he made two dummy transfers from two of our customer's accounts? Didn't you think that was a bit obvious that he could be using you to do it for real at some time in the future?"

"I didn't think and anyway, I didn't stand and watch — I couldn't, I knew it was wrong."

"Precisely, Matthew; it wasn't only wrong, it was downright criminal and you stood by and let him do it."

"I don't know how he could have done it. He gave me the discs back before he left for Brussels and they were the only ...."

Matt Sampson didn't finish his sentence as the second realization dawned on him.

"Oh God, he must have copied the discs while he was using them to test how easy it was to break into an account."

"Which, young man, I never authorized!"

Matt looked nervous.

"What happens now?"

"I don't know, laddie. I'm going to have to notify the police, but first, you and I are going to go to Davy's office.

The office was open when they arrived and Matt's suspicions were soon confirmed when he had turned on his friend's computer.

"Yep, he's definitely copied one disc and I'll bet that the one on the desk there is a copy of the other."

"Right, laddie, my office now. You will stay with me until the police arrive. No doubt, they will want to interview you first before they carry out a full investigation. After I've notified them, I'm going to check with the conference organizers to see if David actually went to Brussels and I'll get Jean to phone his flat in Esher — the conference ended last night and he was supposed to be writing a report for me at home today. I suspect, however, we will get a negative to both inquiries. You say you think he was going to try two accounts for my supposed test?"

"Yes, boss."

"Well, we've only had Mr Meickelberg spot anything missing yet, so we must hope we can trace the other account before a second person finds the same thing. Is there any way you can find out if he did another account?"

"No, I don't think so — the software just enables the accounts to be opened. It doesn't record which ones."

"Right, I'm going to lock his office with my master key before we go back to mine. You will wait with me — I'm not letting you out of my sight."

Matt Sampson was beginning to look very shaky and a little annoyed. *He* wasn't the criminal, after all.

"I'm not going anywhere, boss. I'm as upset as you about what's happened. I had no idea what Dave was going to do, I swear."

"That's not how Her Majesty's Constabulary may see it, laddie. You could even be regarded as an accomplice. In any case, after they've finished with you, I'm going to have to suspend you on full pay, Matthew, I'm afraid."

The police had more news when they arrived — another person had suffered an identical loss from their account at the London Provincial. Eric Skjöldebrand, a retired Swedish banker and oil magnate, living in Weybridge in Surrey had contacted New Scotland Yard direct when his accountant had queried the huge transfer an hour earlier than Solomon Meickelberg. Being virtually a total recluse in his late seventies, he had made just the one phone call and had left the matter entirely in the hands of the police and his accountant.

Superintendant Bill Tamplin of the Yard was thorough, directing his team of one chief inspector, two detective sergeants and numerous constables to interview as many of the bank's staff as possible. The process was painstakingly slow and would eventually take the rest of the day and part of the following morning. Needless to say, Bill Tamplin interviewed Matt Sampson himself and though seemingly a kindly man in his fifties, he nevertheless was direct and to the point and spared no punches as to the trouble the young computer technician was in. Bob Mckellar had vacated his office for the purpose. The all-important interview started at ten-fifteen with a young female detective constable in attendance. The bank's solicitor had also requested to be present. Procedure normally dictated that such an interview should take place back at the Yard but Bill Tamplin decided that the matter was too important to waste any valuable time — they had brought a suitable recording device to ensure all the evidence would be collected correctly.

"Right, young man," Bill Tamplin began. "What can you tell me about all this?"

"Well, like I told Mr Mckellar, Matt Sampson told me that he'd been asked by him to carry out a test of the bank's security for the possibility of any online fraud."

"Is that normal practice at the bank?"

"No, I'd not heard of it being done before."

"Did you check with the senior executive that the request was genuine?"

"No."

"Why not — you've just said that it was not normal practice."

"I don't know; Matt is senior to me, so I thought it had to be O.K."

"Mr Mckellar says you made up some discs for the purpose and gave them to David Marks. Is that correct?"

"Yes, but ...."

"And did he perform the test with you present?"

"Yes."

"Did you not realise what he and you were doing was illegal?"

"Yes, I suppose so, but ...."

The questions were coming thick and fast now and Matt was getting flustered.

"Why did you leave the discs with Mr Marks?"

"So he could carry out the test for Mr Mckellar."

"Which we now suspect was when he made the transfers."

"I suppose so."

"Why do you think he did it — ten million Euros seems to be far too much money for one man to need?"

"I don't know; maybe his gambling debts had got out of hand."

"He gambled?"

"Yes, he liked the horses."

The superintendant grinned.

"Oh come on, he'd have had to have been a pretty poor punter to rack up a debt of that size."

"Yes."

"Do you think he was working for someone?"

"I don't know."

"Had you seen him with any strange characters recently?"

"No."

"Had he been anywhere unusual in the last few weeks?"

Matt Sampson hesitated.

"Well?"

"He'd just come back from a holiday in Portugal — only returned to work last week. He'd been given leave by the bank after a bit of a traumatic divorce from his wife."

"Where in Portugal?"

"Lisbon."

"Did he say what he'd done there?"

"Relaxed and played the casinos, I believe."

"Did he meet anyone?"

"I don't know — he didn't mention anyone."

"So, within a day or two it looks like he's just made one of the biggest bank frauds in history."

Matt Sampson said nothing.

"And you, young fellow, helped him do it, eh?"

"Do you think I would still be here, Superintendant, if I was complicit in the fraud? I had no idea what he was going to do?"

"That may be for a court to decide, but I suppose at least you did give all the details of your part in the scam without being asked. That will stand you in good stead later on."

"I'm not a criminal; I'm not."

"We will see, won't we? Now, to more practical matters where you may be able to help us and the bank."

"What?"

"Well, we obviously know the two account holders whose money has been taken but is there any way of knowing where the money went to?

Matt's head was really pounding now; it was the most awkward question yet.

"You look a little confused — shall I repeat the question?"

"No, I understand."

"Well, can you find out where the money has gone?"

"No."

"Why not? Surely Mr Marks must have had a receiving account. We've checked his own bank accounts and they seem to be in dire straits; one heavily overdrawn and the other virtually at zero."

Matt was sweating profusely now. His throat was dry and he tried to speak.

"I-I, er ...."

"Yes?"

"I designed the software on the discs so that the accounts couldn't be traced. After any transfer, a subroutine immediately wiped clean the details of all accounts used. David said that Mr Mckellar wanted the test to be as realistic as possible and to use all the latest techniques. I just didn't know he was intending to do it for real — if that's what he's done. You don't really have actual proof that he did it, do you?"

"No, but I'd say we've got a pretty strong case against him, wouldn't you agree?"

Matt said nothing — he needed a drink. The superintendant was relentless.

"When was the last time you saw Mr Marks?"

152

It was a change of tack and a bit easier to deal with.

"Friday."

"When, Friday?"

"About nine, I guess — when he brought me the discs back."

"Ah yes, the discs. That kind of fits, doesn't it?"

"Yes, like I told Mr Mckellar, he must have copied them before he gave them back to me and then he ...."

"And then he went and did the deed; transferring ten million Euros to God knows where. The timings fit perfectly with the bank's record on when the money was taken from the two accounts — and you still maintain that we have no real proof? What kind of odds would you give for that happening, eh?"

"I don't know, Superintendant."

"Well I do, young man; I do, and they're pretty long."

Matt gave a shrug of his shoulders. The policeman turned his face to the voice recorder.

"This interview is terminated at 10.43."

He then tried to put on his best fatherly expression.

"Right, Matthew Sampson, you will now go home and await further questioning. You are now officially on police bail. Do you understand what that means?"

"I don't leave the country?"

"No, son, much more than that; you will report daily to — er, let me see — ah yes, Windsor police station at nine a. m. sharp where, also, you will surrender your passport as soon as you get home today. If you fail to turn up, each day, a warrant will be issued for your arrest. Now do you understand the conditions of your bail?"

"Yes."

"And, Mr Sampson ...."

"What?"

"Do not try to make contact with your friend. We are tapping his phone and watching his flat so we'll know instantly if anyone tries to make that contact."

"Yes, Superintendant," replied Matt, looking at the bank's solicitor. "Will there be anything else?"

"No, I'm done with you for the moment. Just go home, and if there's anything else that comes to mind that's relevant, you call me immediately — right?"

"Right."

Matt and the solicitor rose from their chairs and turned to leave the room. Bill Tamplin called the computer expert back.

"One final thing, Mr Sampson."

"What?"

"You might like to use your free time to see if you can trace what has happened to the money and also where Matt himself may have gone to."

"Would it look good for me?"

"It may do, son; it may do."

By the Tuesday lunchtime, it was clear to all at the London Provincial, bank employees and police alike, that David Marks was indeed the perpetrator of the country's biggest online fraud of the year. This fact had been trebly confirmed when it was discovered that he had never attended the conference in Brussels; neither returned to Glendower Mansions in Esher the day before nor appeared for work as scheduled that morning. When Scotland Yard checked all exit points from the country and found no record of such a person having left the country, the conclusion was reached that he had simply vanished off the face of the earth. Finally, with all these facts at his disposal, the details of the online scam were released by Superintendant Bill Tamplin in time for the London evening papers and the rest of the world's media. David Richard Marks had become Scotland Yard's number one wanted man.

Matt Sampson did not leave his maisonette in Windsor from the time he arrived back from the bank early the previous afternoon, spending his time trying to find a way of identifying the accounts his friend had used to receive the money, but without success — his own software had just been too good. Secretly, he was quite excited by the whole affair and impressed by his friend's outrageous courage and enterprise. He was, however, convinced like Bill Tamplin, that David must have had help and guidance to be able to carry the whole operation out — that was, of course, in addition to that which he himself had unwittingly provided. That excitement was tempered by the fear of prosecution for his 'part' in the heist, and he had spent the twenty-four hours wrestling with his conscience to reassure himself that there had never been any intention on his part to defraud the bank and two of its wealthiest customers of such vast sums of money.

The main six o'clock news on all major TV channels carried the breaking story and Matt Sampson's heart skipped a beat when he saw his friend's mug shot staring back at him from the screen — the mug shot that he had been so used to seeing on the identity card that David had always kept clipped to his shirt pocket. That admiration he had earlier felt for his friend suddenly returned with an added twist, as he watched and listened to the details of his crime. The thought that had been lurking somewhere in the deep recesses of his mind had suddenly surfaced as he realised that, if he got away with it, his best friend would have riches beyond anybody's imagination. As he sat in his small lounge, glued to his television, he put that thought into words.

"Davy boy, I think you may just owe me a thing or two. Don't you dare forget your old friend if you get away with this."

He sat back in his chair and smiled. Part of him now hoped that his friend *would* get away with his crime, if only for the sheer audacity of it, and any thoughts that he had been deceived by David began to disappear from his mind as that part of him that upheld honesty and decency as essential parts of the human character was taken over by more primeval thoughts of greed and envy. He had a right to a percentage of his friend's ill-gotten gain. In some sort of strange reversal of moral principles, he reckoned that that was only right and just.

12

Personal Recruitment

Colin woke very late on the Tuesday morning; his sleep had been uninterrupted as his body released itself from the tensions of the previous day. After rising, he was very much left to his own devices and it was not until early evening that Jardigo caught up with him as he took a walk down to the summer house near the lake. He had a frown on his face.

"My friend, we have news from London."

"Oh?"

"Yes, Henry has been in touch to report that the press and TV have been informed of a large bank fraud at the London Provincial Bank."

"Oh no!"

Colin had stopped still in his tracks. They were half-way down the gentle hillside to the lake.

"Yes, but do not worry, Colin — you are safe now. No one can know anything about you. The police have named a David Marks as their chief suspect — I don't think you know him, do you?"

Jardigo turned and grinned at the impostor. Colin did not seem amused.

"Oh, very funny, Jardigo. What else have they said?"

"Not much, Henry says; just that one of their computer experts has been suspended on police bail and that they're checking all exit points from the country for this David Marks. I suppose you must know who the computer whizz kid is, eh?"

"Yes, he was the one who helped me with the transfers — he wrote the software for it and ...."

Colin turned away and looked back up at the castle.

"And what, my friend?"

"And he is — or was — my best friend."

"Ah, I see," said Jardigo. "He must be a very clever man that one; the police have no idea where the money has gone to."

"Yes, he is; he made sure all evidence was destroyed after the transfers."

Though they had resumed their walk, Jardigo suddenly stopped again and placed both his hands firmly on Colin's shoulders.

"Ah, so he knew what you were going to do, then? That is not good, my friend."

"No, he did not; he thought I was carrying out a security exercise for one of the senior executives. He had no idea I was going to do it for real."

"But he will know now that you deceived him?"

"Yes — along with millions of others throughout the world."

They walked in silence for a few yards until Jardigo suddenly put his arm round Colin.

"You know, my friend, I think I could use the services of this friend of yours. What is his name?"

"Matt, er, Matthew Sampson."

"And what does this Matthew Sampson like to do in his spare time?"

"He plays a bit of football at weekends but, like me, I suppose his main passion is horse racing."

"And gambling, eh?"

"Yes, but he never places big bets."

"And is he married?"

"No, he's never had much luck with the opposite sex — he's not the world's most physically attractive guy. You know what computer geeks can look like."

"Geeks? What is this?"

"Anorak?"

Still Jardigo looked baffled by the terminology.

"I mean he is totally wrapped up in his computing to have much common sense or awareness of what goes on around him in the world."

"Ah, I understand."

As they finally reached the summer house and eased themselves into the loungers, it finally dawned on Colin how Matt's services could be of use to Jardigo's operation.

"Are you thinking what I think you're thinking?"

"What are you thinking, my friend?"

"That you might want to employ Matt on a permanent basis like me and use him to perform some more online transfers?"

"Maybe, but I could also have some other uses for him."

"Like what, may I ask?"

"No, you may not, Colin — at least, not until I've thought the idea through properly."

"But it would involve computer hacking of some sort?"

"Possibly."

Colin suddenly shook his head.

"What is the matter, my friend?"

"He's too honest, Jardigo. He'd never agree to join you."

"No? You did."

"I was in debt to you — he's not."

"But maybe he can be bought, eh?"

"Not Matt, and certainly not by you, Jardigo."

Jardigo didn't immediately pass comment on Colin's remark and seemed slightly put out as he headed for the refrigerator.

"Have another drink, Colin."

"No, I'm fine."

"No, I insist. I'm going to open a bottle of champagne. We haven't really celebrated your success yet, my friend."

"Just a glass, then."

The two men drank in silence for a few minutes. Colin felt nervous about how the conversation was going. His thoughts transferred for a moment to his friend back in England.

"You know I've must have put Matt in real trouble, don't you, Jardigo?"

"Yes, I suspect he will need a good lawyer, but at least your disappearance confirms that you, or should I say, David Marks is the real and possibly only culprit."

"Even so, he must be going through hell at the moment and he had no idea that I was using him."

"Yes, it will not be nice for him."

"I still don't think, however, that his parlous position will be enough for you to persuade him to join the cause."

"I won't be doing the persuading, Colin."

"So who, then? Henry?"

"No, not Henry Madison."

"Then who?"

"You."

"Me?"

"Yes you, Colin."

"No way, Jose!"

"But yes, my friend; you are the only one who could do it. He trusts you, yes?"

"Not now, he doesn't — he must hate me more than anyone else in the world."

"Greed and envy, my friend; greed and envy."

"What?"

"Well, isn't it obvious? First, he will be so envious of you that you appear to have got away with one of the biggest crimes ever and second, greed can be a great motivator — just look at what happened to you."

Colin shook his head.

"Aren't you forgetting something?"

"What?"

"They'll be watching him day and night. How on earth would I make contact with him?"

"I've been thinking about that."

"And?"

"And he's not under lock and key, is he?"

"How do you mean?"

"I mean he's still allowed to go out sometimes."

"So?"

"So, you go to wherever he lives and watch for him. Where does he live?"

"Windsor."

"Ah, where the castle is, eh? Is it better than mine?"

"Yes."

"Really? Ah well — maybe someday I own it!"

"You were saying about watching him?"

"Yes, you follow him and pass him a note or something — maybe even talk to him face to face. He may go to a bar or a restaurant and you can casually strike up a conversation."

"He'll be watched and they'll see me. It's a stupid idea, Jardigo."

"Oh yes, and who will they see?"

"Me?"

"And who are you now, Colin? Even your friend will not recognise you, let alone anyone else."

Colin went quiet again. Despite his fears and misgivings, it seemed to make sense.

"He just wouldn't agree, I just know it."

"But it's got to be worth a try, my friend."

"I'm not sure I want to do it, Jardigo. Couldn't you use someone else?"

"You are the only person who could do it and besides ...."

"What?"

"You work for me now, Colin, and if I ask you to ...."

"I've paid back my debts to you, Jardigo."

"Possibly, but once you joined my operation, you joined for life, my friend. Remember, I own you, Colin Fenner. I created you and you are no longer master of your own destiny."

Inside, he knew it was useless to try to argue with Jardigo — he held all the aces; one of which he then produced and waved in front of his face.

"And remember, Colin, I can ask Sancha Castilla to reverse your facial alterations, and return your original passport to discard you like old rags back into society as the wanted criminal Mr David Marks."

He was cornered and beaten.

"O.K., O.K., I'll do it."

"Good, now let's finish the champagne, my friend."

As usual, the *Linden Tree* was packed with Sunday lunchtime drinkers. It was the first time that Matt Sampson had visited his favourite watering hole in Windsor since his forced suspension from work. It had been nearly a fortnight and it had been a living nightmare, with frequent visits by the police, from humble detective constables all the way up to Superintendant Tamplin himself. In addition, a tearful Gaynor Marks had phoned him three or four times to see if he knew where her ex-husband had gone to and to use his shoulder to cry on. Apart from the odd visit to an out-of-town supermarket for food and essential supplies, he had ventured no further than his local paper shop less than a hundred yards from his front door. Such visits had been something of an ordeal for him, owing to the cold reception and whispered comments from other customers and the curt service from the owner, with whom he had been friends for a couple of years at least. That Sunday, the 21st of July, he had decided he would not be denied one of his favourite pleasures any longer. With the weather warm and sunny, he knew he could hide himself away in the isolation of the *Linden Tree's* vast rear garden that backed onto the Thames. However, despite this isolation, he suspected that at least one other customer at the *Linden Tree* that lunchtime would be a detective from New Scotland Yard.

Matt Sampson spotted the policeman early on his arrival at the pub, a favourite gathering place for nearly every Hooray Henry in the area and he nodded politely as he passed him on his way outside. He found himself an empty table right by the water's edge while the detective seemed content to remain inside, only occasionally glancing in his direction through one of the open windows. For almost the first time since his suspension, Matt began to feel reasonably relaxed in a public place, with only a threesome of Hooray Henries for close company at a neighbouring table. He couldn't help but overhear their conversation.

"I say bloody good luck to him. I wish I had the balls to do something like that."

"You haven't got any, Clarence, dear boy."

"Balls? He hasn't got the brain for it, anyway."

"He had help as well — some computer whizz kid was in on it, you know."

"So why haven't they arrested him yet, then?"

"Well, you're the lawyer, Rodders, old boy — you tell me."

"No evidence that he knew what he was up to, so difficult to make a case, unless ...."

"Unless what?"

"Unless they catch him making contact with this Marks fellow or his bank balance suddenly shoots up."

"From his share, you mean?"

"Oh, well done, Clarence — you have got some grey cells after all, old boy."

Matt had just about had enough and to make matters worse, he could swear that one of the Hooray Henries was staring at him with more than a casual passing interest. He was just about to stand and move to a different table when he found that a tall blond-haired man he'd noticed earlier at the bar had joined him at his present table.

"Mind if I sit here, sir?"

The man had a northern accent which Matt found difficult to place.

"No, I was just going anyway."

"Oh just stay for a few minutes — I'm new to the area and could use some information."

The man had sat down by now and Matt began to study him. Apart from his bleached blond hair and a pair of thick sunglasses, he had two other distinguishing features — a moustache of a somewhat darker hue and a lurid scar that ran from his mouth to one ear. He seemed pleasant enough to Matt and his presence was not unwelcome as it formed a distraction from the neighbouring table's conversation.

"Alright, can I buy you a drink?" he asked, attempting to at least be friendly.

"No, I'm fine."

"You say you're new to Windsor — what do you do, then?"

"I'm an actor."

"What on TV?"

"No, I do impressions."

"Impressions? Who do you do?"

"One or two people."

"Anyone I'd know?"

"Probably, but ...."

"But?"

"But I'm not sure I can remember all their idiosyncrasies."

"Try me."

"O.K."

"Well?"

"I wanna' tell you a story."

"Max Bygraves?"

"Got it in one, er ...."

"Matt — Matt Sampson and you are ...?"

"Colin Fenner."

"Nice to meet you, Colin."

"To meet you nice, eh? My Bruce Forsyth isn't very good, I'm afraid."

"Who else do you do?"

"How about this one."

The man paused and looked hard at Matt.

"Did you go to Lingfield for the Hawaiian evening, Matt?"

The voice was now posh East End.

"Wha ...?"

"I said, did you go to the races at Lingfield after I left you?"

"Dave?"

"Shh, my name is Colin Fenner and we are being watched from the veranda up there. In a moment I am going to leave you and you will find that I have dropped a cigarette packet on the ground under the table. When you are sure that you are not being watched, pick it up and put it in your pocket. And, Matty, please do not be alarmed — I only want what's best for both of us, and if

165

you value your life, please do not mention this conversation to anyone. It has not happened, you understand?"

"Ye-es."

"Now enjoy the rest of your afternoon."

And with that, Colin/David walked casually away to disappear among the drinkers thronging near the rear of the *Linden Tree*. It would be nearly ten minutes before Matt reached down and picked up the empty packet of Benson and Hedges — not because the suspected detective was watching him, but because his body was frozen rigid with the incredulity and enormity of what had just occurred. He had just had a conversation with his friend David Marks and currently, one of Europe's most wanted criminals. As he slowly brought his mind back to the reality of the situation, he suddenly found himself torn between rushing to inform the police and his admiration for his friend's bravado. He knew what he should do, but something was preventing him from doing it, and that something was contained entirely within five simple words: '*If you value your life.*'

It had been relatively easy for Colin to find Matt. He had arrived in England three days earlier and had checked into the *Royal Oak*, less than half a mile from Matt's maisonette. He had seen him for the first time on the Saturday when he had walked to the local shop. It had taken three and a half hours sitting in his hired car that morning just a few short yards from his friend's front door. A similar surveillance had led Colin to the *Linden Tree* the very next day, even using the tailing detective as his guide. He had set the ball rolling and time would tell if his erstwhile friend was as game as he thought he was for the next part of Jardigo's plan. As he saw it, Matt had two choices: tell the police, or meet him again as detailed in the note inside the cigarette packet.

Matt didn't open the cigarette packet until he was back, locked inside his maisonette. He had spent a nervous forty minutes trying to give the watching policeman the impression that he was still enjoying his lunchtime drink and that nothing untoward had happened. Resisting the temptation to leave as soon as his friend had gone took all his patience and four more whiskies.

The note was simple enough, but deliberately cryptic for any eyes other than his.

> *'The leafy course on the 23rd for your next career*
> *move and investment in your future.'*

Matt immediately turned on his TV to BBC1 and the Ceefax page for the week-ahead's racing fixtures. He knew what *'leafy course'* meant and there it was — an evening flat meeting at Lingfield Park, or *Leafy Lingfield* as it was sometimes called by the racing press. He smiled at Matt's play on words with regard to a possible business course on the Tuesday. The first race of the seven-race card was scheduled to start at 5.50 p.m. *'Career move'* and *'your future'* struck a chord after his thoughts of compensation from his friend David or, what had he called himself? Colin Fenner — that was it. Well, Mr Fenner, I'm in the mood for offers, especially if they get me out of this hellhole of an existence with the imminent prospect of prosecution or the sack, at least.

Tuesday couldn't come round quick enough for Matt and he spent a lot of his time thinking of a way to get to Lingfield without being followed, particularly by the same detective who had probably recorded his apparently casual meeting with the tall blond-haired man with the dark glasses and scar at the *Linden Tree*. Though he hadn't used it yet — there hadn't been the need — there was a way of leaving his maisonette without using the front door. The one bedroom of his first-floor flat had a sash window that overlooked the overgrown concrete yard which contained nothing more than six or seven dustbins for the residents of the three-storey property. Its rear fence, though high, was eminently climbable and behind its left-hand end there led a narrow passageway between two similar properties. This alleyway ended up in Pelham Crescent which was less than a quarter of a mile from the town centre. With his car parked at the front of his own building, he would have to use public transport to get to Lingfield as he dare not risk being seen by any policeman in their normal position, thus defeating the whole object of his 'back-door' escape. As he saw it, there could be two problems with his plan. First, there was a fair drop to the ground from his bedroom window and second, the police might have any rear exit covered with someone watching the alleyway. Matt guessed that the second problem might be less of a worry than the first which would need some extra preparation. A dustbin or two moved to a position directly under his bedroom window might provide the solution and cushion his jump somewhat. To allay any fears about the first problem, he decided there and then to take an afternoon walk and go the long way round to Pelham Crescent, thus inspecting the alleyway and rear fence to his backyard for any potential worries.

An hour later, he arrived back home after an extended three-mile walk — deliberately made longer in order to confuse anyone following him as to the real purpose of his afternoon stroll. He had seen no one; either anywhere near the alleyway or, indeed, at the front of his building. It seemed to him, at last, that the police had begun to step down their 24/7 surveillance.

He set off early on Tuesday afternoon; it would be an hour to Waterloo from Windsor station, followed by thirty minutes on the tube to Victoria and finally another train to Lingfield, forty-five minutes south from the city. Apart from landing on a dustbin rather awkwardly, thus bruising an elbow, the first part of his escape went without a hitch. Having set out at three o'clock, he was pleased to find that it was only just after five-fifteen when the train pulled into Lingfield station. There were still thirty-five minutes to the first race. Though he had never come by train before, he knew that it was only a five or ten minute walk to the course. He stopped just once — to withdraw £500 in cash from an ATM in the High Street; something he had been reluctant to do in Windsor in case the police had started to wonder why he needed so much cash.

As he joined the small crowd of racegoers making the half-mile walk from the village centre to the course, Matt occasionally glanced nervously over his shoulder to see if he could spot any likely tail. To his relief, there was not a single likely person in sight — everyone was in small groups with nothing more than the exciting prospect of a warm evening at the races on their mind. The talk was all about champion jockey Willy Bentham who had a full book of rides at the meeting. Matt began to relax — he was here to enjoy himself for the first time in over a fortnight, and with the added excitement of seeing his friend again, he *was* going to enjoy himself.

The runners were already in the parade ring when Matt arrived just ten minutes before the first race, a six furlong sprint for two-year-old maidens, and there was a short-priced favourite — a filly aptly named *Summer Fun*. Ridden by the champion jockey, she was a shade of odds on to win her first race. Matt wasted no time with the niceties of inspecting the horses and made his way swiftly to the bookmakers in front of the main stand. So far, he hadn't noticed anyone tall and blond-haired with sunglasses and knew that his friend would find him in his own time anyway. His thoughts were soon disturbed by Barry 'Bismarck' Dennis who was, as usual, on duty at the Surrey course and bellowing the odds in his familiar Essex voice.

"Four to one bar one! Let's get this favourite beat — I've got a wife to subsidise!"

Matt smiled at the Romford bookie's humour as he took his place in the small queue of patrons anxious to listen to his wit and charm.

"Five minutes, gentlemen — and ladies. Get your bets on now. They won't wait for you."

Matt had made up his mind; a hundred at 10/11 would net him nearly another ton and *Summer Fun* looked to be the only horse worth backing. It was soon his turn.

"A ton on number three, Barry, please."

"That's one hundred on the favourite, Mandy. Thank you, sir, and good luck."

Matt took his ticket and moved away — the potential winnings were £190.90. He glanced at the track where the first of the runners was making its way past the front of the enclosures and down to the six furlong start away in the distance to Matt's left. With his member's ticket, he found a good vantage point high up in the stand directly opposite the winning post. It was always difficult at Lingfield, even with binoculars, to tell who was in front until the last couple of furlongs, but the spot he'd chosen was perfect for photo finishes, and there was a big screen directly in front of him for the early part of the race in any case.

"What are you on, mate?"

The voice had come from behind him, and it was familiar.

"Don't turn round yet, Matty — I may look different and I don't want to scare you."

"The favourite."

"Me too, mate."

A body to accompany the voice suddenly appeared at Matt's side. He glanced to his right. It was Dave, and yet it wasn't. His hair was long and brown and tied, like his own, in a pigtail at the back and both cheeks were covered with gruesome looking tattoos. The scar was still there but his right eye was now covered in a black eye patch. He looked for all the world like a modern day pirate, lacking only a black tricorn hat to complete the image.

Seeing his friend's stare, he said,

"Just a temporary disguise in case I was spotted at the *Linden Tree*, Matt. The hair is a wig and the tattoos can be wiped off with the right fluid."

"Did you do that yourself?"

"I'll come to that later, mate. I gather I've put you in some sort of trouble."

"*Last two moving forward; the favourite's already in.*"

"Yeah, suspended from the bank and under police watch 24/7. I even had to climb out of a first floor window and over a fence to get here tonight without a tail."

"Good, so you appreciate how difficult a position we're both in?"

"Yes — but why didn't you tell me what you were up to?"

"Tell you? You must be joking. I couldn't trust you not to go blabbing to the police, could I?"

"*All in!*"

Matt did not reply.

"*Orders and off!*"

"From your silence, I suspect I can trust you now, eh? Want part of the action?"

"Let's just watch the race, Dave, er, Colin. I've got a hundred riding on the favourite."

"I've got two grand on her."

"Wha ...?"

"*Two furlongs to go and the favourite hits the front. She's running all over them. Willy's already looking round for non-existent dangers.*"

Twenty seconds later *Summer Fun* had romped home by eight lengths with Willy Bentham easing her to a canter a few strides from the line. Matt's mouth was still open.

"Did you say two grand?"

"Small bet, Matt," replied Colin with a grin. "I would have put more on but I don't want to draw attention to myself."

"I think your disguise will do that for you."

They had made their way down to the line of bookmakers by now but Colin seemed reluctant to go and collect his winnings, ushering Matt down to the rails a good distance from the grandstand and any other racegoers.

"Let's go and talk," he said.

The evening sun was shining directly into their eyes so they turned to face the stands, resting their backs on the white plastic rails. Matt was first to speak.

"So why did you do it?"

"Why? That's a long story and the less you know the better at the moment, until I ...."

"Until?"

"Until I can be sure that you're on my side, Matt."

"Well, at least tell me about this disguise and your new name. How did that come about?"

"Necessity, old boy. You are now looking at Mr Colin Richard Fenner — that's what my passport says. I have two new bank accounts and a new home."

"Where?"

"All in good time. Let's just say I have a new employer and I live with him now."

"I thought so — I just knew you had to have had help. You couldn't have planned the fraud all by yourself."

"No, Matty, I had help from more than one quarter, eh?"

"You mean ...?"

"Yes, you."

"So how did you come to work for this new employer?"

"Well, let's say I owed him some money."

"Where did you meet him?"

"Where do you think?"

"Portugal?

Colin grinned.

"Now, Matt, before we take this conversation any further, I want to know what you're going to do."

"What do you mean, do?"

"Well, for example, *if* this all blows over and you're not sent to prison, what will you do then?"

"I'll almost certainly be out of a job with the bank, and do you really think anyone else would employ me with my record? I mean who would take me on knowing that I had the power to defraud them. It's hardly something that's going to be forgotten about. My name's all over the front pages at the moment."

"Precisely — you would need to change your identity like me."

"Probably, but that costs money and so what am I going to live on?"

'*This is going well*,' thought Colin.

"You could come and work with me?"

"Doing what?"

"This and that?"

"Meaning?"

"Oh come on, Matt, what do you think?"

"More fraud?"

"Possibly — and other things. My employer could use someone like you with your talents, if you get my drift."

"Yes, don't worry, I can see what you're driving at; I'm not that stupid."

"Well, what do you say?"

"I say I need a drink and the next race is coming up."

"Alright, but are you interested? At least tell me that."

"Yes, of course, I'm interested — what have I got to lose with my career in ruins?"

Colin Fenner smiled and put an arm round his friend — his first recruitment was almost complete.

Neither man had any further winners that evening and both took the decision to leave after the penultimate race. After several whiskeys, Matt had finally given his friend his word that he would join him in whatever business he was in, not that he'd really taken much persuading. He'd actually played it a little coy in case he should have given the impression of being too keen. Secretly, he was only too glad to take his friend up on his offer because, as he kept reminding himself, he owed him. With Colin still in residence at the *Royal Oak*, Matt accepted his offer of a lift back to his maisonette in his hire car. They took the back roads to the A21 and thence to the M25 where they would exit at junction 13 and follow the A308 to Windsor. Initially, Matt thought nothing of it when Colin drove past the exit, simply commenting,

"Gonna' take the M4, mate?"

"Not exactly, Matt."

"So which way are we going?"

"Depends where you think we're going, Matt, my boy."

"Well, Windsor, I presume."

"What for?"

"To go home, of course, you idiot."

"And where exactly is your home now, mate?"

"What the hell are you driving at, Dave?"

Colin took his eyes of the motorway for a second as he stared at his friend.

"I know we're alone, Matt, and no one can hear us, but you really must get into the habit of calling me by my proper name — O.K?"

"O.K., but you haven't answered my question."

"Well, I'll try, old son. First, you have made a life-changing decision this evening to come and work for my new boss and second, because of that decision, you can no longer maintain your present identity."

"Why not?"

"Oh come on, Matt, if you leave the country, as you will have to, you'll be spotted a mile off. Remember, you're still under police bail and a suspected criminal. We have to wipe all traces of your former life away. Putting it simply, you have got to disappear off the face of the earth and leave the authorities to draw their own conclusions."

"Which would be what?"

"That you took your own life while under the stress of your extreme and frightening situation. Your body would never be found and you would soon be forgotten; filed under missing, presumed dead."

"So is your boss in Portugal, then?"

"Clever boy!"

"So where are we going? All the stuff I need is back at my flat and it's all happening a bit quick for me."

"And what stuff is that?"

It was getting dark now and they had already passed the M4 interchange. Matt knew his reply was a little fatuous given his new situation.

"Passport; credit cards; driving licence; clothes and so on."

"Yeah, right," said Colin. "You are joking aren't you?"

Matt said nothing for a few moments. He was absorbing the real consequences of his earlier decision. Was he really not going home? He hardly heard what his friend said next.

"From now on you are Peter Samuel Williams and we are just going to collect your new papers and to make some alterations to your appearance. Welcome aboard, Pete!"

"What?"

"I said, welcome aboard, Pete."

"No, before that."

"Well, we can't just change your name when the police have your photograph at every sea and airport in the country, can we? We need to change what you look like as well."

Matt grunted his acceptance of the obvious.

"So where are we going, then?"

"Initially, Luton."

"And what's in Luton?"

"Not what — who?"

"Alright, who?"

"A couple of my boss's special operatives who are skilled in these kind of things — one to make some cosmetic alterations; hair colour and so on and one to give you a new passport and credit cards. My boss has flown the same person over from Spain that changed my visual appearance and she is good, Matt, believe me she is very good. She is called Sancha Castilla."

"She?"

"Yes, Jardigo employs many different people from all backgrounds and occupations; men and women."

"Ah! Ah!" exclaimed Matt/Peter. "So he's called Jardigo?"

"Yes, you might as well know now you have made the decision. His full name is Jardigo Rodriguez Batista and he lives about fifty miles from Lisbon, as you will soon see. When we reach Luton I will tell you everything that has happened to me since I left the bank on that Friday."

"So what happens after we are done at Luton?"

"We leave the country."

"How on earth am I going to be able to do that?"

"You will see, Peter. Jardigo can arrange things even when they seem impossible. Most things can be accomplished if you have enough money."

"And this Jardigo has enough?"

"Oh yes, mate, he has enough."

Matt said very little more on the remainder of the journey up the M1; his mind was in a whirl and struggling to cope with the enormity and reality of what he had elected to do. The only fact that gave him some comfort was that the alternative might have consequences which would be far worse. Before he had met up with Colin that evening, it was what he'd told himself he wanted to do anyway, and all he needed was the courage to see it through — there was bound to be a crock of gold for him at the end of the rainbow.

13
Breaking Bail

Number 42 Bedford Road was a modern semi-detached house situated in a quiet suburb of Luton and it was one of three 'safe' houses in England rented on a long-term basis by Jardigo for his various needs. After a solid night's sleep, Matt's alterations were rather easier to accomplish than Colin's had been — his hair being reduced to half inch stubble, in stark contrast to his normal shoulder length style which, together with a very good fake tan to his once pale and sallow complexion, gave him almost a Foreign Legion type appearance. Finally, like his friend David Marks, Matthew Sampson no longer existed and in his place now walked Peter Samuel Williams who had been suddenly been reborn after his tragic demise in a fishing tragedy a year earlier. Being out of Windsor and away from any possible tailing police, Colin had returned to his original disguise, with the exception of the scar, it having been replaced by a tattoo of a simpler and less flamboyant nature than those he had sported at Lingfield.

By ten o'clock, both men were anxious to set about the task of getting out of England and back to Portugal. After a long chat the night before, Peter now knew more or less as much as Colin about Jardigo's operations and despite his new passport and identity, he was in for a bit of a surprise when Colin began to explain the plan for their escape from the country. They had just set off in Colin's hire car from the house in Bedford Road.

"Jardigo was insistent that we should not use any usual exit point from this country, Pete."

"Why not? We've both got new identities and passports."

"True, but he wants there to be absolutely no chance that either of us might lead the authorities back to him in Portugal. He is simply covering all bases. And besides ...."

"What?"

"Both our passports use the identities of men who are already dead and it would only be a matter of time before one or other of them was spotted. Any random check of the numbers against the national database would set the alarm bells ringing. Apparently, they do this random check on about one in every hundred entries or exits from the country."

"Yeah, good point. They'll already be looking for me as well, you know."

"Why? I thought you said you left your flat unobserved."

"I did but one condition of my bail was that I report to Windsor police station every morning at nine — I clearly missed this morning. It won't be very long before the news will be out and all strange characters of my height and build would come under suspicion despite my facial alterations."

"So, Jardigo is right, mate — and we use his special plan."

"Which is?"

"He runs a small shipping service from Portsmouth to Oporto — import/export of items that he doesn't want anyone to know about. People can be smuggled in on one of the freighters as well."

"Yeah, but we'd still have to go through passport control."

"Not if we don't join the ship at Portsmouth."

"So where, then?"

"Somewhere in the Channel. For a small fee, the captain will drop anchor at a convenient place and wait for a small fishing vessel to come alongside. He will ask no questions if the money is right — and it will be, you can be sure of that."

"And where do we get this fishing boat to take us out to the freighter? Has Jardigo paid someone else as well?

"Of course — we're booked on an evening's fishing trip aboard the *Mary Louise* at six o'clock, which will be setting sail from the little Devon seaside village of Palimpton, situated about eighty miles west of Portsmouth. The skipper will leave with two men and return later tonight with none. He will ask no questions and tell no lies."

Kevin was basically an honest man, but after the smooth-talking American had talked to him in the *Dog and Duck* the previous Sunday, he had accepted an offer he couldn't refuse — five hundred pounds up front and a further two thousand when the job was done. Palimpton fisherman, Kevin Rogers was the owner of a small off-shore fishing boat and the task was simple enough — take two men for an evening's fishing the following Wednesday and rendezvous with a small freighter called the *Bartolomeu Dias* which would be lying at anchor about a mile off shore. The transference was to be carried out under cover of darkness, the freighter's captain launching a small motorised dinghy for the purpose. It would be the easiest £2500 he would ever make.

When Wednesday morning dawned, the weather looked set fair for the evening's business but by mid-morning, Kevin was having second thoughts. If he was caught, it would almost certainly mean the end of his freedom — he was well aware of the penalties for people smuggling; those for contraband were bad enough. By noon, he had walked into Palimpton's small one-man police office — nothing more than an extension to the village's post office and explained all leaving out the details of the upfront payment which he had carefully stashed away in a secret compartment on his boat. Sergeant Alwyn Jones began his questioning with his usual wry humour.

"I'd have done it for a grand, Kev."

"What in your rotting dinghy?"

"I'd have got the police launch from Plymouth."

"Yeah?"

"No, Kevin, I'm joking. This is a serious offence that you were about to commit."

"I know, and that's why I've come to you."

"Yes, but what I don't understand, Kev, is why you didn't come straightaway when this Yank made you the offer."

Kevin Rogers was silent.

"Because, Kevin, it will not look good in my report, especially as your inaction would seem to imply that you were going to go through with the assignment."

The sergeant paused.

"Unless ...."

"Unless what?"

"Unless you cooperate with us and go ahead as the American originally instructed."

"And will that stand me in good stead?"

"I don't know, Kev, but it can't do your case any harm if we catch what must be two illegal immigrants who are trying to leave the country."

"I'll do it, then."

"Good, now are you sure there's nothing else you've got to tell me?"

"No, why should there be?"

"Because my knowledge of cases like this would suggest that the organ grinder hires the monkey with a down payment — a hundred now, a hundred later when the job's done, for example."

"He didn't give me any money upfront; he just made one or two veiled threats against my family, that's all, Alwyn, and the promise of two grand when it was all over."

"I see, well you'd better give me as much detail as you can about this American and the name of the freighter. No doubt the authorities will want to interview the ship's captain when he docks, whenever and wherever that will be. After I've got all the details for my report, you are to proceed about your daily business and await the arrival of the two men just as instructed. And Kevin ...."

"What?"

"You say nothing to anyone, right?"

"Right, just so long as Tracy and little Ben are going to have protection."

"Of course, you don't need to worry about that. Palimpton is too small a place for any strangers to go unnoticed for more than a few hours. I suspect that several people will have seen this American in the area already. Now let's have his description and anything else you can remember about him."

After leaving Luton, Colin and Peter headed north on the M1 — Jardigo's instructions had been that the hire car should not be abandoned just anywhere, but returned to an outlet a long way from the Devon coast, thus preventing the police with any possible link with their final whereabouts in England before they made their escape via sea. Within two hours, Colin had returned the hire car to the rental company close to Birmingham's New Street Station and by one o'clock they were safely aboard the Plymouth-bound express. With a four hour trip ahead of them, calling only at Cheltenham, Bristol and Exeter, both men seemed to be in need of sleep and the journey went quickly without any alarms or mishaps on the way.

It was twenty past five when the train pulled into Plymouth and Peter was clearly worried that they were not going to make their six o'clock meeting with the *Mary Louise* in Palimpton, a good twenty miles west down the Devon coast. His friend soon put his mind at rest when he announced that the anonymity of public transport was not going to be necessary for the final leg of their journey — the journey by three different buses would have taken an hour and a half in any case. The alternative arrangements soon became clear when they were hailed by a familiar voice the minute they alighted onto the platform.

"Hi guys! Your car awaits you."

It was the tall, freckle-faced American, Henry Madison. With Colin doing the introductions, they were soon on their way with Jardigo's top operative in the UK. Travelling down many winding country lanes, Henry had time to finalise the details of their 'fishing trip' that evening.

"The boat's skipper is called Kevin Rogers."

"How did you find him?" queried Colin.

"Oh, Palimpton is handily situated for a rendezvous in the English Channel and it was easy to find out which pub the local fishermen drank in. I arrived on Saturday, and by Sunday evening, I had found our man in the *Dog and Duck*, one of only two inns in the village. Listening to the locals' conversation told me a lot about those people who were struggling for money and Mr Rogers was only too keen to help."

"Are you sure he can be trusted?" asked Peter.

"Two grand says he can — and if not ...."

"If not, what?"

"I think I made him aware of the consequences of reneging on his contract. Need I say more?"

"No, we understand," replied Colin.

They could see the sea again by now and soon the road sign announced that they had reached their destination. Suddenly, the road began to wind steeply downhill until, within a quarter of a mile, it opened up into a wide concrete apron, lined on either side by two rows of fishermen's cottages and the odd trinket shop or artist's studio.

"We'll park in the car park at the visitor's centre further up," said Henry. "We're just here for the scenery — right, gentlemen?"

"Of course," said Colin. "Where's the *Mary Louise*, then?"

"Oh, no doubt, it will be out of sight of the main harbour — probably around the small headland. Kevin Rogers is due to meet us in the car park at ten to six."

Peter looked at his watch — it was 5.45 p.m. He felt uncomfortable. It was alright for Dave/Colin — he'd had a couple of weeks of this kind of life, living on the edge.

The car park was reached by a narrow concrete track and at that time of the day, Henry said, it would be quite busy, so they could park and wait, hidden among the other cars without causing any suspicion — after all, they were just there for the views. It was not to be long before the American began to suspect that everything was not entirely as it should be.

"I don't like this," he said, as they pulled into the open area marked with spaces for a dozen cars. They were all empty except for one in the far corner adjacent to the beach. Two men were sitting in the front seats — they appeared to be watching a small fishing boat anchored a few yards offshore.

"We're not stopping, guys," he suddenly announced, immediately turning the red Golf GTI round and heading back the way they had come. Peter and Colin said nothing.

"Sorry, guys, but I think our friend Mr Rogers has done the dirty on us."

"How do you know that?" asked Colin — their speed was increasing now as they shot through the main village and back up the hill they'd come down a few minutes earlier. They could hear the sound of at least one car in hot pursuit behind them.

"Hold on, guys!" shouted the American. "This is going to get a bit hairy."

They had a lead of a few hundred yards by now as the powerful V6 Golf reached the top of the hill.

"We're gonna' have to ditch the car, I'm afraid — they'll have spotted the make and licence plate. I'll lose them in the next village."

Dorsey Fenton was bigger than Palimpton and consisted of a maze of narrow lanes and streets, perfect for hiding a car which, hopefully, the chasing police would ignore and drive on for the A387 a few miles further inland, fully expecting their suspects to head for the main road network and freedom.

"We may gain a few precious minutes head start. Then we'll have to make alternative arrangements and take another route out of the country. Now put your heads down and pray!" Henry Madison smiled and winked.

The Golf's superior manoeuvrability had given them the upper hand by the time they had reached Dorsey Fenton, and they had soon parked the VW in a quiet spot several streets away from the main road. They knew they would have to be quick as a sizable proportion of the county's police force would soon be out looking for them and the red Golf. To add to their problems, Dorsey Fenton did not look like the kind of place where you could easily hire a car. The American, however, did not seem overly concerned as they tried to walk casually away from their dumped car.

"So what now, Henry?" asked Colin.

"Plan B."

"Which is?"

"Just wait and see. In the meantime, I think we need a nice cup of your English lifesaver."

"Huh?"

"A nice cup of tea!"

Colin and Peter looked at each other as if to say: '*He's gone stark raving mad now.*'

"Here we are: *The Rustic Spoon.* I think this will serve our needs."

"But ...?"

"But, nothing, Peter — just think for a moment. What will the police expect us to do after dumping the car?"

"Get another one, Henry?"

"Precisely, so we do exactly the opposite."

"Which is what?"

"Nothing."

And so it was that the three fugitives from justice took an early evening cup of tea in a quaint little cafe, mingling quite naturally with the more genteel holiday makers and residents of Dorsey Fenton. Whatever their fate was going to be, it was nothing when compared to that which awaited Mr Kevin Rogers, ex-fisherman of Palimpton, Devon. In a few days time, his unmarked body would be found washed up on a beach a mile east of his home village. The *Mary Louise* would be discovered at anchor offshore and his death would be put down as a tragic fishing accident, even though Sergeant Alwyn Hughes would have his suspicions that his demise was not all that it seemed. The captain of the *Bartolomeu Dias* would be arrested on his arrival in Portugal but would be released when no evidence could be found that he had been involved in any people smuggling. Jardigo's shipping operations would be able to continue as before and no connection would be established between him and Kevin Rogers.

14

Plan B

Colin and Peter were clearly not amused with Henry's apparent lack of concern for their safety and freedom from justice. Neither seemed to have much enthusiasm for their Devon cream teas, despite the American's relaxed attitude after he had returned from a welcome freshen-up in the gents.

"Well guys, enjoy your teas — you can't get anything like this in the States."

"We're not hungry, Henry; we're more concerned about getting the hell out of here. The police will be swarming all over this village in a minute," replied Colin, angrily.

"Patience, my friend — help is on the way."

"So what's this Plan B of yours?" asked Peter.

Henry Madison smiled coyly.

"Ever heard of Brentor?"

"No, obviously not," said Colin.

"Well, it's about twenty minute's drive from here."

"So? We don't have a car and, anyway, what the hell's there?"

"A private airfield," replied Henry, smiling. "Jardigo insisted that an aeroplane should be available this evening just in case Plan A went wrong."

"So why didn't we use that in the first place instead of the rendezvous by boat?"

"Because, dear Colin, it is more difficult to leave this, or any other country by plane — there are things like air traffic control and clearance to cope with. It is not easy to just turn up at an airfield and fly off into the sunset."

"So how are we going to do it, then?" interrupted Peter.

"We wait until after dark — the pilot has been briefed by Jardigo and hopefully we can get you airborne without anyone knowing. There should be no one else about at the airfield by then to monitor your take-off."

"What do we do till then? We can't stay here all that time."

"No, Peter, this café closes at seven-thirty — that's in twenty minutes. By then, we will be well on our way to Brentor airfield by car."

"What car?" asked Colin.

"Your pilot will be with us in a few minutes — he's driving down from Brentor this very minute after I called in just now from the rest room out back. Now eat your teas and relax."

Five minutes later, and a tall man about Colin and Peter's age suddenly appeared in the doorway of the café. He signalled to Henry with a brief thumbs-up sign. The three men tried to look nonchalant as they followed the pilot and driver outside where he soon introduced himself as Nigel Dutton — he was immaculately dressed in a white cotton suit with pale blue open-necked shirt. He had swept-back black hair and his general bearing and opening remarks suggested he had seen service in the RAF at some stage in his career. Henry reciprocated with the introductions.

"You've picked a fine night for the sortie, chaps. The crate's fuelled and ready to go. Top secret mission, eh? Me the monkey: Ask no questions ...?"

The car was parked a few streets away and, to say the least, it was not what Colin and Peter had been expecting. The beige and cream VW Camper had clearly seen better days and looked more like something an aging hippie from the flower power days of the sixties might have driven — and not the preferred mode of transport for the smooth-talking elegant pilot who stood before them.

"Fear not, chaps, modesty is needed tonight. Who's going to notice one more camper van parked anywhere in open country. There must be thousands in

Devon at this time of the year. Your boss was insistent I be inconspicuous and he's paying me well, so who am I to argue, eh?"

Henry Madison quickly made his brief goodbyes as he left the two young men with their pilot. Once again, his parting words indicated that he would see them again soon. Neither Colin nor Peter bothered to ask him how he would fare when faced with the prospect of being hunted by the police — he seemed used to operating above and beyond the law and would, no doubt, be able to disappear without a trace until needed again by Jardigo for the next important operation in the UK.

The private jet had obviously seen better days and was parked just off the far end of the runway at Bentor aerodrome when the VW camper pulled into a lay-by beside the quiet B road that ran the full length of one side of the airfield. When they arrived at ten to eight, it was the only aircraft out in the open; Nigel explaining that three or four others were in the hangar they could see about a quarter of a mile distant. A low wire fence and hedging seemed to be the only attempt at security for the aircraft and hangar and would not prove an obstacle to reaching their transport less than fifty yards away. The lay-by was perfect for waiting inconspicuously till dark descended in a couple of hours. Initially, Nigel Dutton was curious as to Colin and Peter's need for their unobserved escape from the country.

"So do you both work for Mr Batista?"

"Sort of," replied Colin.

"Am I also right in thinking that Colin and Peter aren't your real names?"

"Why do you think that?" asked Colin, cautiously.

"Well, you're either both wanted by the police, and therefore can't leave the country by normal means, or you're travelling on false passports and would be stopped at passport control."

Peter was more forthright than his friend.

"Well, Nigel, whatever our reason is for this means of exit from the country, it is no real concern of yours — you understand?"

"Of course, and I apologise for seeming a bit nosey. Why should I care when I'm being paid so handsomely by Mr Batista? Henry Madison often hires my plane for moving packages to and from Portugal, but this is the first one where the packages have been human. I don't normally ask too many questions and I won't pry anymore into your affairs, chaps, I promise."

"Thank you," said Colin. "We appreciate your discretion. Now I, for one, am going to get some shut-eye if you guys don't mind. Wake me up when we're going to make a move."

"Sure," replied Nigel. "It won't be till after ten."

They sensed rather than saw the police car pull up behind them — its blue light was not flashing and it had stopped quietly and without fuss. Nigel Dutton, who had remained awake reading, coughed gently.

"We have company, gentleman."

Both his passengers stirred.

"What?" said Colin.

"I said we've got company, so just act normal; we're campers, remember?"

The uniformed officer was standing beside the driver's door by now. Nigel wound his window down.

"Good evening, officer."

"Good evening, sir, and just what are we doing here?"

"Just taking a break; I don't suppose we can park here for the night, can we?"

"No sir, we can't — it is an offence to stay overnight in a lay-by. Where are you off too?"

The constable's accent was pure West Country — he and his colleague were clearly local. Nigel knew he had to be careful as they would know the area like the back of their hands. The second constable was walking round the VW camper, torch in hand and inspecting the vehicle carefully.

"Just touring, officer — we we're going to cut across country to the North Devon coast, but it got a bit too late, so we decided to stop for the night."

"I see, sir, can I see your driving licence and insurance, please."

Nigel reached inside the glove compartment and handed the necessary documents to the constable.

"Mr Nigel Dutton, sir?"

"Yes, officer."

The constable bent down and peered into the rear of the camper.

"Thank you, sir, and your two passengers; their names, please."

Colin was quick to answer; his accent was pure Yorkshire.

"I'm Colin Fenner and my friend is Peter Williams."

The constable made a note of the names. He opened a rear door and said,

"Would you two mind stepping out of the vehicle for a moment, please."

The sweat was beginning to ooze from Peter's face; this was not good, but both men obeyed passively. They joined each other next to the constable who shone his torch in their faces.

"And where are you both from, please?"

Again Colin was quick to respond.

"I'm from Leeds and Pete here is from Norwich — we're on a few days holiday touring the south and west."

"I see, sir, and do you have any identification on you?"

"Just our passports and credit cards."

"May I see them, please?"

Both men reached inside their back pockets. The officer took them and again made a brief note. He handed them back and said,

"Thank you, sir, everything seems to be fine — we've had reports of three men in the area who might have been trying to leave the country illegally; one is an American, but we don't have details of the other two yet."

"Oh really?" Colin feigned surprise.

"Yes, sir, now you'd better get moving — there's a campsite about five miles further on near the village of Penny Westwell; you can't miss it."

"Thank you, constable."

The policemen returned to their patrol car and waited while Nigel set the camper in motion and they pulled away. Nobody said a word as the police car followed some fifty yards behind. They had no choice but to try and find the campsite. After a few hundred yards, Peter finally broke the silence.

"Now what?"

"We head for the campsite and hope they then leave us alone. When they've had enough of us, I'll double back on the other side of the airfield where I know a track I can park on. The only difference is that it'll be nearly half a mile to the old crate from there."

"What about the camper — the police might find it now they've got its registration."

"I'm sure I can hide it somewhere. It only needs to be there until about nine tomorrow morning as I should be back by then with a quick turnaround in Portugal; I'm landing at another private airfield outside Lisbon. If there are problems, I can always just abandon it and pretend it broke down."

They had reached a crossroads and Nigel turned left for Penny Westwell. He glanced in his rearview mirror.

"They've gone, chaps; they took the Plymouth road."

"Thank God for that," said Peter.

"Yeah, just so long as they're both not the Sherlock Holmes type," replied Colin.

"How do you mean?"

"I mean that they could easily run our passports through their national computer and discover that both of us are actually dead men walking."

"We'll be in Portugal by then," said Peter.

"Maybe, but we could still be traced, and it might make restrict our future movement."

"So let's hope they can't be bothered, then."

"Anyway," said Colin. "They don't have our addresses."

"They have mine, chaps — I may have to join you if they come asking questions. You might let Mr Batista know of my possible problems, alright?" remarked their driver.

"Sure thing, Nigel — he'll see you alright," said Colin. "Believe me, he has enough money to overcome any problem, no matter how big."

"Are you not married, then?" asked Peter.

"Not now."

"You were?"

"Yes, up until three months ago."

"Really? Colin here has just gone through a divorce, too," said Peter. "I'm still single and happy."

"Welcome to the club, fella'!" exclaimed Nigel.

They could just make out the lights of a small hamlet ahead.

"Should be able to turn round ahead and take the other road back to the airfield, boys," he continued.

"What was she called?" asked Colin.

"Who?"

"Your wife."

"Hilary."

"Nice name."

"Yeah, but we weren't really suited to each other — married at twenty-one and didn't really know each other."

"What led to the divorce?"

"I'd had enough — she became less than passionate in one particular area, if you get my drift."

"Any kids?"

"Nah, I moved too many times for us to settle down with a family. The RAF rarely post you anywhere for longer than a year or two."

"How long were you married?"

"Fifteen years."

"Where does she live?"

"You're asking a lot of questions, Colin."

"I'm just comparing notes; I haven't met anyone about my own age that's gone through a divorce."

"She lives near Banbury in Oxfordshire — I was stationed there up until I left the RAF a year ago, in the hope I could keep the marriage alive. I even took a civilian job in Banbury working for a bank, but it didn't help and after six months, I walked out and moved to Plymouth; bought myself a small private jet out of my RAF pay-off."

"Must have been a good pay-off."

"Had some private money as well — my parents were loaded. Hilary eventually got some of it but I still have a sizeable chunk left."

Up until then, Peter had remained silent while the two ex-married men had been chatting and his sudden interruption nearly caused his friend to choke.

"Colin and I used to work in a bank."

"Oh yeah, which one?"

"Barclays," said Colin quickly, digging his friend sharply in the ribs.

"Mine was the Oxford and District; a much smaller operation."

The pilot paused briefly; they could just make out the airfield ahead which was now on their left.

"Did you read about the online fraud at the London and Provincial? Bloke got away with millions and nobody knows where the money has gone to."

"Yeah, I saw it on TV the other day," replied Colin.

"Seems like there were two of them and both men are now missing. I bet they've already left the country, just like you're trying to do, eh?"

"I expect so," said Colin.

"Still, good luck to them, I say," said their driver. He winked at Colin and Peter.

To their relief, Colin and Peter sensed the conversation was finally coming to an end. They were also both thankful that Nigel had been unable to make out their contorted facial expressions in his rearview mirror under the dim light of the VW. For himself, Colin knew that it was only a matter of time until he would have to reveal his and Peter's real identity — but better to leave that to Jardigo when they arrived in Portugal, if he saw fit to involve their pilot more in his operations. Soon, the camper began to slow as it started to negotiate a narrow track which branched off on their left and Nigel began to concentrate on finding a suitable place to stop. Their ordeal was over, at least for the time being, and their driver's thoughts returned to the main task of the evening.

"Right, as I remember it, this track goes for about half a mile towards the airfield and then stops at the entrance to a small plantation of trees. We'll hide the campervan in there and get to the plane on foot."

The walk to the private jet on foot sometimes proved to be difficult with a series of thick bramble hedges to negotiate before the perimeter fence was reached. All three men would sport a few battle scars for a few days afterwards and each would need some repairs to their clothing. It had been easy to conceal the VW camper in a small copse of hawthorn bushes — none of it could be seen from the track and only small portion of its dull paintwork from the airfield side. Given that it would be extremely unlikely that anyone would approach the copse from that direction, Nigel was reasonably certain that it would not be discovered before his return. After dusting various pieces of woodland from their clothes and cleaning up a few minor scratches, Nigel soon had the 1970s Lear jet's engines running and his passengers safely aboard the six-seater. The two fugitives from justice could see from the bare interior that the jet had seen better days and as their pilot made a few last minute checks, Colin asked,

"So how much did you fork out for this piece of shit?"

"More than you might imagine."

"So, how much?"

"Three quarters."

"Of a million?" asked Peter.

"Yep, and that's cheap — today's equivalent model sells for four times that new."

"You're not telling me the RAF gave you that good a pay-off."

"No, I told you my parents were wealthy."

"Were?" queried Peter.

"Yes, they died last year in a coach crash while touring South America on holiday."

"So what did they do?"

"Dad was a successful author — he wrote thrillers under the name Christopher Salmon and Mum was an ex-ballerina who ran her own stage school in North London."

"Your dad wrote *Operation Blue Sky* and *On the Edge?* "

"Yes, and as you know, they were both made into successful films."

"Wow!" exclaimed Peter. "No wonder you were able to afford this — he must have been a multi-millionaire before he died."

"Not quite — only the really best-selling authors make millions and Dad wasn't quite up there with the top ones. You'd be surprised how little some good writers get for each book; just pence in a lot of cases. You have to sell a shedload of books to make a million. The vast majority of authors write for pleasure rather than to make a living. I guess Dad was luckier than most. Now, let me finish my checks, otherwise we'll be in the Channel before you know it. It's going to be tricky taking off without clearance from the ground. At least we've no problems with weather — it's a beautiful clear and still night."

"Won't we be picked up on the radar from somewhere?"

"Maybe, but we'll be over the continent in minutes, so who cares?"

A minute or so later and the Lear jet taxied smoothly onto the grassy airstrip and within another couple, they were airborne and heading south towards the sea. At precisely 11.23 p.m., aircraft GW-437B left the United Kingdom airspace and five minutes later crossed the French coast, identified by the twinkling lights of a small town close to the sea.

The flight took nearly four hours and the night sky had lightened a little when they landed at the isolated landing strip set high up in a range of mountains about thirty miles from the Castelo no Monte. Jardigo himself was there to meet them, along with his deputy, Rafael and his driver, Leon. Henry Madison had clearly relayed the news of the alternative plan to his boss who effused warmth and seemed somewhat relieved to see his new friend, Colin, back safe and sound. Whatever Nigel's plans had been with regard to his own return to England, they were soon overruled when the three weary men climbed down the steps onto the dirt runway. The headlights of the black Mercedes showed the tiredness in their faces.

"Welcome! Welcome! I am so glad to see you all — Colin, and it's Peter and Nigel; am I right?"

The two men mumbled their tired acknowledgements.

"Now, Senhor Nigel, you will please rest for a while at the castle until you return to England."

"But I need to get back quickly before the police discover my vehicle. They are well aware that I am involved with these chaps' disappearance. We were stopped before we came and half the police in southern England are looking for Colin and Peter."

"That maybe so, but I may also have another well-paid job for you, my friend, if you are interested?"

Nigel seemed hesitant.

"How — how well-paid?"

All three men had joined Jardigo now on the short walk to the waiting limousine and the billionaire seemed reluctant to answer Nigel's question. The tall handsome pilot was drawn, almost against his will, towards the car. He had wanted to do nothing more than say goodbye and climb back aboard his plane, but something in Jardigo's tone had prevented him carrying out his wish. He had silently acquiesced to the offer of hospitality at the castle — his rational thoughts replaced by those of greed and the possibility of financial gain. He was being led like a lamb, unable to resist the temptation that Jardigo had somehow laid in his path. That temptation became irresistible on the drive to the castle. While Leon drove in silence with Rafael beside him acting as navigator down the winding mountain roads, Jardigo had joined the other three men in the capacious rear of the limousine. He was soon apprised of everything that had happened that day and showed his pleasure that Peter had agreed to join his operation.

"You won't regret coming to work for me, Peter, my friend. I have much need for someone with such skills with computers. Though you didn't know what was happening at the time, you are now no doubt aware that you have made me a little richer over the last few days. I will show you my gratitude later today when you see the bank account I have opened for you in your new name. I can guarantee you will be pleasantly surprised, my friend."

"I would say that ten million was more than a little richer," said Peter.

"A drop in the ocean, my friend; a little test to see if the fraud could be pulled off."

"It was just a test?" asked Colin. "It didn't seem like that to me."

"No? Well, I have greater plans; just you wait and see, my friends."

Nigel had remained silent for most of the time while Colin and Peter had related their stories but now he interrupted the conversation. The penny had clearly dropped at last.

"I knew it, I just knew who you two must be — the two bank employees who robbed the London and Provincial, eh?"

"That's us," said Peter. "All part of Jardigo's plan."

Nigel smiled and continued.

"And this job you want me to do, Jardigo? Is that part of one of these greater plans?"

Though the others couldn't see it in the dim light, Jardigo's face had taken on a sly smile. He was tickling another fish that had swum to the surface. He had the bait ready to dangle at the end of his line.

"Not exactly, but you are a skilled pilot used to collecting things for me when transporting goods by sea or over land takes so long. After what I've heard about you today, I would say you were not only a skilled pilot but also a very resourceful gentleman."

No one saw the pilot blush. The tickling was efficient and it was working.

"From the UK?"

"And elsewhere."

"And how much would each such transportation pay?"

"Nothing, my friend."

"Nothing? Are you having a joke with me, Mr Batista?"

"No joke, Nigel — and please call me Jardigo."

"Alright, Jardigo, but you said earlier that the job would be well-paid."

"Well, my friend, there will be more than one job — many more than one, so why not be paid on a monthly basis. I give you a salary and you do whatever I ask, using those talents you clearly possess."

"You mean you're offering me a full-time job?"

"Of course."

"But I live in Plymouth."

"So you come and live with me at my castle."

"Oh, I see; I hadn't realised what you meant."

"Well, does it appeal to you? I understand from Henry Madison that you no longer have any real ties to England and no family to keep you there."

"You are well-informed."

"I have to be when it concerns the people I really want to work for me."

"I'm flattered."

The bait was in the fish's mouth and the net was closing.

"And if I refuse your offer?"

"Well let's just say that now I know a lot about you, Senhor Dutton, that knowledge could be used to reverse that refusal."

"Is that a threat?"

"Not exactly; I'm just showing you the alternatives and like Colin here, a year's contract, renewable on both sides is all you would be committing yourself to."

"How much?"

"What, for the year?"

"Yes."

"It will be the same as what Colin and Peter will both be getting."

Now Peter, who had nearly drifted off to sleep, was all ears.

"Which is?" asked Nigel, desperately trying to hide the excitement in his voice.

"Half a million Euros."

"You are joking, aren't you?" asked Nigel, incredulously.

"I never joke, my friend. So what do you say?"

"A year?"

"Yes, initially — it gives us both time to see if the arrangement suits."

"Then I say thank you very much — I accept your offer."

"Good."

Nobody said anything further for a few seconds until Colin suddenly remembered his own bank balance.

"And that's on top of the upfront bonus I got when I started? I think these two guys deserve the same."

Even in the dim light, Colin could see from the expression on Jardigo's face that he had overstepped the mark.

"That, my friend is not for you to say!" he snapped. "These gentlemen beside you will find out about their new bank accounts in due course."

"Yes, I am sorry; I spoke out of turn, Jardigo. It won't happen again."

"No, it won't my friend. Remember *you* work for me and your life is not your own."

After this last remark, the conversation immediately dried up with Nigel, for one, pondering what he had let himself in for. He, Peter and Colin would find out later the true reality of their commitments to Jardigo's cause. For the time being, they were all overwhelmed with the financial gains that lay ahead.

15

A Philanthropic Vision

Having not got to bed until after five that morning, the three Englishmen did not surface until early afternoon for a late lunch. It was a help-yourself affair of cold meats and salads on the rear veranda. Peter and Nigel were clearly anxious to discover more about Jardigo's operation and their own roles in it. With strong black coffees to hand after their fill of the excellent food, they began to question Colin.

"If he's such a wealthy man, Dave, why does he need even more money?" asked Peter.

Colin glared at his friend; Nigel looked confused.

"Dave?"

"Whoops! I forgot, mate."

"Forgot what?" queried Nigel.

"That we both have new identities and that was my old name, Nigel," replied Colin. "You must have known that we wouldn't have tried to leave the UK under our real names, especially after what we had done."

Colin paused and then smiled.

"And anyway, Peter and Colin *are* now are real names."

"Yeah," said Nigel. "I remember one of the men was called David Marks, right?"

"I really couldn't say, Nigel," replied Colin.

"Alright, but why does Jardigo need all this money? Looking round the castle on the way down to lunch, I should say he has everything a man could ever want. I saw some genuine old masters hanging on the walls."

"Yeah, and he has a secret vault somewhere that contains billions in cash and gold — literally billions," said Colin.

"So why want more? It can't just be greed."

"He wants to give a lot of it away to the poor of the world."

"What, like a modern day Robin Hood," said Peter.

"Sort of — he calls it a redistribution of the world's wealth."

"And how does he do this redistribution, then?"

"I don't know, Nigel. I haven't been involved in that side of the operation."

Peter looked dubious.

"So how do you know his intentions are genuine?"

"I don't, but that's what he told me when I first joined him."

"It could just be greed, then," remarked Nigel.

"I suppose so."

"Maybe he just used the idea to make his offer to you more appealing, Colin," said Peter.

"He, or at least I, didn't use it on you, mate."

"No, you didn't, but with me it's different."

"How so?"

"I'm just here for the money, Col — it is pure greed with me, and anyway, I *am* one of the world's poor!"

"Sounds like we all are when compared to him," said Nigel.

An hour later, Jardigo had joined his three most recent recruits for a stroll around the grounds. He was immaculately dressed in a cream cotton suit, penneck shirt and straw boater; Somerset Maugham style. With the afternoon sun still just on the rear of the castle, their boss had decided to take them to see the magnificent aspect of its twin turrets, with its manicured lawns and ornamental fountain fronting the elegant early nineteenth century facade. Unlike the rear aspect of the castle with its cloistered veranda, there was little evidence of its former use as a medieval monastery. Jardigo told them that the square lawn at the front was a 250-metre walk round the perimeter on the neat gravel path. He often did it four or eight times, he said, to keep fit and his record for the two-kilometre walk was a creditable eighteen minutes and ten seconds. They had completed two circuits when the conversation turned from a history lesson on the castle and the surrounding area.

"Now I have you three here working for me, I'm going to tell you a little more about what I have in mind."

"Ah, your master plan, boss," remarked Colin.

"Sort of, my friend."

"First of all, each of you, in your own way, has proved to me that you have certain characteristics, not the least of which is your greed for money."

The three Englishmen stopped walking.

"Oh yes, my friends, you are greedy. What kind of men do I have here in front of me, eh?"

"What do you mean?" said Nigel.

"I have two gamblers and someone not afraid to spend enormous sums of money — your plane was £735,000, was it not, Senhor Dutton?"

"Yes, but ...."

"And Peter, not even your friend Colin here knows how much you are in debt to one or two online casino sites, does he? Your skills with computers haven't helped you much there, have they?"

Colin looked at his friend.

"But you always bet small when you come to the races with me."

"And so he does, Colin, but when a man is in the privacy of his own home, who knows what he does."

Peter looked aghast.

"How on earth do you know what I do in private?"

"Oh, you will soon learn that I can find out most things about people I want to hire, my friend."

Jardigo paused to look at Colin.

And finally, we have Mr David Marks, who is now Mr Colin Fenner and who lost a six-figure sum at a Lisbon casino a few short weeks ago. I don't think you can comment on Mr Matthew Sampson's private gambling habits."

Colin turned his face away from Jardigo's powerful stare. Nigel Dutton had other thoughts.

"So am I going to have a new identity?"

"Yes," replied Jardigo. "Eduardo is working on it as we speak."

"Who's Eduardo?" asked Peter.

"He is Rafael's assistant — you met Rafael last night, or at least, this morning. I will make all the introductions at dinner this evening."

Colin turned back to look at Jardigo.

"So tell us about your plan."

"O.K., now that you can see what has driven you to work for me, let me explain my vision for the future."

He cleared his throat and turned to look in the direction of the Portuguese capital. He had the air of an actor who had rehearsed his lines many times for his big speech.

"There are many poor in my home city — many, many poor, my friends. There is poverty there the like of which you cannot even begin to imagine, as there is in every other city in this so-called civilised world. From New York to New Delhi; from Sao Paolo to San Francisco — nowhere escapes this canker on society. I haven't even mentioned anywhere in the third world in our two largest continents — Asia and Africa — where poverty is the norm and not the exception."

"There are charities that help with that," said Nigel.

"Yes and what percentage of that money actually gets through into people's pockets, eh?"

"I don't know."

"Well I'll tell you, my friend — virtually nothing, that's how much. No, I'm talking about a redistribution, not through organised schemes where these so-called charitable organisations cream off the lion's share anyway, but through direct handouts into people's pockets."

"Sounds fine in principle," observed Colin. "But how on earth can you do it?"

"Not me, my friends — you. You three are going to do it for me under my instructions. Together, we are going to flood the world with money.

"What? We just take a load of cash and dump it on the first shanty town we come across?" remarked Nigel, with a grin.

"Precisely, my friend. Why do you think I needed a pilot used to flying difficult missions?"

Nigel looked incredulous.

"You don't mean what I think you mean, do you?"

"Why not? What could be simpler?"

"Because there could be riots like when food parcels are dropped."

"Maybe, but the kind of aid I'm proposing will not only feed the people, it will also help build a better society for them on a long term basis. Drought and famine are a way of life in some parts of the world and handouts of food are only a temporary solution. They need long term finance to counter the bad times when they come."

"So what would be our role in all this?" asked Peter.

"I was just coming to that. Your knowledge of the banking system can be used to help countries in other ways, making it a two-pronged assault on poverty."

"How?" asked Colin.

"Well, although I said charities waste and redirect money in the wrong way, there are other organisations that are out there on the ground that need the money direct, whether it's building roads and communications or essentials like providing pure drinking water. These organisations have bank accounts, don't they?"

"Yes," replied Colin.

"So you two will inject these accounts with mysterious donations."

"Why don't you just give them the money upfront? Why does it have to be so secretive?"

"Isn't that obvious, Colin?"

"Not to me."

"Well let me put it this way — would your great Robin Hood have gone up to the Sheriff of Nottingham and given him a thousand pieces of silver, instructing him to distribute it to the poor or use it as he saw fit for the benefit of the local society?"

"No, of course not," replied Colin. He could see the other two men smiling in the background.

"And why not?" asked Jardigo.

"Because the Sheriff would arrest him on the spot and probably behead him within hours."

"And why would he do that, pray?"

"Because he was an outlaw and a thief."

Jardigo stood back and laughed.

"Need I say more, my friend?"

Colin felt stupid as his friends joined their boss in laughing at the irony of their situation.

"So you see, Colin, in order for my plan to continue for as long as is necessary, secrecy is paramount. If we're all in jail, and all my assets seized, no one benefits, right?"

"Right," said Colin.

"So, gentlemen, what do you think of my plan?"

"Bold," replied Nigel.

"Very philanthropic," said Peter.

"And you will each have an equal role to play," said Jardigo. "Peter and Colin to investigate the necessary bank accounts and Nigel to make the cash drops, but you will all help each other."

Jardigo paused and his grin became wider.

"You will be my Three Musketeers."

"And where are you going to start?" asked Nigel.

"Right here in Lisbon and the operation, code name Friar Tuck, will involve you all doing some ground work and a lot of walking, my friends."

"Where?" asked Peter.

"*Os Campos do Preto.*"

"Right and where's that when it's at home?"

"It means *The Black Fields* in Portuguese and it is a shanty town just on the northern edge of Lisbon — it is home to over 4000 men, women and children."

"No, really? But this is Europe in the twenty-first century."

"Exactly, Peter and it's the same the whole world over."

Colin's East End roots suddenly caused him to break into verse.

> *"It's the same the whole world over.*
> *It's the poor what gets the blame.*
> *It's the rich what gets the pleasure.*
> *Ain't it all a bloomin' shame?"*

"What the hell is that, Peter?" asked Jardigo.

"Just a traditional English rhyme."

"It's very apt, my friend; I think I may adopt it as my anthem in future."

"Just ignore him, Jardigo, he often quotes useless pieces of information," said Peter.

"Nevertheless, it expresses exactly how the poor of this world must feel about their situation," said Jardigo. "Unfortunately, it doesn't express very positive views about them. I aim to change that, my friends."

So, finally, Jardigo's plan had been revealed, and as the three new recruits to his cause continued their stroll around the castle grounds, they found that their spirits, each in their own way, had suddenly been lifted by his philanthropic vision of the future.

16

The Black Fields

That evening at dinner, Peter and Nigel were introduced to the castle's staff, as Colin had been before on a previous such occasion. Again, their introductions were greeted with warm applause — word had clearly got round on the grapevine as to the details of their exploits the day before and of Peter's abilities with a computer. None of the resident staff seemed either to overeat or drink too much and the dinner was concluded in almost exactly an hour at eight o'clock. Jardigo was a strict disciplinarian with regard to the day to day running of the Castelo no Monte and that rigid routine applied to meal times and the health and well-being of his employees, who he ruled with a paternal rod of iron — he was firm but fair. As some had found to their cost in the past, he could make anyone who crossed him or failed to carry out his orders suffer serious consequences. Talk sometimes circulated that he had once put a member of staff in hospital for disobeying a curfew that he had imposed. As the three Englishmen were about to go to the well-equipped relaxation area for a few games of pool, Jardigo approached Nigel in the corridor outside the dining hall.

"Senhor Nigel, I need to have a few words with you in private in my rooms. Would you please follow me?"

"Right, of course. I'll catch up with you chaps later."

The instruction had been simple and friendly but it had also been spoken in the tone of a Headmaster addressing a pupil. Nigel felt a little nervous as he followed his boss up to the second floor of the west turret that they had seen from the front earlier that afternoon. On reaching the apartment, it was soon clear to Nigel that Jardigo's did not live as extravagantly or in as much luxury as his untold wealth would normally dictate. There seemed to be just five rooms in total: a bedroom; a kitchen; an open-plan living area; a bathroom and a small study. The living area, whilst spacious, was sparsely furnished with cheap, modern items and the only evidence of Jardigo's wealth was the massive TV and entertainment centre that occupied one wall from floor to ceiling. Nigel drooled when he saw the quality of the equipment.

"Yes, Nigel, I like to relax in here with the best that money can buy."

"I can see that, Jardigo."

"Now please sit down — I need to talk to you."

Nigel took the single armchair while his new boss stood in the centre of the room.

"This sounds a bit ominous," said Nigel, nervously.

"Oh no, not at all, my friend — I'm sorry if I gave you that impression."

"So what's it about, then?"

"A couple of things. First, I need to make sure that you are one hundred per cent behind my operation."

"You bet I am — why do you ask?"

"Well, unlike Colin and Peter, you haven't really committed any huge crime yet — a bit of people smuggling, but nothing that a skilled lawyer couldn't get you off."

"So?"

"Let me finish, Nigel. Also, as far as I know, you don't gamble and are not in debt to anyone — in fact you are very comfortably off with a six-figure bank balance after your parents' deaths."

"You know about that?"

"Yes."

"So how does that make me different? I don't go bragging about it."

"It makes you different, Nigel because, unlike the other two, you could get up and walk out of here and still be relatively wealthy. Colin and Peter have large debts and need to earn good money — they could not afford to leave and in any case, where would they go? They are two of the most wanted men in

Europe right now, so they are bound to stay and give me their utmost loyalty, if ...."

"If?"

"If they know what's good for them."

"I see, and you think that you don't have my utmost loyalty, too?"

"I don't know, my friend — you tell me."

Nigel leant forward in his chair and rested his chin on his hands.

"I don't suppose there is a way of convincing you at the moment, except to say that when I give someone my word, I don't go back on it, of that you can be absolutely certain. Other than my word, I suspect the consequences of me pulling out and running back to England would be too frightening to imagine. Am I right?"

Jardigo's wry smile and silence gave the pilot his answer.

"So it looks like you're stuck with me for a while, Jardigo," said Nigel.

"Good — it sounds like you understand me. Am *I* right?"

"Reading you loud and clear, skipper. You said there were a couple of things."

"Yes, Nigel, we need to give you a new identity and, like your friends, make one or two alterations to your physical appearance. I don't know if you are aware — and I'm surprised you haven't asked about it — but we will be giving your private jet a makeover, too."

"I hadn't forgotten about it, if that's what you mean. I don't seem to have stopped since I put her down at the airstrip up in the mountains. When you mentioned my salary, it kind of became less important for the time being."

"Well rest assured that it's safe and hidden away in a mountain cave and guarded day and night. It will soon bear some new markings that will not be traceable back to your old self or anyone in England. It will also have a new documented history, too."

"And a lick of paint?"

"Naturally, the colour scheme will be new."

"So who am I to be?"

"Your new name will be Anthony Taylor and you will have short brown hair and a couple of tattoos to go with your profession of freelance pilot. We do not have to be so drastic with your alterations as we had to be with Colin and Peter."

"Brown hair, eh? I can cope with that, and Tony Taylor has the ring of a film star about it — good for attracting members of the opposite sex."

"You won't have much time for that, my friend."

"Only joking, skipper; I've had enough of women for a while."

"Good, now your papers and credit cards will be ready sometime tomorrow after we have made the alterations and taken your photograph. In the meantime, you must try to think of yourself as Anthony Taylor — waking or sleeping."

"Gotcha!"

"Now I have some work to do, Anthony, so you may go and join your colleagues."

"Please, call me Tony — only my mother calls me Anthony."

Colin and Peter were clearly having an argument over the rules for pool when Nigel/Tony joined them in the play area on the ground floor in the east wing and they hardly noticed his return until he interrupted the heated debate.

"What's up, chaps? Bit if a dogfight, eh?"

"Just a minor disagreement, Nige; you don't get a free shot just because I coughed at an inappropriate moment, do you?" replied Peter, indignantly and looking for support. He got a strange reply from the pilot.

"Are you talking to me, fella'?"

"Well I wasn't talking to this idiot."

"Well I'm afraid my name isn't Nige or Nigel if that's what you meant."

"Yeah right," said Colin.

"No seriously chaps, you are looking at Mr Anthony Taylor, but my friends call me Tony. You can call me sir or skipper, if you prefer."

"Oh," said Colin. "You have your new identity. Is that what the boss wanted to see you about?"

"That and one or two other things."

"Like what?" said Peter.

"He just wanted to be sure that I was really committed to his operation."

"And are you?" queried Colin.

"Of course; you guys know I am. Who wouldn't be on our salaries?"

"Well he must have had some doubts about you, Nigel; sorry, I mean Tony," said Colin. "He never interviewed me about my commitment."

"Nor me, Tony," said Peter. "Other than some veiled threats about the consequences of pulling out of the contract."

"So did you reassure him?" asked Colin.

"I think so — he was just concerned that I didn't necessarily need the money and he'd done his homework alright on my financial situation. He even knows exactly how much my plane cost. But hey, what the hell, I'm gonna' get even richer, as we all are. Now let's play some pool."

"No second thoughts about your new identity and the loss of your real one?" queried Colin.

"No, not really — it's good fun having a second life to enjoy. It's like being reincarnated without dying. Just think of the fun to be had by going incognito if we ever go back to Blighty."

"You might, but we can't, Tony. Remember that cop took the details of our new passports and, no doubt, the police will soon put two and two together about our real identities, especially when they find your abandoned campervan."

"True," said Tony.

"Come on you two, let's hit some balls," interrupted Peter. "Hundred Euros a game; winner stays on."

"Make it a thousand and I'm your man," said Colin.

"Once a gambler, always a gambler, eh Col," said Peter.

"Oh I can give it up anytime, you know."

Peter gave his friend an old-fashioned smile.

"Of course you can, mate; of course you can."

Their first mission was simple enough; each man would distribute one hundred envelopes to a selection of the residents of *Os Campos do Preto*. In every envelope there would be a wad of five thousand Euros — more money than a *Black Fields* family would see in one or two years. The distribution would take place in the early hours of the morning and under the guise of a local charity, indicated by colourful tabards and shoulder bags advertising the charity's name, just in case anyone was about to see the envelopes being delivered. The envelopes would have a biblical text on the outside, suggesting that the envelope contained a free bible, a book so revered by the largely catholic population of Black Fields that the envelope would not just be thrown away, like many others which often just contained leaflets advertising things that were well out of the reach of the recipients of the envelopes. Each of the three hundred envelopes would have one of ten different texts on the cover, and each text would be painstakingly written by hand by some of the castle's staff. An additional note would say that the envelope must not be opened until the following Sunday in an acknowledgement of the gift from God. In this way, 1.5 million Euros would find its way directly and safely into the hands of those who most needed it. The distribution would take place the following Thursday — August the 3rd.

Os Campos do Preto was a good distance north of the city centre; its sprawling mass of corrugated iron shacks and rough concrete box-type houses had been steadily forced further away from those areas of Lisbon that even the most adventurous tourist might visit, and its southern boundary was now at least six miles from the so-called recognised population of the Portuguese capital. Very few of its permanent residents possessed any identification papers and there was a mixture of several nationalities among their number — Portuguese and Spanish being the most prevalent, but with a liberal proportion of North Africans as well. Even though it was after two in the morning when Jardigo's driver dropped the three delivery men at the start of the track that led from the main road down to the *Black Fields*, the stale aroma of the cosmopolitan cuisine still lingered in the warm night air. Leon issued instructions that he would return at first light to collect them; they had instructions to be quick and to avoid the niceties of letter boxes (if they existed), relying rather on the cruder dissemination of throwing the envelopes onto the front porch, or any flat area that doubled as such. From their drop-off point at the junction of the track with the main road, they had about a quarter of a mile before they reached the first of the shacks. As they walked, they talked quietly about their mission.

"The sooner we get rid of some of these envelopes the better, chaps; my bag weighs a ton," remarked Captain Tony, as Colin had nicknamed the pilot.

"It shouldn't take us long; I bet we're back at the road in an hour," said Colin.

"And how do we ensure that we don't double up? We won't be able to see much in this light; there's no moon tonight," observed Peter.

"We take a section each, chaps," said Tony. "Jardigo said it didn't much matter if we didn't cover the whole town. I'll take the west side; Peter takes the east and Col can go straight down the middle. If Pete and I keep to the outer edge of the town, we can work inwards, but to be honest, looking ahead, we'll be lucky to cover more than just a small fraction of the shacks — there are thousands of them, judging by the lights that can still be seen."

"We copy, skipper; I just hope there aren't too many untethered dogs about," said Colin. "We disturb one of those and we could have a stampede of ravenous hounds on our hands, let alone waking everyone up."

Peter and Tony did not reply as the first of the shacks had suddenly appeared crouching in front of them, barely seeming high enough to allow a grown adult to stand upright inside. All seemed peaceful enough as they quickly nodded to each other and went their separate ways.

Colin found his route followed a ruler-straight dirt avenue which seemed to be better kept than most of the side tracks that led off it, and by walking in the very centre of the road, he was able to almost distribute the envelopes in pairs; one left followed by one right. He made quick progress and within twenty minutes, he had delivered nearly half his allocated quantity. From the very moment he had started his walk, it had been deathly quiet, and when he heard the first noise, he immediately sensed that something might be wrong. He had just tossed another envelope to his left, and out of the corner of his eye he spotted movement in front of the previous shack, followed by the tearing of paper and a grunt of delight. The shack itself was still in darkness. Within seconds he heard the sound of heavy footsteps advancing from behind him. He turned round to see the two men suddenly appear in the gloom; one appeared to be carrying a rough piece of wood. Each was hurriedly stuffing notes into their trouser pockets.

"Dê-nos o saco!" shouted the one with the stick. Colin was frozen to the spot. He had learnt enough Portuguese to understand the final word in the man's command — they wanted his sack.

"English," he stammered.

"Ah, Inglês!"

"The bag, senhor!"

'Stick man' moved menacingly forward. The odds were stacked against Colin. Without bothering to weigh up those odds or even a moment's thought for the value of the bag's contents, he released its strap from his shoulder and let the bag fall to the ground beside him. Almost simultaneously, he ducked to his left, fly-half style and ran past the two men before they could move to stop him. He didn't stop or look back until he was back at the junction with the main road, where he finally paused to catch his breath and review his situation. They had not followed him, preferring instead to count their windfall and, no doubt, to collect any other envelopes they could find. It wouldn't take a genius to realise that there must be many more such packets lying in front yards all over the shanty town. They would soon be very rich men and Jardigo's intention of a fair and equal distribution would have partly failed. He wandered around for several minutes wondering what to do next. Should he wait till Leon returned with the Mercedes? How long would the others be? Then another thought came to him — and he couldn't think why it hadn't come to him before. He had to warn them. They might not be so lucky, as he had been, and Tony, with his military background, might well try to resist the robbers with nasty consequences. Without considering any possible dangers to himself, Colin wasted no further time and ran back up the track, heading first for the right-hand boundary of the town; he had decided that Peter might need help rather than Tony. He hadn't gone more than a few yards when his friend emerged from a side alley. He still had his bag on his shoulder.

"Whatcha, mate!" he called out. "I've finished."

"I've been robbed!"

Peter approached his friend and glanced at his bare shoulders.

"You're shaking, Dave."

Colin did not correct his friend's usage of his former name. At that particular moment in time, their new identities didn't seem to matter, and as Peter put his arm round his friend's shoulder, he blurted out his story.

"There were two of them — came at me from behind. They must have followed me and seen me throw the envelopes. I saw them open one and stuff the cash in their pockets. One had a piece of wood, Pete."

"It's alright, mate, just try and get yourself together. Where's Tony? Have you seen him?"

"No, I didn't stop after I dropped the bag and ran. I've been back up at the road for the last half an hour or so, I guess."

"Well, we'd better try and find him, mate," said Peter.

The two men headed back to the main track that led into the shanty town, and from there, they skirted its left-hand boundary. They did not have to go far before they spotted a figure stumbling towards them — there was already an orange glow in the eastern sky and the darkness was lifting quickly. A few seconds later, and Colin's fears for Tony were realised as he staggered towards them, blood pouring from a head wound and one arm hanging limply at his side. He had met the thieves, and it was all too clear that he had tried to resist them. That his resistance had failed was evidenced by his lack of a bag. Colin ran forward to help him.

"Easy, skipper; you've been in the wars."

"Bit of a dogfight; bandits at one o'clock," he mumbled, a couple of broken teeth hindering his speech.

"We'll get you back to the road, Tony; Leon will be back there soon. Get you patched up."

"Gave as good as I got — think I landed a couple of decent blows. Whacked me on the elbow — arm busted. Feel a bit dizzy, chaps, need help to walk straight."

Colin and Peter took a position on either side of the wounded pilot and supported him as best they could, using the shoulder strap from the one remaining bag to tie the limp arm to his side. Moving cautiously and slowly, they made their way back up the track to the main road where the sight of the waiting black Mercedes immediately lifted their spirits after their ordeal. The attempt to carry out Jardigo's first philanthropic mission had failed miserably — destroyed by man's greed. Very few residents of the shanty town would discover any windfalls later that morning, having been robbed by two men who would never be discovered or even identified — they had enough money to disappear to any place on the planet where no one would ever find them. Jardigo's desire to provide some of the very poor of the world with a fair and equal share of his money had not allowed for the evil of man's greed. It would be a salutary lesson to the wealthy philanthropist for the organisation of such missions in the future.

17

Old Habits Die Hard

There was no need to take the injured pilot to a local hospital as the castle possessed its own medical facility of sorts. Two of Jardigo's earliest recruits had been a qualified doctor and an auxiliary nurse who between them soon patched Tony up; his left arm had a simple fracture just above the wrist and would heal in four to six weeks. His head injury, though bloody, needed a few stitches but there was no serious damage to the skull. He would spend the next few days in the medical centre, recuperating and recovering from his injuries. The other two crusaders spent most of the following day in bed and did not emerge until an hour before the scheduled time for dinner. A note had been slipped under the door to each of their rooms. It read,

When you are sufficiently recovered
from your ideal, please join me
on the rear veranda.
Jardigo

It was remarkable that, without any prearranged coordination, both men appeared on the veranda within five minutes of each other, looking reasonably refreshed, at least in the physical sense. The visit to the *Black Fields* had, however, left other scars that would take longer to heal. Jardigo and Rafael were enjoying a pre-dinner drink when Peter arrived first. His boss was immediately on his feet to shake the computer technician's hand.

"Peter, my friend, thank you for joining us; you must be exhausted. This is not how I had hoped your time with me would start. I am sorry you had such a bad time of it last night."

"Yeah, thanks — I'm only a humble back-room boy and I'm not used to such robbery and violence."

"Leon tells me you did not see the bandits."

"No, I was lucky, I guess, but I saw what they did to Tony — and Colin looked a nervous wreck when he went to bed. He'll be able to fill you in."

"Ah yes, I hope he will join us soon, and I will talk to Tony over the next few days when he's feeling better. He was lucky, you know — these bandits don't often leave their victims in the land of the living."

Peter hung his head.

"Come, have a beer, my friend and try to forget what happened. You may rest assured that I will do everything to find these men. Ah, here's my other hero — welcome, Colin."

"Peter's friend had appeared behind him. He looked pale and nervous.

"Whatcha, mate," said Peter. "How do you feel?"

"Alright, I suppose. I could use a drink, though."

Jardigo handed Colin a bottle of beer and said,

"Please sit down. I need to hear your story."

Two more beers and twenty minutes later and Jardigo was fully in the picture about his disastrous first attempt at random philanthropy. He was philosophical in his appraisal.

"Ah the evil of men; it will always be there even when we try to do good. All men should be treated equally, eh? Unfortunately, some men think they should be treated better and it's all down to greed."

"Perhaps, in future, such a distribution needs to be organised differently," observed Colin. "Maybe, mass cash handouts need to be targeted more specifically."

"Maybe, maybe not," said Jardigo. "In any case, we must hope that some of the residents of *Os Campos do Preto* still managed to receive some of the money. It may do some good when they spread their new-found wealth amongst their own families. At least I have made a start."

He paused and looked at Colin.

"Now Colin, do you think you would be able to recognise the two men who stopped you?"

"I doubt it; it was very dark and I was too scared to take much notice. I just dropped the bag and ran, Jardigo."

"Of course, my friend, and you did right."

"Maybe Tony will be able to help you more; he obviously spent more time in their company than I did."

"I will ask him later. Now, drink up and let us go and eat. After dinner, Peter, I have something to show you that may be of particular interest. Colin, I think you will need to relax in your room this evening — watch a few DVDs — take your mind of last night."

"Yeah, as long as the films are not action-packed and violent, eh, Col?" said Peter, with a broad grin.

The room was below ground level and reached by a wooden staircase behind the main kitchens of the castle. As Peter followed Jardigo into the dimly lit stone-faced corridor that led from the staircase, he was reminded of the former history of the building. Colin had told him that the present castle had been built on the site of an old monastery and the area that his boss was now leading him into had all the hallmarks of its former use. The corridor was lined on either side with small monastic cells; some fronted with old oak doors and some open to view. In olden times, no natural light would have filtered into the cells, even during the day, and solitary meditation would have taken place with the senses of sight and hearing rendered useless. Now, the corridor had electric light to guide them on their way.

"It's just at the end here, Peter. I think you'll like it."

They had reached what appeared to be the end of the corridor — it had been about fifty yards long and one final room was directly in front of them, spanning the complete width of the corridor and the cells on either side. A modern steel door filled its entrance.

"Here we are, my friend."

Jardigo pushed open the door and fluorescent light filled the corridor as Peter followed him in. After his eyes had refocused to the sudden brightness, Peter's jaw dropped in amazement.

"Oh my God!" he exclaimed. "What the hell is all this?"

"Your new workspace, my friend. Do you like it?"

Peter's eyes scanned the room's interior, taking in the mixture of mainframe computers and laptops, arranged in a U-shape on modern work tables and benches. In all, he counted eight monitors staring back at him and numerous keyboards and all the other equipment associated with a high-tech computer suite.

"It's better than I had at the bank."

"Yes, I hope so — you have a complete network here with some of the world's most powerful computers."

"And that's an IBM Columbus at the back, isn't it?"

"Yes, one of the world's best and most powerful supercomputers, I'm told. It is the main hub of the network and just what you need for you new job, I hope. Of course, if you think you need something better, you will have to let me know and I will get it for you."

"It must have cost millions," gasped Peter.

"Yes, it did, my friend — many millions."

Peter's face suddenly took on a puzzled expression.

"There's no one working here at the moment?"

"No, Peter, you will work alone. All this is for your sole use. I don't think there's anyone else at the castle that would have a clue how to operate any of this equipment."

Peter walked forward; he was like a little boy in a sweet shop and he could have what he liked.

"All mine," he murmured. "All mine, to ...."

He turned back to face his benevolent boss.

"To do what exactly?"

"To help you with your next task, my friend."

"Which is?"

"All in good time, Peter. Tonight is not the time to speak of that — I shall tell you that when you've had a chance to assess what you have got here and what you could do with it."

"Anything, I should say — absolutely anything. What you have here could run a major international corporation employing tens of thousands of people."

"Really? How interesting."

Jardigo smiled and walked over to an array of steel cupboards to the left of the computers.

"These storage cabinets contain all the software and peripherals you will need and there is a stationery cupboard here, too. I have ordered a water machine and a coffee maker for you as I guess you may want to spend long periods of time down here. I can also arrange for your meals to be sent down, if you wish. There is a bathroom and toilet in one of the cells outside. That cell and the computer suite both have power and light. Only you and I will have keys to this room and the network is totally self-contained and does not link to the castle's ordinary computer."

"I understand, so can I ...?"

"Can you start?"

Peter nodded excitedly.

"Of course, my friend — the sooner, the better."

Jardigo reached inside his pocket.

"This is your key. From now on, this room and all the equipment is your responsibility and, as I said, if you think you need something else, just go ahead and order it and charge it to my personal account."

Peter did not reply — he was already in a world of his own as he sat down in one of the expensive leather swivel chairs.

"I can see you want to try out your new machines, my friend, so I will leave you now."

Jardigo turned for the door and then stopped.

"Oh, I forgot to mention that there is another cell behind the stationery cupboard. You will find a single bed in there should you wish to spend any nights down here. However, it would be nice to see you at least once a day, Peter, O.K?"

Jardigo thought he detected a mumbled acknowledgement as the IBM supercomputer whirred into life.

At that particular moment, elsewhere in the castle, Peter's friend had also just switched on a computer. It was of a much smaller variety and it was about to be used for an entirely different purpose.

Colin had deposited 10,000 Euros in his online casino account — at least ten times what he had been accustomed to before his change of identity. At least half of his original debts had been accumulated by using such sites. Now, it didn't matter; that evening's deposit was a small fraction of his new-found wealth and in the coming days, his bank balance was likely to be multiplied many times over. It was not his role to give away any of *his* money. He'd always found the anonymity of online betting sites suited his personality — no prying eyes could see how much he was gambling and no one could pass comment when he won or lost — especially when the loss was heavy. Also, it never felt that he was playing with real money as nothing changed hands physically, unlike in the bookies or in real casinos. It kind of lessened the mental anxiety when he wagered a large amount. Above all, it gave him tremendous excitement as he watched wheels spin or balls roll a few inches in front of him. Sometimes, he kept his eyes firmly shut or looked away from the screen until his fate had been completely determined. There was nothing worse than knowing a split second before the ball stopped on a roulette wheel that it was nowhere near your number. The whole process of private gambling relaxed him and gave him a strange sense of power. It needed courage to place huge sums of money on the roll of a dice or the spin of a wheel, even though most people would argue that all it needed was blind stupidity and a suicidal view of life. Colin had always had this devil-may-care attitude; the 'in for a penny, in for a pound' or the 'got to be in it to win it' approach to gambling and he was not about to change with his six-figure bank balance waiting to be tapped into. Ever since he had been a young boy, he had gambled mentally on even the most trivial of things — the colour of the next car to pass him in the street; how many starlings there were perched on a overhanging wire and it had given him huge satisfaction when he'd got it right. To make money at it made the challenge meaningful and concentrated his mind on his selection. Unfortunately, he had always reckoned he could use his intellectual powers in games of pure chance — he had never really understood simple probability. To him, if a six hadn't come up in twenty rolls of a dice, or a favourite number on a roulette wheel hadn't appeared for ages, it was more likely to come up the next go than its established odds. He would just never accept that the probability of individual events was completely unaffected by what had happened before. When red came up ten times in a row at roulette, he would argue that the wheel was biased. In short, Colin was the bookie's favourite kind of gambler and since his love of winning outweighed his fear of losing, he was destined to gamble till he took his last breath — he had as much of an addiction as an alcoholic or someone hooked on drugs. The only difference, especially now that he was single, was that his gambling did not have a detrimental effect on anyone except himself.

That particular evening had started well. Playing roulette, and using a combination of favourite numbers and 'predictions' based on previous spins, he had nearly doubled his casino account balance in the first half an hour. When next, on a mere whim, he placed 1000 Euros on sixteen, his excitement also doubled when the ball came to rest on his chosen number. He had won another 35,000 Euros. Though he rarely kept with the same number twice in a row, he chose sixteen again, this time placing 5000 Euros on its red square. He clicked on '*Spin*' and closed his eyes, opening them just in time to see the ball fall into the sixteen slot. He blinked at the screen as the recorded applause erupted from the computer and '*Congratulations!*' flashed across the screen. He had won 180,000 Euros and the only dampener to his excitement was his usual thought: "*Why, oh why didn't I put more on?*' He was always like that after any kind of win — he was just never satisfied and often, that would be precisely his downfall in subsequent bets. He would try to win what he thought he had been entitled to; what he should have won if he'd placed the larger bet. He knew it was stupid and it rarely, if ever, worked, but he just had to do it — he hated thinking he had missed out on a bigger win. This evening was to be no exception and within another half an hour, he had not only lost all of his accumulated winnings, he had dipped into his bank account to the tune of another 50,000 Euros as well. If it hadn't been for the gentle tap at his bedroom door, he would have probably continued that evening — his bank account still contained over 400,000 Euros, which he may well have lost entirely, given the frustrated, yet adventurous mood he was still in. The knocking was persistent.

"Come in!" He called out, closing his laptop sharply in his frustration.

"It's only me, mate — I just had to come and tell you."

Peter stood in the doorway.

"I'm not disturbing you, am I?"

"No, Pete, I was just googling some things. What's up?"

"You have just got to come downstairs, Col."

"Downstairs? I am downstairs, you clown."

"I mean in the basement — the old monastery cellars."

"Why, what's there?"

"Just come and I'll show you."

"O.K. Just let me put some shoes on. Why the secrecy?"

"You'll see — I want it to be a surprise."

A few minutes later, Peter led his friend into his new computer suite. His reaction was similar to his of an hour or so earlier.

"Wow! What the hell is all this for?"

"It's for me to use."

"It looks expensive, Pete."

"It is, believe me, it is."

"So, what's it for?"

"I'm not exactly sure yet. Jardigo has given me licence to investigate what it will do over the next week or so."

"But what do you think he's going to use it for? You must have some idea, surely."

"Well, I suppose he wants me to do something similar to what you did back at the bank."

"Raid a few more bank accounts?"

"Possibly, but ...."

"But?"

"I was going to say that may not be its entire purpose."

"Oh, why?"

"There's far too much equipment here for that, if that's all his plan is. You could do what we, or should I say you did before with one reasonably powerful laptop. You just need the right software."

"So what else, then?"

"I'm not really sure, mate, but whatever his plan is, he wants me to execute it."

"Does that worry you?"

"No, not worry as such, but it's certainly exciting to think that all this stuff is for my sole use."

"Is that what he told you?"

"More or less."

"You know what I think," said Colin, after a moment's reflection.

"What?"

"I have a funny feeling that you're right and he isn't only interested in stealing money, whether from banks or not."

"How do you mean?"

"Well, you've said yourself that that could be accomplished with much less equipment so there's got to be something else."

"I've just said that, Col, so what are you driving at?"

"I think he's after some information or he wants to control something."

"Control? What, like people?"

"Maybe, or businesses."

"You mean rob a multi-national company?"

"Possibly — but, as I said, not just of money."

"What then?"

"Secrets?"

"But why, Col? After all, if all he wants to do is rob the rich to give to the poor, why would he need secrets?"

"I don't know, but I've started to sense he may have a slightly different plan in mind — a plan that isn't as philanthropic as he makes it sound."

"What makes you say that?"

"It's just a feeling and anyway, just stop to think for a moment."

"I have been."

"Well, has it not occurred to you that he has been a very wealthy man for a very long time, so why hasn't he given any money away to the poor up until now? Why does he need even more?"

"He's greedy for more?"

"Precisely, and does that strike you as being the kind of human quality you would normally associate with a philanthropist?"

"I suppose not."

"And what about all the veiled threats he has made to us about the consequences of reneging on our contracts. Does that strike you as the kind of Christian behaviour of such a supposedly well-intentioned man?"

"No."

"You've heard the stories about how he always gets his way and what may have befallen those who dared to cross him in the past."

"Yes."

"Well, I'm beginning to draw my own conclusions and take quite a different view of our boss and host."

"You don't trust him, do you, Col?"

"No, I don't and you shouldn't either, especially with anything he may ask you to do."

"So what do we do, then?"

"Nothing — we watch and wait. I'm sure he's up to something and I want to be prepared for when he does it."

"Well, we can't leave, that's for sure. We can't go anywhere; we're wanted criminals."

"True, but we can be careful."

"And carry out what he asks us?"

"We'll have to."

"Even if we were to put lives at risk?"

"What do you mean, Pete?"

"Well, I for one don't mind robbing banks and so on, especially when the money could be put to better use, but I would draw the line at anything where someone might get hurt. We were close to getting hurt ourselves last night. Like you, I think that Jardigo would stop at nothing to get his own way, even if it meant that in the long run, he was helping someone else. There are limits to that kind of philosophy. It's the difference between being reactive and proactive. Robin Hood didn't deliberately set out to harm people; he just wanted to protect his own and see that justice was done."

"Justice for the poor inevitably means that the rich will suffer, though, Pete."

"Yes, but only financially and in no other more sinister way. They have a right to justice, too."

18

Doubts and Questions

Colin didn't return to the online casino that night. The exchange of ideas with his friend about Jardigo and his intentions had worried him a little and he decided perhaps that discretion was the better part of valour. He might need a healthy bank account if their boss was not quite all that he seemed. Instead, he decided to pay Tony a visit in the medical centre, situated at the rear of the castle on the second floor. If he was well enough, it might be interesting to hear his views on Jardigo. They hadn't really discussed each other's views of him since the pilot had joined the operation less than twenty-four hours previously. He'd tried to persuade Peter to accompany him but the computer expert was too wrapped up in his investigations of his new equipment.

Tony was propped up in bed, his arm swathed in plaster and his head bandaged heavily. A small television hung from the wall in a corner of the room and though it was switched on, Tony's eyes seemed to be closed in sleep when Colin poked his head round the door.

"You awake, skipper?" whispered Colin. "It's only half-past nine."

Tony opened one eye and raised his right arm in acknowledgement.

"Nah, mate — just resting my eyes. There's nothing on TV that I can understand."

"I'm not disturbing you, am I?"

"No, come on in, chap."

Both eyes were now open and Colin walked forward to help the injured pilot into a more comfortable position.

"Thanks, Col, I'm glad of the company. It's boring just being laid here — the doc says I need to let my body recover from the battering, so I'm trying to be a good little soldier. It has its advantages, though."

"Yeah?"

"Yeah, especially if the lovely young thing, who's looking after me, gives me a bed-bath."

"You're partly recovered, then?"

The pilot's face broke into a grin. Colin pulled up a chair and sat next to his bed.

"So what's new, Col?"

"Not much; Peter's been given a computer suite down in the old cellars, so I doubt we'll see much of him in future. He'll be in his element down there."

"More online fraud, I suppose?"

"Maybe."

Colin paused.

"You don't seem sure."

"Can I ask you a question, Tony?"

"Sure, fire away."

"Now that you've met Jardigo, what do you actually think of him?"

"Think of him?"

"Yes, you must have wondered what he'd be like after Pete and I told you a bit about him."

"Well, he's not exactly how I imagined him."

"Go on."

"You two made him seem like your typical wealthy philanthropist."

"And isn't he?"

"I'm not sure, mate. On the surface, he makes his intentions seem that way, but underneath, I'm not so sure. Take last night, for example and his method of distributing to the poor."

"What about it?"

"Well, the more I think about it, he must have known there was a strong possibility that something like that could happen. He put us in danger, Col — I could have been killed, and though he apologised profusely to me, I had a funny feeling that ...."

"What?"

"That I was expendable."

"We all are, Tony."

"And there's another thing — and this must have bothered you two as well."

The pilot paused to gather his thoughts.

"What thing?"

"How many philanthropists do you know are also out and out criminals as well, answer me that?"

"He only robs those who can afford to lose the money."

"That's not what I've heard."

"Oh?"

"Yeah, I've heard that he runs protection rackets in Lisbon and not only against wealthy businesses. He also exerts pressure on the poor, struggling ones as well."

"Who told you that?"

"Leone."

"And who is Leone?"

"My nurse."

"So are you regretting coming to work for him?"

"No, not really, I'll just close my eyes to certain things and ...."

"And take the money?

"Precisely, Colin — after all, what have we got to lose?"

"Our lives?"

"Only if we go against him, and I'm not about to do that. Are you?"

"No, not if I can avoid it."

"Anyway, you've known him longer than me; what do you and Pete think of him?"

"Much the same, except I still think his philosophy is a worthy one."

"And Pete doesn't?"

"Maybe; I'm not sure. He's going to be too busy playing with his new toys to worry overmuch about the finer details of Jardigo's operation. He's got a new electric train set and he's not about to give it up."

By this time, Colin seemed to sense that they had just about exhausted their individual views of their boss and he started to change the subject.

"So, when are you going to be up and about again, skipper?"

"Doc says I can get up tomorrow as long as I take it easy."

"What about flying your plane?"

"A few weeks, I guess. I need two strong hands to fly the old crate. She can be a pig in rough weather. Jardigo's going to take me out to the mountain airstrip sometime early next week to show me the alterations to her paintwork. They even have a natural hangar up there — a huge cavern, hollowed out in the mountain side with everything on hand inside to run and service small aircraft. I can't wait to see what's there. I've never seen it on my trips in and out of there."

"Has he told you what your fist mission will be yet?"

"No, other than helping him to fetch and carry goods to and from the UK, like I've done before."

The pilot yawned.

"Sorry, mate, I'm bushed. Think I'll get some shuteye, if you don't mind."

"No problem," said Colin. "It's been a helluva day, one way or another."

"Thanks for coming to see me and, Col?"

"Yes, skipper?"

"For God's sake, don't worry. We three musketeers will be alright. One for all and all for one, eh?"

"I hope you're right, skipper. Now I will bid you sweet dreams, and keep your mind off that nurse of yours; you're supposed to be resting."

Tony just about managed a smile as his heavy eyelids closed once more — he was almost asleep before Colin left his room.

The following Tuesday, Jardigo and Rafael were to be found taking their leisurely breakfast as usual on the rear veranda; the day was unseasonably dull and cool for early August. Jardigo's deputy seemed a little fidgety and preoccupied.

"Something is troubling you, Rafa, is it not?" asked Jardigo, suddenly. "You've hardly touched your breakfast. Are you sick?"

"No, boss, I have heard things."

"What kind of things?"

"I have heard murmurings of unrest from the Englishmen."

"Ah yes, I have heard these rumours, too. It is nothing to worry about, my friend."

"But I am not sure they are fully committed to the cause, Jardigo. I have seen them whispering to each other."

"They are perhaps homesick, Rafa."

"Maybe, but I think we need to watch them carefully."

"Then organise it, my friend — I have some jobs for them that will keep their minds occupied for a while. I think I maybe need to remind them that their contracts require nothing less than a hundred per cent commitment from them, eh?"

"And what the consequences are if they stray from that commitment?"

"Yes, a gentle reminder of that, too," said Jardigo, with a wink. "Now would be a good time, I think, for me to have a little chat with our English friends. Go and find them for me and tell them they are to join me down at the summer house in one hour."

"Yes, boss."

Peter was the first to be notified of the meeting with Jardigo; Rafael knew there was only one place he would be, and at first, he had difficulty in getting the computer expert to understand his message.

"Senhor Williams, you are please to go to the summer house at ten — Jardigo wishes to speak to you."

"Not now, Rafael, I'm in the middle of some important work. Tell him I'll see him lunchtime."

Rafael smiled at the young Englishman's audacity — he needed persuading, he thought. Without raising his voice, he said,

"Please remember who you are, Senhor Williams and when I, Jardigo's deputy, give you a command, you do not question it. You will report to the summer house at ten. If you do not, it will be a disciplinary matter and I will not be held responsible for any consequences of your disobedience. I am merely passing on your boss's instructions."

"Oh, alright, I'll be there, but it is most inconvenient. Why couldn't he have given me more warning?"

"That is not for me to say, Senhor. You must take that up with him, but I give you a word of warning ...."

"What?"

"I advise you not to take the same attitude with Senhor Batista that you have just tried to take with me. He will not like it. Compreende?"

Finally, Peter began to show some humility.

"Yes, Rafael, I apologise if I was a little disrespectful but I am in the middle of some important investigations that Jardigo asked me to carry out."

"Of course, Senhor and I did not take offence."

When Rafael approached the other two Englishmen with the same request, neither was anything less than courteous and acquiescent with their response. By chance, the three men were able to join up with each other as they strolled down the grassy slope that led down to the summer house by the lake. The sun had started to appear from behind the clouds and the morning was getting warmer. Despite this, Peter was still somewhat moody and annoyed at the short notice of his summons.

"This is most inconvenient, boys. I can't leave my work just like that."

"Chill, Einstein," said Tony.

"It's alright for you two; you've done nothing but that over the last few days."

"You want this broken arm, then?"

"Sorry, skipper. I wasn't thinking."

They were in earshot of the summer house by now and Colin whispered,

"I wonder what he wants."

"I haven't the foggiest," replied Tony. "But it must be quite urgent; we were all given less than an hour's notice."

"Probably his next mission," said Peter.

"Well, I can't help yet," said Tony. "Doc says another three weeks at least before I can operate the controls. At least Jardigo is going to take me up to the strip tomorrow to see what they've done to my plane. I shall start to feel like a pilot again, I hope."

Directly in front of them, Jardigo had emerged from the summer house — he raised his arm in a friendly wave.

"Well, at least he looks happy," whispered Colin.

"Welcome, my friends!" he called out. "Come and join me, please."

Inside the summer house, three sun loungers had been arranged in a semi-circle facing the lake. Jardigo pointed to them and then took up a standing position with his back to the water. The three Englishmen sat down in silence. There was an uncomfortable formality to the meeting.

"Now I expect you are wondering why I have summoned you all here at such short notice, my friends."

"The thought had crossed my mind," replied Peter.

"Ah, Senhor Williams, Rafael told me you were not too happy at being disturbed. That is good. I am pleased to see you are working hard but I must remind you, and the others, that you work for me and will do my bidding without question or argument."

The three men looked down at the floor. They felt uncomfortable and unable to hold Jardigo's icy stare. His eyes seemed to penetrate their very souls. Suddenly, as if sensing their nervousness, he turned his back on them and looked across the lake. In a voice only just loud enough for them to hear, he said,

"I have heard rumours, my friends — rumours that do not make me happy."

"What rumours, boss?" asked Colin, with suitable deference to their positions at the castle.

"You will be silent until I have finished, please."

Jardigo continued to face the lake. Tony looked at Colin and raised his eyebrows. His face had a worried expression.

"As I was saying, I have heard rumours and these rumours would suggest that some of you may not be entirely convinced about our cause."

Jardigo turned back to face the three men.

"Is this true?"

The direct question caught them off guard and nobody said a word.

"You may speak now," said Jardigo.

Tony tried to be diplomatic, if a little evasive.

"I think we're all a little bored at the moment, especially me and we are anxious to start work proper."

"Well, I've got plenty to do," mumbled Peter.

"That doesn't really answer my question."

He looked directly at Colin.

"What about you, Senhor Fenner, are you fully committed to what I'm doing?"

"Of course, boss."

"Does that go for all of you?"

"Well ...."

"Yes, Senhor Taylor, you have something to say?"

"I was going to say that we all are committed to helping the poor of this world and relieving very rich people of money which lies wasting in untouched bank accounts, and which they have no use for, but ...."

"There is a but?"

"I think we are not happy when the acquisition of that money entails the use of violence, or threats of violence."

Jardigo's stern face seemed to darken further.

"And who has used violence, my friend? Have I?"

"I don't know," replied Tony. "We have heard rumours, too, about some unusual tactics they may have been used in the past."

"Really? Do you have proof?"

"No."

"Then you should not listen to rumours, my friend."

"You threatened me," said Colin, boldly.

"Did I, Senhor Fenner? What did I say?"

"I don't remember exactly."

"And did I threaten you with violence?"

"You said that if I didn't come to work for you and didn't pay my debts back, you would give me pain — I recall you used that word in the members' bar at the *Las Vegas* casino the night we first met."

"I see, and did I say physical pain, Colin, my friend?"

"No, but that's how I interpreted it."

"Then you are letting your mind run away with you — you must be watching too many gangster DVDs."

"So what did you mean?"

"Pain can be emotional as well as physical. If you hadn't allowed me to wipe your debts clean, you would have had a painful life trying to cope and live to the manner you were used to, no?"

"Probably," replied Colin, weakly.

Jardigo turned to look at the other two Englishmen.

"And did I threaten you with violence if either of you had refused to come and work for me?"

"No, boss," replied Peter. "It was Colin who persuaded me, anyway."

"Senhor Taylor?"

"Er, no; you just said that if I refused, you could reverse that refusal. You didn't say how."

Jardigo smiled and turned to face the lake again. Colin stood up and said,

"Can we go now, or was there something else, boss?"

"Yeah, I could do with getting back to my computers," added Peter.

Jardigo turned round to face them.

"No, not unless you have any other criticisms of my mission or the methods I use to carry it out."

The three men looked at each other.

"No, boss, you have reassured us," replied Colin.

"You should not need reassuring, my friend, and please all of you remember that I pay your wages and can toss you out on the street to face the real world and the inevitable consequences when the police catch up with any of you."

Jardigo paused as his eyes moved from one man to the next.

"And, gentlemen?"

"Yes, boss," replied Tony.

"That *is* a threat, but it does not require violence — just a severance of your contracts. You understand?"

"Yes, boss," came back in a three-way unison.

"Oh, and before I forget," added Jardigo. "I would like to chat with Colin and Peter after lunch, down in the computer suite. I have a job for you to do."

As the three Englishmen wandered back up to the castle that morning, it was clear that only Colin remained really sceptical of Jardigo's true intentions. Peter and Tony seemed reasonably content with his attempt to allay any of their fears. The pilot seemed to have a simple philosophy, which he expressed as soon as they were out of earshot of the summer house where their boss had remained to enjoy a cold drink and a cigar.

"Why should we worry, chaps? He's paying us film-star wages. I suggest we keep our heads down below the parapet and do as we are told and leave the thinking to him."

"Yeah, I agree," said Peter. "I wish we'd been brave enough to ask him some more questions, though."

"Like what?" queried Tony.

"Like why I've got so much powerful computer hardware."

"And why he hasn't given any money away before," added Colin.

"Oh come on, Col," replied Tony. "That's hardly a case for doubting if his philanthropy is genuine or not. He has to start sometime."

"Well, I didn't like his attitude to us. Did you notice when he stared into our eyes? It was scary and as though he was trying to hypnotise and control us."

"Just face it, Colin, he *does* control us, mate," said Peter. "Like Tony says, he pays our wages and can cut us loose anytime he likes. I, for one, am going to toe the line. I broke bail, remember?"

"Don't worry, I hadn't forgotten, Peter," said Colin. "However, I'm still not convinced he's a genuine philanthropist but I suppose I'll just have to go with the flow like you pair."

"From where I'm standing, there's not much else we can do, mate," said Tony, finally.

For once, Rafael seemed anxious to join the three Englishmen for lunch, making a beeline to where they were sitting in the dining hall and even encouraging another employee to vacate their chair so that he could sit next to them. Though he did not join in their conversation, it did mean that they felt unable to talk about Jardigo, and the conversation was limited to memories of England and snippets of news they'd seen or heard on television. As they were leaving, Jardigo himself also made a point of accompanying them and, as he had indicated earlier, it was clear that he wanted to talk to Colin and Peter on their own down in the computer room. He was carrying a long cylindrical cardboard tube under his arm.

"No time like the present, my friends. Let us go downstairs and I will discuss with you what I would like to do next."

Tony seemed relieved that he was not required.

"Well, I'm off for my weekly check-up at the medical centre, so I'll catch you chaps later."

The two friends nodded briefly to Tony and duly obeyed the invitation as they followed their boss, each with their own sense of apprehension. What did he want with them? Was this the next part of his plan? Was it going to involve more skimming of bank accounts? What was in the cardboard tube? It looked like the type of container that held plans or blueprints. Jardigo was quick to reveal its contents after they had entered the computer room.

"Now my friends, bring that empty table into the centre of the room where the light is good," he said, excitedly. In robotic silence, Colin and Peter pushed and dragged the heavy steel table away from its neighbours as Jardigo opened the tube to reveal its contents.

"Take a look at this," he said, as he unrolled the large plastic-backed map.

"A map of Africa, Jardigo?"

"Yes, Colin."

"Never seen one that big and detailed before," observed Peter.

"No, I had to have it specially made by a cartographer in Lisbon."

The two Englishmen moved closer to the table to study the map, which measured about five feet by three; its detail was extraordinary and seemed to contain everything that could possibly be known about the world's second biggest continent.

"So is this related to your next mission, boss?" asked Colin.

"Yes, if you two can make it happen for me, my friends."

Peter smiled and nodded at Colin.

"Some of the poorest countries on the planet, mate."

"Well observed, Peter, and we are going to help one of them."

"How?"

"By doing what we tried at *Os Campos do Preto*."

"Which failed miserably, Jardigo," pointed out Colin.

"I know, but this time we do it in daylight, so everyone can see it and not just bandits prowling after dark."

"We're going to Africa to hand out bundles of cash? I think not, Jardigo — we'd be robbed and killed at knifepoint."

"No, you will not have to set foot on the ground, my friends. We make the delivery by air."

"Tony's plane?" said Peter.

"But what do you want us to do?" queried Colin. "You don't need all this equipment just for that, surely?"

"No, the computers will be used for another mission I have in mind, but I do need your expertise right now for the African drop."

"How?"

"There are several things. First, I want you to find a country for me — one with the greatest need; one that is the easiest to fly over and one that has a suitable area for such a drop. You may need to investigate further with more detailed maps online. Secondly, I need to know what currency to send, and that is where your banking knowledge will come in useful, Colin."

Colin nodded. He was encouraged; it all seemed reasonable so far. Surely they would not face attacks in the air.

"And thirdly, if I need to buy the local currency, how would I do it — without attracting attention to the castle?"

Neither man said anything. Jardigo looked pleased as no objections had seemed to be immediately forthcoming..

"So, can it be done, men?"

Peter looked thoughtful, as his friend replied,

"Yes, it can be done; the only difficulty, as I see it, will be obtaining the cash, unless ...."

"Yes?"

"Unless we use US dollars, or maybe Euros — I seem to recall that one or two African countries are only too welcome to have certain international currencies."

"I had thought about that, but I want the money to go directly to help the ordinary poor people, even though it would be easy for me to arrange, as I probably already have enough of such currency here at the castle. However, would they not have problems exchanging it for food and so on?"

"Maybe," replied Colin. "We would have to investigate that."

"Fine, then investigate. You have some time yet; Tony will not be ready to fly for nearly a month."

"Have you asked him if he thinks it's possible?" asked Peter.

"Not yet; I want you two to talk to him about it when you have decided which country to help."

Colin gave a little shake of the head.

"No, with all due respect, I think we would need his advice *before* we select the country."

Peter nodded.

"Yeah, Col's right, it would be stupid to choose a country that's too far away, with all the problems of refuelling that that would entail; let alone being able to get safely and quickly back to Portugal."

"O.K. then, you'd better speak to him today," said Jardigo. "I will leave the finer points of the organisation entirely to you three, and there is just one last thing."

"What, boss," queried Peter.

"You three and I are the only people who are to know about this — you understand? You talk to no one."

"Yes, Jardigo," said Colin.

"Good, I will leave you now to start your research. I would like a full progress report in exactly one week from today."

As soon as Jardigo had left the room, the two men wasted no time in offering up their individual opinions on their boss's unusual mission. Their views were clearly mixed concerning the effectiveness of such a daring and direct approach for providing aid to the poor.

"Well, I think he's flipped his lid," said Colin.

"So why didn't you say so when he was here?" said Peter. "You seemed all for the idea."

"Because you know what he's like if you ruffle his feathers and anyway, I didn't actually tell him I thought it was a good idea; just that I thought it was possible."

"You've got to admit that it's bold, though, Col."

"Oh it's that alright — I just don't think he's thought it through properly."

"I think the idea is that that's our job."

"And if we say it can't be done, Pete?"

Colin's friend shrugged his shoulders.

"He'll make us do it?"

"Precisely, my friend," replied Colin, mimicking their boss. "But before we get into that, we need the skipper's views," he continued.

"Damn right we do. It all hinges on him."

"And that's another thing I found curious, Peter."

"What?"

"Why didn't he have Tony at the meeting; he could have got his opinion there and then."

Peter thought for a moment about the ebullient pilot.

"Probably because he would have been more forthright than you and spoken his mind openly. Then you would have had some support for your doubts and so felt able to join in and express those doubts, making it seem as if there was a majority of us against the plan. Clearly, Jardigo didn't want that scenario."

"So he deliberately didn't invite Tony?"

"Yes, because it is always easier to convince two than three. He's leaving that to us and because we didn't express any objections, he can assume he has the two of us already on board. He's a very clever man."

"Devious more like," said Colin. "He's a manipulator."

"Of course he is; just look how we were all manipulated before we made the decision to come and work for him, and he's done the same thing again, not ten minutes ago. He knew we wouldn't object openly, just as he knows we'll convince Tony of his plan."

"He won't need much convincing — he can't wait to fly again in his newly refurbished jet. He'd probably fly into a war zone to relieve his boredom and frustration."

Peter grinned.

"There might well be one or two of those in Africa at the moment. Also, Jardigo's taking him to see his plane tomorrow. I would say that was just about perfect timing, wouldn't you?"

"Give him the promise of an exciting mission and then pull an ace out of the pack in the guise of his gleaming new toy?"

"Exactly, mate."

"So we'd better go and find him," said Colin, finally.

"Best try the medical centre first; I'm he sure that's where he said he was going."

They didn't have to wait long outside the centre; Tony's appointment with the doctor concluded within minutes of Colin and Peter's arrival. He was grinning from ear to ear.

"You look happy, skipper," said Peter.

"And I am chaps. Doc says I'll be out of plaster sooner than expected."

"Good," said Colin. "We need to talk to you urgently. What are you doing now?"

"Nothing much, I was going to get some exercise and go for a walk."

"Right, we'll join you. What we have to say needs to be in private."

"O.K., roger that, chaps — top secret, eh?"

"Sort of, skipper," whispered Colin.

"Let's head down to the lake, then," said Tony. "Quiet there."

They had related most of Jardigo's plan before they had got half-way to the lake with the pilot merely grunting incoherently at each detail. Finally, after another non-committal response, Colin said,

"Is there any chance you're going to give us your opinion, Tony?"

"Sorry, mate, just taking all the facts on board. Didn't realise you were so anxious for my views on the mission."

"Well?"

"A bit crack-pot, chaps."

"Can it be done?"said Peter.

"Depends where in Africa."

"What's the Lear jet's range," queried Colin.

"With not much wind, about 4500 kilometres — enough probably to get to somewhere like northern Nigeria and back; further with refuelling. But that's not the real problem."

"Oh?"

"Not easy to just open the main door and drop things, chaps. It may be a small aircraft but it's still a jet with a cruising speed of 420 knots. Got to be very careful when you open the cabin at that speed."

"So it's not possible?" observed Colin, hopefully.

"I didn't say that. It can be done with some modifications to the fuselage."

"Like bomb doors?" said Peter.

"Yeah, or something similar. The drop would need some kind of control if the boss wants the distribution to be even and well-directed over the area you choose."

"You'll need to help with that choice, Tony," said Colin.

"Yep, not mountains or water, for example."

"Parachutes?"

"What for — us?"

"No, for the bundles of cash."

"Nah," replied Tony. "Would it matter if the packets split open?"

"Probably not," replied Peter. "It would help with the even distribution."

They had reached the lake by now and Colin stopped to put a hand on Tony's arm.

"So, be honest, skipper, will it work?"

"Yeah, I should say so, if I can have the right alterations made to the plane."

"Well, money's no object there," replied Colin.

"Then all you chaps have got to do is decide on the country and find a way of getting the right currency. Then we need to choose a populated area which is accessible, with my advice, of course. And remember ...."

"What, skipper?" said Peter.

"Africa is a vast continent; I've known pilots lose their bearings and disappear, just like in the Bermuda Triangle."

19

Into Africa

The only thing he recognised was the basic shape. The Lear jet had been completely transformed from its dull grey and standard black markings of a private operator to the gleaming white and red of the worldwide carrier, DHL. With the easily recognisable logo of the famous international company emblazoned in bright red down the length of the fuselage, Tony's jet stood waiting for him on the matt red tarmac of the cavernous hangar's floor. Jardigo strode forward as two men in dirty white overalls bowed and nodded to their boss.

"Come, my friend, let me show you inside."

"I'm gobsmacked," said Tony. "That must have cost a small fortune."

"They have spared no expense for you."

"Why DHL? Isn't it a bit dangerous using an internationally recognised logo?"

"Oh no, Tony, the plane is already fully registered with them. I had Peter create all the paperwork online for you."

"You mean that I'm one of their pilots?"

"Of course, even down to your photograph in their personnel section. Peter was quick and efficient yesterday evening. It is a perfect disguise for any of my import/export operations as well as the flight to Africa."

Inside, Tony was quick to spot that six seats had become four with the passenger cabin shortened slightly from the rear.

"We have enlarged the rear hold and given you an extra fuel tank. The engineer says the range should be increased by at least twenty per cent."

"That's what the extra dial is for on the dashboard, presumably," said Tony glancing forward.

"Yes."

"Very impressive, I must say."

"The engines have been given a complete overhaul; one of the mechanics reported that she wasn't really airworthy, you know — it could have developed a serious fault at anytime."

"She was overdue a service, but I just never got round to it."

Tony moved to the rear of the cabin and peered through into the hold.

"You've even put some parachutes in there."

"Yes, and I hope no one ever has cause to use them, Tony."

"There's just one thing, Jardigo."

"Yes?"

"If we're going to make drops, whether it's cash or not, we're going to need some kind of bomb door in there. It would be too dangerous to just push any packets out of the passenger door."

"Colin came and told me this morning and the engineers are working on a vacuum-release design right now."

"Brilliant, then I think it's all systems go, boss."

"When do you think you'll be fit to give her a test flight?"

"The doctor says in two or three weeks."

"I understand from Colin that you're helping him and Peter organise the drop."

"Yes, we're meeting again tonight to see if we can come up with a country."

The People's Republic of Mafoso appeared to be right on the limit of the Lear jet's range. With Senegal to the north and Guinea to the south and west, it possessed an western border on the Atlantic coast of less than 200 kilometres in length and while it could give refuelling problems, Tony was clearly in favour of the small country for the cash drop.

"It's flat, has a seaward approach and we could be in and out of there in no time."

"How does coming in from the sea help?" said Peter.

"Because we'd be less likely to be spotted before the job was done and although Mafoso probably doesn't have radar detection, we wouldn't have to fly over any North African countries that would have. We could fly west from here and then fly south over the Atlantic till we reach the Mafosan coast. From there, by the look of the map, it would be less than 150 kilometres until we were directly over the centre of the country."

"That's all fine, skipper, but there is a major problem with Mafoso," observed Colin.

"Two problems, mate," added Peter.

"Yeah?"

"First," said Colin. "They have their own currency — the Mafosan Pound and, second ...?"

He turned to look at Peter.

"Second, Tony, the country is still in turmoil after two rebellions in the last six months with mass genocide of one particular tribe."

"And it's not possible to get hold of enough of the currency?" queried the pilot.

"Colin says not," replied Peter. "They have raging inflation of several thousand per cent."

Colin nodded.

"So that's three problems?" remarked Tony. "But wouldn't they desperately need something like US dollars, then?"

"Possibly," replied Colin. "Peter and I need to do some more research. It is certainly one of the poorest countries on the continent."

"Well, I haven't seen any other area of Africa that fits the bill from my point of view," said Tony. "So it's got my vote."

"It gets mine, too if we can be sure that the people can use dollars," said Peter.

"At least the war has stopped for the time being," added Colin.

"Anyway, surely they have banks that can exchange the money?" said Tony.

"Not many, skipper — I've checked, and mainly only in the capital, Filare," replied Colin.

"Well, we'll just have to keep looking, chaps — we've still got the best part of a week before we need to report back to Jardigo," said Tony. "But as I see it, The People's Republic of Mafoso will probably be our best bet. It's poor, small, flat and easily approachable; the only downside is the currency. Surely that should be the least of our worries."

The following week, Jardigo seemed pleased with the men's report, and though the currency issue had not been totally resolved, he was democratic in his final decision. The meeting took place as Jardigo took his daily walk around the castle's front quadrangle. His three researchers had spent two circuits going through other possibilities, but all of them seemed to have irresolvable issues, whether geographical or otherwise.

"Well, I am happy, my friends. I have enough cash in US dollars to make the drop worthwhile. Let us vote on it."

The three Englishmen ceased walking to look at their boss.

"Well, I'm for it," said Tony.

"Colin?"

"No, I think it could do more harm than good."

Jardigo didn't ask the banker to elaborate.

"Peter?"

"I'll abstain, if I may, boss."

"Well, I make that motion carried, two votes to one. Mafoso it is."

"I hope the money isn't wasted, that's all," remarked Colin.

"It won't be," replied Jardigo. "I can assure you of that."

"How can ...?"

"No questions, Colin, please. We have agreed democratically on Mafoso so now we all have to be one hundred and ten per cent behind the choice."

"Sure, boss."

"So, Tony, what's the latest prognosis on your fitness?" asked Jardigo.

"If I had my way, I'd rip this f'ing plaster cast off now — it itches like hell. Doc says another ten days should see it off, however."

"Well, today is the 22nd, so I would like for you to make the drop in exactly two weeks; Tuesday, the 5th of September. Will that be alright, Tony?"

"Yeah, I'll be fine — I mostly use my right hand for steering and the left for the switches and so on."

"Excellent, my friends! I will organise the cash into packets which we'll ferry up to the airstrip the night before under strict secrecy."

"May we know how much we will be taking, Jardigo," asked Colin.

Ten dollars for every head of population in Mafoso."

"But that's ...."

Peter didn't finish; Tony and Colin were doing the same mental calculation.

"Yes, a little over 80,000,000 US dollars."

"How many packets, then."

"Each packet will contain a thousand $100 bills, so you can work it out."

"Eight hundred," replied Colin.

"Thank you, Einstein," said Peter.

"Now, if there are no further questions, I have some work to do," said Jardigo.

"Well, there is something that's been bothering me, Jardigo," said Colin, quietly.

"Yes?"

"You haven't told us if there were any comebacks after the failed distribution at the *Black Fields*."

"Comebacks?"

"Yes, surely some people there must have found a lot of cash the following morning. Wouldn't the police have been interested?"

"I have been monitoring the situation — I have a few of my employees who live there and they have kept me informed."

"And?" queried Peter.

"And the situation is under control — police can be bribed."

"I suppose there have been one or two improvements to their lifestyles, eh?" said Tony.

"Yes, and one or two parties as well, my friends."

"I'll bet," said Colin.

Jardigo smiled and said,

"This meeting is at an end, my friends; now go and relax. The 5th will come round all too quickly."

And quickly it did, though Tony's cast still had not been removed when the time came for his brief test flight the day before the actual day of the mission. Fortunately, however, enough mobility had returned to his left hand and wrist to make flying the small jet reasonably comfortable. Later, he would not be involved in the more arduous task of supervising and correcting the flow of packets from the aircraft, if it was found necessary to override the automatic device now constructed in the base of the fuselage. The test flight went well, with Tony accompanied by one of the engineers responsible for servicing the aircraft, and announcing on his return that, '*the old bird had flown like a dream.*' They had managed a hundred mile circuit up over Lisbon and the Atlantic, with speeds in excess of 420 knots.

The following morning dawned clear and sunny with very little breeze to concern Tony and the three men were up early, with Jardigo scheduled to drive them personally up to the mountain airstrip at eight-thirty sharp. It was a forty minute drive from the castle and gave Jardigo a chance to issue some last minute instructions.

"The packets should be released as evenly as you can. My engineers tell me that the lever is quite sensitive and has a safety feature that only allows ten packets to exit per release. There is then a twenty second delay before it will allow the next batch to go — you understand?"

"Yes, boss," said Colin. "Tony filled us in last night and Peter is going to operate it while I move the packets towards the chute."

"You'll need all your strength, Colin, and you'll need to work quickly, with Tony coordinating the releases from the front."

"Yeah, we've set up a code, Jardigo," said Tony. "I'll give them a time window and I'll count it down on each run."

"Good, because there's no earthly point in releasing packets miles from any pockets of population."

"We know," said Peter. "We're going to head for the capital, Filare first and make a few circular passes over the most heavily populated areas. I've given Tony some detailed maps of the areas involved — wonderful things these Google maps, you know."

"And where else have you identified?" asked Jardigo.

"There are a couple of towns in the north of the country which we'll fly over on our return journey."

"Good, you seem to have organised the mission well."

They were in the mountains now and only Tony and Jardigo had ever been on the route to the airstrip in daylight, causing Colin to remark,

"You mean to say this is where we landed?"

"Yes," said Tony. "Just wait till you see it properly; it's fully equipped with the hangar hidden in the mountain side."

Five minutes later, after Jardigo's Range Rover had crested one more rise, Colin and Peter saw the hangar clearly for the first time.

"Wow, it's right out of a James Bond film!" observed Peter.

"Yep, chaps, it's even got its own fuel depot," said Tony.

"I have two tankers I use for refuelling and your jet is full and ready to go, my friends," said Jardigo.

"And there she is, chaps," said Tony, pointing out of the front window of the luxury 4X4.

"Interesting colour scheme, skipper," remarked Peter.

"Yes, today you are employees of one of the world's largest air freight and logistics companies."

"Who, unfortunately, is going to lose an entire consignment of one of its best customer's goods over a poor and desolate African country," said Tony with a wry smile.

"I shall not file a complaint, my friends!"

"Good, because when today is over, if I may be so bold, Jardigo, I think we'll deserve a bonus, eh?" said Colin.

"We'll see, we'll see."

Jardigo pulled the black Range Rover to within a few feet of the white and red Lear jet. He turned off the engine and looked at his watch.

"It is now 08.55. Please remind me how long the flight is each way?"

"Provided the weather is much the same over Africa as it is here, I should say about three hours fifty. It should take about an hour and a half to make the drops so ...."

Colin did the calculation for him.

"We should be back here by 18.00, give or take a few minutes, boss."

"Or a few weeks, if we don't make it," joked Peter.

259

"Then I shall be here to greet you from about five. You will maintain radio silence for the entire mission, you understand?"

"Absolutely," replied Tony. "I'm literally flying by the seat of my pants today. No interfering flight controllers to tell me what I can and can't do. Pure heaven, chaps."

"Now go and make some poor of this world a little happier, my good friends. I will pray that the mission is a complete success."

Apart from the sight of one commercial airliner heading east to west a few miles in front of them off the North African coast, the flight down the Atlantic seaboard was uneventful and smooth.

"Bang on schedule, chaps," said Tony, as he turned the Lear jet on an easterly course towards the West African coast — Tony had maintained visual contact with land for the entire flight south.

"Roger, skipper, it is 12.33 hours," called out Peter from his rear seat.

"Man the bomb bay, Flight Lieutenant Williams!"

"Are we there, then?" said Colin. "I must have dozed off; the flight was so smooth."

"Look lively, Flight Sergeant Fenner!"

"Demotion, Col."

"Target ETA is 12.55. Prepare the first batch."

"Roger that, skip," replied Peter, who had already released his harness and was at the door to the rear hold. Colin stretched himself and peered out of a side window.

"Is that Mafoso below us?"

"I hope so, chaps, unless your maps are wrong."

"It looks a barren wilderness — no green anywhere."

"They've had drought after drought, Col," said Peter from the rear of the jet.

"Well, there's one good thing — if we run of fuel and have to put her down, it's as flat as a pancake down there," said Tony.

"And that's a good thing?" said Colin.

"Only kidding, boys — now hold on; I'm going to take her down a few thousand feet and we don't have much distance to do it in. Hold onto your stomachs; it'll feel like you're on a roller coaster."

The engine noise began to change to a high-pitched whine as Tony eased the stick forward, throwing both passengers forward into the back of the seats.

"Ouch!" shrieked Peter. "You might have given us more warning."

"Oh, didn't I tell you to keep seated with your safety harnesses on till we'd levelled out? Oops, I'm so sorry!"

"Bastard!"

Colin and Peter lunged for their seats and quickly put their harnesses back on.

"Mind your language, Flight Lieutenant or you'll be on a charge back at base."

"Sorry, skipper," said Peter. "I wasn't questioning your parentage."

The Lear jet began to level out.

"Right, nearly done; we're down under a thousand feet now. Everything is looking good. Filare is ten minutes away. Get the first ten packets lined up — it is safe to leave your seats, gentlemen."

The two men crouched either side of the rear door, now open to reveal the packets covered in a kind of clear plastic.

"Well that's not going to hold the notes together; the packets will just spit open on impact and be blown all over the place," observed Colin.

"That's only the outer protection. Inside each packet are ten smaller packets which are in stiff vacuum-sealed plastic that will survive the impact," called Tony from the front. "The outer covering will probably break off in the air anyway."

"He thinks of everything," said Colin.

"He can afford the best minds," remarked Peter.

"Get ready, men! Filare is directly ahead. I'll take her left round the perimeter and then give you the signal."

"Copy that!" called out Colin.

A couple of minutes late and they felt the jet change course.

"Hold tight, I'm going a little lower," shouted Tony.

This time, the descent was gentler and the jet soon levelled out once more.

"Code amber!"

"Roger, skipper!"

Seconds passed; Peter's hand was sweating as he held the chrome-plated lever.

"Code green!"

Peter pulled the lever and the first ten packets slid from their position and down through the release valve. He began counting.

"Ten, nine, eight .... three, two, one."

"Code green!"

Over the next ten minutes, they released 250 packets, with Colin keeping an accurate tally, until Tony shouted,

"Code red!"

"Roger, skipper! Nearly a third dropped now," said Colin.

"Right, we'll do the southern side of the town and dump any left after that over northern Mafoso. Hang fire while I turn her round."

They'd released another 320 packets on the second pass over the Mafosan capital when Tony called out,

"Code red, chaps! I'm going north."

It was 1.33 p.m. and they were right on schedule.

They reached one of the towns that Tony had identified on the map within ten minutes and he quickly issued the first instruction.

"Code amber!"

This was followed by another apparently innocent command.

"Drop all but thirty packets!"

"Roger, skipper!" shouted Peter. Colin smiled and said nothing. It was a strange order.

"Get ready!"

The jet lost height smoothly and began to level out.

"Code green!"

Peter pulled the lever and Colin started his count. As he did so, he mentally put aside three stacks of ten packets and in just over seven minutes, he shouted,

"All done, skipper!"

They felt the aircraft regain height and bank left.

"Where are we going to now?" called out Peter.

"Home!"

"We've still got these thirty packets, though," replied Peter.

"I know," said Tony. Colin smiled again. He knew what it meant.

"It's insurance, Pete," continued their pilot. "One million US dollars each is not bad for a day's work."

Colin and Peter had returned to their seats by now. Peter leant forward.

"But we can't just take it, Tony. Jardigo will know when we walk off the plane with it — there's no way we can hide thirty packets in our clothes."

"We're not going to take it off. If you look at the back of the hold you will see a couple of big plastic storage boxes which I have always kept there. Both have padlocks, so we simply store the cash in one until I can find a way of transferring it back to the castle. It shouldn't be hard to bring it back, even if I have to do it a few packets at a time. I should have several opportunities over the next few weeks as I do more and more jobs for Jardigo. Who's going to notice me carrying the odd rucksack?"

"You crafty bugger," said Peter.

"Insurance, that's all."

"Against what?" asked Colin.

"Against Jardigo's operation going tits up, Col, and we have to make a run for it. If the police start investigating him and discover our real identities, our bank accounts would probably be frozen and we wouldn't get very far without any money. The cash is there for that kind of emergency. You chaps had better start putting the cash in the blue coloured box — it is open. I'll give you the key and you can lock it when you've done."

With the Lear jet now safely back over the Atlantic and heading north, Colin and Peter quickly stashed the thirty packets neatly in the storage box and covered them with some old sacks. As Colin returned the key to Tony, he remarked,

"Though what we're doing seems eminently sensible given our somewhat unusual situation, it is still stealing, Tony."

"Yeah, right," replied the pilot. "Like who cares?"

"If he ever found out, he'd ditch us, you know," said Peter.

"Or worse," added Colin.

"It's a risk worth taking. Call it wastage, if it makes you feel better about it."

"Wastage?" queried Peter.

"Well, you don't think all the money we've dropped is going to go to where it was intended, do you? I bet a sizeable proportion will never be found and will just lie hidden in dense undergrowth. After all, we've literally just thrown it to the wind today."

This seemed to ease their worries and they began to relax — the day had been exhausting enough and hunger pangs had become more of a concern.

Apart from some now empty water bottles, they had had no refreshment since breakfast at the castle.

Tony landed the Lear jet at 18.20, a few minutes later than expected and after taxiing to the hangar, the three men disembarked onto the tarmac to be greeted by their boss. Rafael was at his side.

"Welcome back, my friends! You have done well and I shall see you are well rewarded for your efforts."

Colin and Peter exchanged knowing looks.

"How did the mission go?" asked Jardigo.

"A complete success," replied Tony. "All eight hundred packets were dropped over Mafoso in the areas designated."

By this time, Jardigo's deputy had climbed into the plane. Tony suddenly looked nervous. Jardigo waited until Rafael rejoined them a minute or so later.

"All empty, boss," he said and nodded at Tony.

"Good, now I expect you men could do with something to eat. We have a banquet tonight, my friends, to celebrate today's achievements. It will not be long before the world is also celebrating your good deeds to help the poor."

20

The Final Straw

Very few foreign visitors, let alone reporters had ever made it into Mafoso, especially in the recent months of coups and bloodshed. It was well known that the communist-backed ruling Congress Party had been guilty of several incidents of ethnic cleansing amongst the indigenous tribes of the region. Though he hadn't been able to see much from the air, Tony had suspected that the occasional reduction in visibility over Filare had not been due to any natural weather phenomenon, but rather to the clouds of smoke still rising from burning buildings on the ground. Rather like the veil of secrecy that existed over Mafoso's political situation, this man-made fog had seemed to keep any prying eyes from viewing the country from the air as well, just as the news black-out had done for the world's media for weeks on end.

Given this wall of secrecy that blocked the rest of the world from knowing about the internal affairs of the small African country, it was not altogether surprising that it would be nearly a week before anyone would learn anything, other than Jardigo and his men, about the unusual delivery made by Tony and his crew. Jardigo had spoken to Colin, Tony and Peter several times, both individually and as a group about the success of their mission and all four men had watched and listened to as many news bulletins as they could. One such group meeting took place immediately after breakfast the following Tuesday. Jardigo, unaccompanied by Rafael, had a rather sombre expression on his face as he joined the three Englishmen on the rear veranda.

"Have you seen the news this morning?" he asked quietly.

"No, boss," replied Tony, looking at his other two companions, who shook their heads in unison.

"I have been watching a central African TV channel and there is news from Filare, my friends."

"Oh?" said Colin. "People are buying expensive goods and are partying?"

"No, Colin, people are being killed."

"What, more genocide?" asked Tony.

"It is not an organised set of killings — this is rather different."

"The tribes are getting their own back?" suggested Peter.

"No, the killings appear to be totally random and are occurring all over Filare between ordinary people. The militia don't seem to be involved, other than to try to quell the riots."

"Riots?"

"Yes, that's what the reporter said; the riots seem to be between neighbouring families of the same tribes."

"What about, boss? Did the reporter give details?"

"What about, Colin? Isn't it obvious, and it makes me so sad, my friends?"

"Greed," said Tony, quietly.

The penny seemed to drop simultaneously for the other two Englishmen. Neither said a word.

"Yes, my friends, it would appear that neighbours are fighting each other over money — money that we gave them. The fights have become full-blown riots in the streets of the capital. Hundreds are dying and their bodies left to rot. The military are unwilling to intervene in something they regard as none of their concern, and it is even being suggested that they are aiding and abetting the situation to further their own desire to continue the ethnic cleansing."

"And they're rioting over the dropped money?" said Colin.

"Yes, it all started, according to the news channel, when expensive barbecues began appearing in some yards, along with new TVs and stereos blasting out music. Neighbours asked questions; others told of their windfalls and others got envious. One thing led to another; from some people accusing neighbours of stealing, to others taking matters into their own hands and attempting to redistribute the windfalls. It would appear that our worries that US dollars would not be useful in Mafoso were totally unfounded. I'm just glad that I only put used notes in the packets."

Jardigo sat back — he looked tired and worried.

"And haven't the authorities become suspicious? They must be curious about the windfalls," observed Tony.

"The packets of money are being investigated, the reporter said, but some of the militia's families may have benefitted, so progress on that score is confused and slow," replied Jardigo.

"It looks like we have caused chaos rather than providing aid to Mafoso," said Colin.

"And caused people to be killed," added Peter. "This is not good, Jardigo, and it's all our fault."

"You cannot be held responsible for man's greed and envy, my friends. You carried out your mission completely to my instructions, so if there's anyone that can be blamed, other than some greedy and evil men in Mafoso, it is me."

"Well, you can't do anything like that again, boss," said Peter. "Or if you do, it must be directed more carefully to those who most need it."

"Yeah, boss," said Tony, forcefully. "I'm not going to fly any more random sorties. We've done two now and it's clear to me that they just don't work."

"Maybe, Tony; I'm not sure, my friend. I need to review the situation over the next few weeks."

"Surely you're not thinking of doing more such drops, boss?" said Colin. "Tony's right; we just can't be responsible for people killing each other."

Jardigo stood up and looked down towards the lake. His mood seemed to have changed in an instant. His body appeared stiff and his next few words had a familiar sinister tone to them.

"I've said I will review the situation, Senhor Fenner. I should not have to remind you that you work for me and will carry out whatever missions I decide."

"But ...."

Jardigo turned and stared angrily at Colin.

"There are no buts, Senhor Fenner."

Jardigo strode powerfully towards the castle.

"This meeting is at an end," he shouted back to the three stunned Englishmen.

Nobody said anything for a few moments; each man was wrapped in his own thoughts about what they had just heard. Colin finally broke the tense silence.

"Well, I think he's flipped his lid."

"Did you notice his eyes?" said Peter. "There are definitely some signs of madness there, you know."

"Well, I am definitely not going to fly another one of his hair-brained missions, chaps," added Tony.

"He'll make you, skipper," said Peter.

"You know what I think?" said Colin.

"What?"

"I don't think he's all the philanthropist he would have us believe. He didn't really seem to be that worried about the loss of life he'd caused in Mafoso, did he?"

"Well, I'm beginning to realise that you just can't chuck money at poverty — it'll never cure the situation in the long run," said Tony. "Now, aren't you glad we've got three million dollar's insurance."

"You mean it's time to make a run for it; take the money and get out of here?" asked Peter.

"I'm not sure yet, Pete," replied Tony. "It would need careful planning — I've got to get the money from the plane first."

"But when you do, at least we've got a perfect escape route. You could fly us anywhere."

"Again, that would need organising. He has guards patrolling the airstrip 24/7."

Colin began shaking his head.

"We shouldn't be too hasty, until we've had time to weigh up all the consequences. In the meantime, I'm prepared to give him one more chance and see what his next philanthropic gesture to the poor is going to be. If it's as stupid and naive as the first two then we make a decision one way or the other."

"Seems sensible," said Peter.

"Alright," said Tony. "But I'm going to get the money from the plane as soon as possible. I want to be ready to go at a moment's notice."

"Agreed," said Colin, finally.

Exactly a week later, when it appeared that the remainder of the world's media had finally got hold of the events in Mafoso, Jardigo chose the same day to gather his triumvirate together down at the lakeside summer house. It was late afternoon and the day had an autumnal feel to it — the three Englishmen's halcyon summer was about to end, too. With his employees sat in a semi-circle in front of him, he began slowly and in a somewhat end-of-term mood.

"Well, in a moment, I am going to tell you about my next and final operation, my friends."

He paused to look at each man in turn. Colin, for one, averted the cool and uncompromising stare. He could see the instability that Peter had observed at their last meeting.

"But first," he continued. "I want to offer you my thanks and praise for all that you have done in my service. I am truly grateful as will many other people be when you carry out your final mission."

"Which is, Jardigo?" asked Tony.

"Patience, my friend — first, I want to tell you a story."

Jardigo cleared his throat.

"I am a very rich man; probably one of the richest on the planet, but I want to become richer and before you comment, it is not about greed."

Tony grimaced.

"No, my friends, it is about power — power and control; power to do things that other people have been unable to do. My attempts at philanthropy have failed miserably, I can see that, but they were only the starter for the full menu and for the main course I will need billions, if not trillions — enough money to right certain wrongs in this world, whether it be erasing oppressive regimes or financing schemes to eradicate sickness and disease. For such ventures, I need not only a global fortune, but also the destruction of certain concerns that have been a stumbling block to progress in the areas I have just indicated."

"What concerns?" asked Colin, as he dared to break Jardigo's oration.

"Please be patient," replied the philanthropist. The eyes were staring and glazed again, his mind wrapped up in the explanation of his crusade.

"All will be revealed shortly," he continued. "I will need your help in this final mission, and when it is finished, you will be paid a fortune for your services — a fortune that will make your current salaries pale into insignificance. Like me, you will number among the richest men in the world."

Jardigo got to his feet and seemed to tower over the three Englishmen like some Old Testament prophet. None of his listeners looked directly at him.

"It will be a two-pronged mission." He continued his speech. "On the one hand, I need money and on the other, those barriers to progress must be torn down. Now, the money is the easy part — robbing more rich men, and possibly some international companies as well, should not be a problem for our computer genius here, but the second part of the plan will need much more skill and daring."

Jardigo paused and performed his usual dramatic turn to face the lake. He continued in a quieter voice.

"There are certain major companies in the oil industry and elsewhere that have, for decades, been too greedy and have exploited the poor of some countries, causing untold misery and even deaths in some cases. In addition, there are certain countries themselves that have kept their poor hidden from the outside world, while those in power have got richer."

"We are well aware of the injustices in this world, but ...."

"Shut up, Colin, you are aware of nothing!" shrieked Jardigo, as he turned back to face his audience. His face was red with anger.

"You three are going to help me right those injustices by punishing those people who have been stumbling blocks to humanitarian progress."

"How?" asked Peter, trying to demonstrate some kind of acquiescence to Jardigo's master plan.

"That is for you to decide, my friends. You must use your computer skills to get me more money and cripple those companies and regimes I shall direct you to."

Jardigo reached inside his light cotton jacket and pulled out a white envelope. He handed it to Colin.

"The details are in this envelope. You will study its contents and report back in one week with your suggestions. That is all for today — I am not going to take any questions now. Just remember, I have the power to destroy many things, including you, so be warned — I will not accept any objections to my dream. Now go and leave me in peace. We will reconvene here at six p.m., one week from today."

Jardigo turned back to face the lake. Colin had been about to say something until Tony had dug him in the ribs with his fist. Peter had started to stride away and was already on the grassy slope behind the summer house. The three men joined up with each other after about fifty yards.

"Time to make that decision," said Tony.

"He's not a philanthropist; he's just a madman, plain and simple," observed Colin.

"It's not about the money; it's about power — he said so himself," said Peter. "He wants to create world chaos so that with his money, he can reign supreme from his castle."

"So you don't believe him when he says he wants to right the wrongs of this world?" queried Tony.

"Absolutely and categorically not, skipper," replied Peter. "What he's proposing would cause more hardship, death and outright chaos than all his so-called injustices put together."

Colin nodded.

"As I see it, he wants to destroy the present world order and ...."

Colin paused. Tony finished his sentence.

"And replace it with one of his own?"

"Exactly," said Colin. "He wants to get enough money together to have the power to do that, and he doesn't care how he does it. It's one thing creaming the froth off dormant bank accounts; it's another thing altogether even to think of bringing down international companies of governments that he doesn't like, let alone believe that he can do it."

"And that's the problem, chaps — he just doesn't see the insanity of what he is proposing," said Tony.

"And that's because, skipper, he's downright insane himself," remarked Peter. "You heard his speech. It was like listening to old Adolf in the flesh."

"So what do we do?" asked Colin.

"We make a run for it, like Tony said."

"Well, you have the last of the money, chaps, and we've got a week to plan our escape — he probably won't bother us if he thinks we're discussing his plan so we can use the time to make our own plans instead."

The castle was in front of them now. Rafael was standing on the rear veranda; arms folded and clearly watching the three men approach. Colin whispered,

"We meet in the computer room after dinner; it will seem natural enough. I will not open the envelope till then."

As Tony and Peter mumbled their agreement, Colin was to add one final comment; a comment that expressed a sentiment that the other two men had been feeling but had been too nervous to articulate.

"We've not only got to stop him carrying out his master plan, you know; we've got to stop *him* as well."

21

Mutiny

Colin's final remark had clearly left its mark on Peter and Tony and it was to be the first topic of conversation when they assembled after dinner that evening in the computer room. His two friends seemed more interested in what he had meant than the contents of Jardigo's envelope.

"What did you mean, Col, about 'stopping him'?" asked Peter, as soon as they had all gathered in the room.

"I meant that if we don't carry out his plan for him, someone else will, and we have to find a way of preventing him being able to do that as well."

"There is only one way, mate," said Peter.

"I know and sometimes that is the only way to rid society of evil."

"And he is evil," added Tony.

Peter hesitated before expressing openly what they had all been thinking.

"We kill him?"

"Can you think of another way?" said Colin.

"We could go to the police and tell them everything," replied Peter.

"And you think they'd believe us? Jardigo is too careful to have left any evidence of his operations. Besides, the local police are on his payroll anyway, and it would be us that would be killed."

"So, after we escape, we go back to the UK and tell the police there — give ourselves up and exchange our knowledge of his operation for mercy and small prison terms," replied Peter.

"Well, I for one am not prepared to take that risk," said Tony. "And that's given that anyone will believe us — we're wanted criminals, remember?"

"Well, I couldn't do it," said Peter. "Could you, Col, mate?"

"I don't know; I'd never thought about it."

"Don't worry, chaps. When it comes to it — as it no doubt will — I'll do it," said Tony.

"You've done something like that before in the RAF?" asked Peter.

"Not exactly, but I have been on bombing raids over Bosnia and elsewhere so I have been responsible for people's deaths, no doubt."

"Under the legitimacy of war, though," observed Peter.

"I think the situation that faces us is as legitimate as any war I know of."

"Well, I think we need to think about ourselves first," said Colin. "I'm not ready to be the hero yet until I'm sure we're going to escape safely."

"Perhaps if you open the envelope, it will give added impetus to Jardigo's possible unfortunate demise," replied Tony.

"Right — are you guys happy for me to read what's there?"

"Yeah, just get on with it, Col," responded Peter, impatiently.

Colin tore open the white envelope and unfolded the single sheet of expensive looking A4 paper. He began to read.

My dear friends,

Here is a list of the five companies that I wish you to cause problems for:

(1) The Anco Oil and Gas Corporation,

(2) The Royal and Commonwealth Insurance Company,

(3) Richard Thompson Media,

(4) The Texas Drilling and Mining Company,

(5) Microdata of Europe.

Secondly, I have identified the following three individuals from whom I want you to 'skim the froth' from their bank accounts:

(1) David D'Angelo, pop star,

(2) Abraham Epstein, property magnate,

(3) Robert Goldman, entrepreneur.

Colin turned the paper over and continued.

Finally, you will investigate ways of bringing down the following regimes:

(1) The Government of South Korea,

(2) The Revolutionary Party of the People's Republic of Mianlong.

(3) The Socialist Party of Sunelia and Martinette.

Good luck, and please remember your individual contracts with me.

Jardigo Batista.

"Stark raving bonkers," said Peter.

"Enough proof for you, Colin?" asked Tony.

"Do you chaps recognise all the names?" asked Colin.

"Most of them," replied Peter.

"Any connection between them?"

"Well, the companies must all be among the world's top ten biggest," replied Tony.

"And the three individuals you mentioned are hugely wealthy," added Peter.

"What about the regimes?" continued Colin.

"Well, certainly two of them are about the most oppressive in Asia," said Tony. "I've never heard of the socialist party you said."

"The only other thing is that Microdata have a policy of never contributing to any good causes. I used to know several guys who worked for them," said Peter. "They are not a good company to work for."

"I'm sure that Anco was the company who had that massive explosion in India a couple of years ago where hundreds got killed or maimed. It was never proved that Anco was negligent, but everyone suspected they were," said Tony.

"So he's chosen according to his rules," concluded Colin. "At least he's given the choices some thought."

"Yeah, with the mind of a maniac," said Peter. "Robbing individual's bank accounts would have been hard enough, but bringing down global mega-corporations or governments, even using the equipment here, is something out of a fantasy novel. It just can't be done, and there's nothing on his list about aiding organisations on the ground, like he once said."

"Any sane person would know it can't be done," added Peter.

"You don't even think we could have skimmed any of the bank accounts?" asked Tony.

"No way. When we did it before, Colin selected the accounts randomly from the bank's computer. With the individuals he just mentioned, we wouldn't even know where they banked."

"So, chaps that is it. He has to be stopped before his warped brain dreams up something even more frightening. At least we have a few days before we need say anything to him," said Tony.

"That meeting will not be as he expects, and you know it, skipper," said Peter. "We plan for our escape and for his execution from this very moment on."

"He will be protected," remarked Colin. "That Rafael always seems to be at his side now."

"He may have to go, too," said Tony with a smile.

"So how will you do it?" asked Peter.

"Oh you don't need to worry about that — the other storage box on the plane contained one or two extra things as well as just tools."

Colin smiled.

"You mean?"

"Yes, all senior RAF personnel are issued with a weapon for self defence and emergency situations. I kept mine, even though I don't officially still have a licence."

"What about flying out of here? Won't that be tricky after you've done the other necessary business?"

"It'll have to be coordinated with military precision and timing," replied Tony. "You know I have use of one of Jardigo's 4X4's whenever I want to go to the airstrip — that's why it was relatively easy to smuggle the cash back to the castle."

Colin seemed ready to conclude their initial discussion, carefully folding the paper and envelope and putting it back in his pocket.

"So, we are all agreed?" he said.

"Yes, mate," replied Peter. "Now, if you don't mind, and like Colin, I am very tired and I think we all need some rest before we meet again tomorrow morning."

"And I'll make sure I go to the airstrip tomorrow afternoon to collect what is necessary," said Tony. The mutiny had begun.

The following morning at breakfast, Peter had news for the other two mutineers. The three men had managed to sit together well away from any of Jardigo's employees, particularly Rafael who normally tried to be close to them so that he could eavesdrop and monitor their conversation.

"We can't meet in the computer room this morning; Jardigo is having some more equipment installed. They started an hour ago."

"What kind of equipment?" asked Tony.

"I didn't stay long to see, but in addition to some more computer hardware, I should hazard a guess at some kind of surveillance gear."

"What, cameras?" said Colin.

"Yeah, and listening devices. I think Jardigo is going to watch and listen in on our research for his plan."

"Well," said Tony. "We must not disappoint him. Whenever we meet there — and we must in order to keep up the pretence — we must do a little play acting just for his benefit."

"And we discuss the real plan outside somewhere?" said Peter.

"Yes, and this morning you might as well join me for a little trip up into the mountains — kill two birds with one stone."

"Who is installing it, mate?" queried Colin.

"What?"

"The equipment — who is putting it in?"

"I don't know — some company from Lisbon. I hadn't seen either of the two guys at the castle before."

Suddenly, Tony coughed loudly and before either Colin or Peter had a chance to say anything further, he stood up dramatically and said,

"Good morning, boss, and how are you this fine morning?"

"I am well, my friends. I see you have started your discussions," he whispered. "I am pleased to tell you that the computer room's upgrade is now complete, Peter."

"Oh, er, thanks, Jardigo," stammered Peter,

"I think you will find the new additions very useful," said Jardigo. "I suspect you will want to take a look after breakfast."

"Well, this morning, we're going to take ...."

Tony quickly interrupted Peter.

"We're going to take our time over the matter you discussed with us yesterday, boss."

"Good, my friends, but not too long, eh? I shall not trouble you further today; I have business in Lisbon and I shall be gone from ten until after dark this evening."

With that, Jardigo bowed slightly and, accompanied by his deputy, walked out of the dining hall. Colin let out an audible sigh of relief.

"You idiot, Peter, you were going to tell him about our trip up to the mountains, weren't you?"

"Sorry, chaps."

"Well, at least he's out of the way for the day," said Tony.

"Looks like Rafael is going with him, too," added Colin. "I bet he's expecting us to go to the computer room for most of the day."

"And so we shall later," said Tony. He looked at his watch. "I make it ten past nine now so I suggest we meet out at the garage at eleven. That will give Jardigo and Rafa ample time to be well on their way to Lisbon before we make our trip."

Colin looked thoughtful.

"I think Pete and I might as well go and stage our first scene down in the cellars. I've nothing else to do and I bet Pete wants to investigate his new equipment — Jardigo would find it rather strange if he didn't rush down to check it out."

"Copy that," replied Tony. "Just don't be late, alright?"

"Roger, skipper."

The scene would be a simple one. After Peter had investigated the new computer hardware, which consisted of two extra computers — neither of which seemed to add much to the overall capacity of the network — the two friends began to act out their pretence. Both had quickly spotted the additional device fitted to one of the fluorescent lights overhead and Peter made play of standing directly beneath the somewhat obvious listening device. If there was a camera, it was well hidden.

"I think we should start with the bank accounts, mate. You try Mr D'Angelo and I'll have a go at Mr Epstein."

281

They sat down side by side at two of the desktops and, over the next hour or so, pretended to google as much as they could about the two men, occasionally jotting down notes on pads beside them. In actuality, they divided the time between catching up on news from the UK and playing each other at various computer games. The pads, if ever checked, would reveal a series of meaningless numbers and letters, purporting to represent bank account numbers and passwords. Finally, at 10.40, Colin announced loudly,

"Well, that's a good start — you'll be able to process these codes later."

"Yeah, I just need to upgrade the software you used before at the London and Provincial. It may take a day or two but I think I can get into Mr D'Angelo's private affairs."

"Good, now let's go and have a break. I fancy a walk in the country till lunchtime. We've made good progress and we can return this afternoon sometime."

The two men picked up their pads and carefully locked them in the desk drawers. The pretence had begun.

Only Tony seemed relatively cheerful on the drive up into the mountains, given the seriousness of what they had decided to do.

"You never know, chaps, but we might become celebrities if they ever find out we prevented a world catastrophe."

"I'll settle for a quiet anonymous life somewhere, living off my fortune. I want no publicity for what we've been through," said Colin.

"I'll second that," added Peter. "I just want it to all be over and done with."

"Changing the subject to the airstrip," said Colin. "Are the guards likely to be there today, Tony?"

"Probably not — there might be a couple of mechanics, but they won't take any notice of me. They've got used to seeing me tinker with my plane and collect the odd thing from the boxes."

"Won't they be surprised to see us?" asked Colin.

"Nah, not if you remain in the vehicle. I'll bring the gun and ammo out hidden in one of my tool bags. I'll get them to refuel the plane as well while I'm there."

Silence descended on the three men for a while until Colin asked the inevitable question.

"Have you thought about how you'll do it, Tony?"

"Well, I think it has to be somewhere where he will be alone with us."

"What about afterwards? How will we get away up to the airfield?" asked Peter.

"We need to be sure that his body will not be discovered for at least an hour," replied Tony.

"You've thought of somewhere, haven't you?" said Colin, quietly.

"Yes, and it should be obvious to you two as well."

"The meeting at the summer house next week?" said Peter. "The lake would be a good place to hide the body."

"Just so long as he doesn't bring Rafa with him," added Colin.

"That depends how much he's in the know about his boss's master plan," said Tony.

"Well, they're always as thick as thieves," said Peter with broad grin.

"But, assuming he does come on his own, when will you do it?" asked Colin.

"As soon as I'm comfortable that I can down him with one shot — I don't want him putting up a struggle or crying out for help. However or whenever I decide to do it, we must be prepared to report some findings back to begin with."

"We'll agree on that later," remarked Colin. "It should be easy for Pete and me to blind him with science and waffle on for ages."

"You may need to. It will be so much easier if he does one of his dramatic pirouettes and turns to face the lake."

They had crested the last rise before the airfield by now and Tony started concentrating on the immediate task. They could just make out the red and white Lear jet parked at the entrance to the hangar.

"I shall park the 4X4 on the other side of the plane, away from the mechanics shed. It doesn't look as if there's anyone about, chaps."

Tony swung the compact Suzuki onto the apron and manoeuvred it past some oil drums and packing cases. The steps were still where they had been left after the last mission, conveniently in place against the plane's side. The 4X4 slowed to a halt next to them.

"Looking good, boys," muttered Tony. "Now stay here; I'll be in and out in a jiffy."

He was less than a minute inside the jet and emerged carrying an oil-stained canvas tool bag. In no time at all, Tony had the Suzuki back on the mountain road and heading back to the castle. They had been at the airstrip for less than three minutes. No one had emerged from the shed or adjoining huts. Tony was suitably jubilant.

"Sweet as a nut, chaps!" he exclaimed as the jeep disappeared from view of the airstrip.

"Thank God that's over," said Colin. "Are you sure no one saw you?"

"Pretty certain; the guys' cars weren't in their usual place."

"So we're all systems go," said Peter.

"As long as you chaps can come up with a believable report for next Tuesday, we have a chance," said Tony.

"We will," said Peter. "We've started our little play already."

"Good, it just relies on Jardigo being on his own at the summer house."

"Are we going to just saunter back up to the castle afterwards and then drive up to the airstrip?"asked Colin.

"No, either Peter or you are going to twist their ankle kicking a ball about that afternoon and I'm going to have to drive you down to the lake in the Vitara. Then, when the deed is done, we can make our getaway quickly. We don't even have to drive back up to the castle — there's a track that leads from the lake to the main road. We'll be long gone before the scheduled meeting was due to be over."

"As I see it, it all hinges on no one being with Jardigo at the summer house," observed Colin.

"If there is, Col, we'll be dumping more than one body in the lake," replied Tony.

"Well, roll on next Tuesday," said Peter. "I can't wait to get out of this place."

"Where will we go to, Tony?" asked Colin.

"Well, it's likely to be dark soon after take-off, so I'm going to make for a small airfield I've used before in La Malona."

"And where the hell is La Malona?" said Peter.

"It's a quiet town in Northern Spain — Basque country, where money talks, and no one will pay attention to three odd looking Englishmen and a DHL Lear jet. Just another case of smuggling that will be ignored after suitable contributions to their fighting fund," replied Tony.

"Then what?" asked Colin.

"That's up to you. We all have new identities and papers, and those can be changed again for the right price if we think it necessary after we escape the castle."

"Thinking about money, how will we be able to take our US dollars with us next Tuesday?" asked Colin.

"I've thought of that," said Tony. "I'll put it into the Suzuki that afternoon when I conveniently pick our wounded footballer up from the top playing field. I can stash the three bags in the space around the spare wheel."

Colin and Peter sat back in their seats. The plan looked watertight.

"Right," said Tony. "Who's for some relaxation in Lisbon?"

"Sounds like a good idea," replied Peter. "I could do with some new clothes."

"You can say that again," said Colin.

"I could do with some ...."

"You want I should shut 'im up, Senhor Fenner?" said Tony.

22

Preventing Evil

The brand new leather sports holdalls had been Tony's idea on their retail therapy trip to the Portuguese capital. When they made their way to the top playing field the following Tuesday at a quarter to five that afternoon, each bag would contain certain necessary belongings and papers, as well as one million US dollars in plastic packets of used notes. In Tony's case, the bag would also contain an extra item in the form of his service revolver. Exactly one hour later, Mr Peter Williams was to be seen rolling in agony on the yellowed grass clutching his right ankle.

"Ah! I've sprained it!" he shouted, almost loud enough for people at the castle 400 yards away to hear.

"Nice one, mate," said Colin, as he strolled nonchalantly over. "You should have been an actor."

Joining the two men, Tony winked and said,

"Can you stand, old chap?"

"I think so, but I don't think I'll be able to walk very far, and certainly not down to the lake for our important meeting with Jardigo."

"Oh dear, how sad, I'll just have to fetch the jeep. You'd better wait here with Col. I'll take my bag with me."

After Tony had trotted away towards the car pound, Colin said,

"Not bad, mate, but I don't think there was the need for all the histrionics."

"I had to make it realistic, in case anyone was watching. I've been in pretend mode all week. It won't be long before I'll not be able to tell fantasy from reality. Anyway, have you seen Jardigo yet?"

"No, not since lunch."

"Tony's taking his time; I'm fed up just lying here," said Peter.

Colin looked towards the castle.

"Here he comes, Pete, and ...."

Colin shielded his eyes from the late afternoon sun.

"Whoops, I think he's got someone with him."

A few seconds later, Jardigo leant out of the Suzuki's passenger window and shouted,

"Are you alright, my friend?"

Colin helped his friend to his feet, and imitating two contestants in a three-legged race with their bags in their free hands, he and Peter hobbled to the jeep. Demonstrating as much difficulty as possible, they eventually clambered into the rear seats.

"We'd better take you to the medical centre, my friend," said Jardigo.

"No, no, I'm fine — it's just twisted."

"Are you sure?"

"Certain."

"Well, we'll get you some ice for it down at the summer house," said Jardigo.

Colin nudged his friend to be quiet.

"I hope you all have some good news for me, my friends," continued their boss.

"Oh yes, we've one or two surprises for you, boss," replied Tony, as the Suzuki approached the summer house.

"Good, I will look forward to your report. Ah, here we are now. Thank you for the ride, Senhor Taylor — most convenient."

This time, when Peter climbed out of the 4X4, he displayed much less difficulty in his movement.

"Oh, it's much better now, chaps. I think I can walk unaided."

"Remarkable," said Tony with a broad grin.

Once inside the cool of the summer house, Jardigo again arranged the chairs in a semi-circle facing the lake and he took up his usual position facing them. Tony made sure he sat in the middle chair and was strangely careful in how he sat down, ensuring that his slightly bulging right pocket was easily accessible. Jardigo could not hide the manic excitement on his face.

"Well now, who's going to start?"

"I will, boss," said Peter — and so began his rehearsed speech. He spoke for nearly five minutes, concentrating in the main on the private bank accounts and a couple of the international companies, with whom he said they had had some success. Colin and Tony made suitably supportive comments, which had also been carefully rehearsed and when Peter finally paused, Jardigo clapped his hands in appreciation. It was the act of a little boy who had just opened his first electric train set for Christmas.

"Wonderful news, my friends — you have accomplished more in one week than I expected."

Colin looked at his companions and raised his left eyebrow — it was the signal for some rehearsed input from Tony; designed to alter Jardigo's mood.

"There's just one problem, boss," he said.

"Oh really, Senhor Taylor, and what is that?"

"Well, none of us are in agreement with you about bringing down the regimes you indicated in you note, I'm afraid. In fact, we are totally opposed to such a scheme."

The summer house went silent as Jardigo glared at the pilot. He seemed to be struggling to put his emotions into words and his face had turned a nasty shade of pre-heart-attack purple.

"I don't need your agreement," he bawled. "Who the hell do you think you are to tell me that you don't agree with me, eh?"

"We're just saying that ...." started Colin, weakly.

"You, Senhor Fenner, are not to say anything!"

What happened next would take less than ten seconds. As the three friends had hoped, Jardigo turned to face the lake, desperately trying to control himself as he wavered on the edge of insanity. His next words were calm and measured and were to be his last.

"I think it is time that I made you understand your responsibilities, my friends. The castle possesses more rooms below ground, other than the ones you have seen so far. You would, no doubt, call them dungeons in your language. I, however, prefer to call them cells of solitary correction, and you will each spend a month there, starting to ...."

He fell forward as the bullet penetrated the rear of his skull, blood spurting in all directions as the three Englishmen sought desperately to avoid its contact. A few spots spattered on Tony's white t-shirt but Colin and Peter remained stain-free. The noise of the gunshot had been deafening causing Colin to remark,

"That could have been heard back up at the castle, Tony."

"All the more reason for getting out of here sharpish. Grab that heavy metal table!"

It took the three of them two minutes and seventeen seconds of rehearsed precision to weight the body down and tip it into the deep and sheer-faced lake. As they ran to the jeep, they glanced up anxiously at the castle on the hill — there appeared to be no unusual movement. Once safely in the Suzuki, Tony remarked,

"We'll just have to hope that anyone who heard the gunshot just put it down to a car backfiring or someone doing a spot of poaching in the woods on the other side of the lake."

"And if they don't?" asked Colin.

"We'll find that out when we get to the airstrip when the mechanic or guards have been alerted to our escape," replied Tony.

"They won't be that quick, surely?" said Peter. "It would take them a good while to discover Jardigo or we three missing, let alone his body."

"Probably, yes, but if they go down to the summer house, the blood-stained floor will be unmissable. Rafael, at least, would have been aware that his boss had a meeting with us there at six."

"How long is it via the back way to the airfield?" asked Colin.

Tony peered down the lakeside track — they were doing less than twenty miles an hour as they negotiated the pot-holed surface.

"Forty minutes from the main road; God knows how much of this track there is. Maybe an hour tops."

"Well, God had better be smiling down on us," said Peter. "He owes us one."

"Does he?" replied Colin. "I'm not sure he views what we've done today or over the last couple of months with the same sense of fair play and justice, mate."

23

Freedom

It was almost dusk by the time they reached the mountain airstrip, and the sight of the green Fiat Punto did nothing to alleviate the tension in the Suzuki. As Tony pulled the jeep up beside the Lear jet, he turned to his passengers and said,

"One of the mechanics is still here. I don't see any guards, though, so we should be alright. Just leave the talking to me if we're approached."

Tony got out and opened the rear door to collect his bag from the spare wheel compartment. The others followed suit and headed for the plane.

"Senhor Taylor!"

The mechanic was about fifty yards away. Tony was half that from the jet.

"He wants you, Tony," muttered Colin. "I think he may have been on his mobile phone when we arrived."

"Keep walking and act naturally, chaps."

"Batente!"

They were at the foot of the steps to the cabin. The mechanic had broken into a trot. He was frantically waving his arms. There was no sign of a weapon.

"Senhor Taylor, batente!"

Tony stopped and peered past his companions.

"It's alright; I think I know what he wants, chaps."

The man had joined them and he was pointing at the starboard engine where part of the inspection cover was hanging down. The mechanic strode past the three Englishmen and proceeded to quickly secure it. He rejoined the three men at the foot of the steps. He looked skywards at the gathering gloom.

"You fly, senhor?"

Tony held up a forefinger.

"One hour."

"O.K., senhor — I wait."

"Obrigado, Jorge."

A mobile phone started ringing. Jorge reached inside a pocket of his overalls.

"Desculpe-me, senhor."

Tony did not stay to find out what the call was about, but ushered Colin and Peter onto the jet. After they had disappeared inside the plane, he slowly pulled the cabin door to. Through the diminishing gap, he noticed out of the corner of his eye that Jorge's face seemed to drop. His left hand went to his mouth as though in shock.

"Buckle up quickly, chaps. I think our helpful mechanic has just received some tragic news."

As Tony raced through his checks and the twin engines fired into life, hammering could be heard on the side of the fuselage. Seconds later, the Lear jet began to taxi forward. Colin looked out of his small side window.

"He's running for the hut."

Seconds later, he called out,

"Oh God, he's got a rifle!"

"Keep down!" shouted Tony. "This could get a bit hairy."

The jet was level now with the huts but Jorge seemed to be having problems with the weapon that was perhaps unfamiliar to him. Suddenly, he took aim and fired. Nothing seemed to strike the aircraft. They were almost at full speed now.

"We're nearly out of range, chaps!" shouted Tony. "Prepare for take-off!"

Colin and Peter were thrown back against their seats as the Lear jet's front wheels broke contact with the ground. Then they were airborne and Jorge had failed to stop his boss's murderers. The call from Rafael had been seconds too late.

"Relax, men," said Tony, calmly. "We are away and scot-free."

"Well, I prayed," said Peter. "I didn't know what I was doing but I prayed, believe me I prayed, boys."

"Oh that must have been what saved us," said Colin, sarcastically. "We owe you our lives, mate."

"I won't have any yet, but you'll find a bottle or two of bubbly in one of the storage boxes. It might be a bit warm but it'll certainly be fizzy," said Tony. "We have just over an hour before we land — if I can find the airfield without guidance from the ground."

In the end, they only drank one bottle of Dom Perignon — just enough to release the tension without causing them drowsiness. Their day was not yet quite at an end.

It was gone nine when Tony suddenly announced,

"It's just ahead, chaps. Prepare for landing — it may be a little bumpy. The strip's not used very often."

"Will there be problems after we land, skipper?" asked Colin.

"Nah, there shouldn't be anyone there at this time. I'll park up, and then it's only about half a mile down a track to the town. I seem to remember there's a decent hotel in the centre of La Malona."

"Good, I'm hungry, thirsty and in need of some recuperation after today," said Peter.

"What will we do tomorrow?" asked Colin to no one in particular.

"Whatever we like," replied Tony. "We are millionaires now."

"Well, I'm not risking going back to England, that's for sure," mumbled Peter. "I may well hang around this town for a few days."

"Going down — hold tight!" shouted Tony.

The Lear jet dipped sharply to its left and the engines' whine got louder. There seemed to be few lights ahead to guide Tony in. He seemed to be muttering something to himself.

"You alright, skipper?" said Colin.

Tony did not reply immediately as he seemed to be struggling with the controls. Colin sensed something was wrong.

"What's up, mate?"

"Can't get her nose up — going too fast! I can't hold ...."

The wreckage of the red and white Lear jet was discovered the following day. Though some people reported hearing a loud explosion the previous evening, the area to the east of the northern Spanish town of La Malona was heavily wooded and interspersed with steep hills and gorges, making recovery of the remains of the three male bodies difficult, even in daylight. Nothing much of interest was found in the jet's burnt-out wreck. Over the coming weeks, it proved difficult to identify what was left of its three occupants, as everything, apart from the aircraft's basic structure, had been burnt to a cinder. The human remains were placed together in a single simple casket and buried in La Malona's public cemetery beneath a simple headstone that bore the following inscription in English:

In Memory of the three occupants of DHL Lear Jet
No. 21875 which crashed tragically on
Saint Teresa's Mount, 26th September 2001
Free at Last
RIP

THE END

www.ingramcontent.com/pod-product-compliance
Lightning Source LLC
Chambersburg PA
CBHW030409030726
47497CB00002B/535